"Who wants you dead?"

Doug asked.

Arielle's body tensed, and she closed her eyes as the impact of the cold question sliced through her. She tried to speak, but the words wouldn't come.

"Damn it, Arielle, toss me some crumbs. Considering the fact that I dodged a few bullets this afternoon, I have a right to know who we're up against."

"That's true," she said. "You have a right to know."

Doug's eyes glittered in the soft glow of the lanterns, challenging her, reminding her of a panther ready to spring.

Bravely she took one breath. Then another. "There was a hit hired on my life. I know that for a fact."

He didn't blink, didn't react. Was he really as superhuman as he seemed?

"Go on," Doug said.

She dug deep for courage. "I know because I hired the hit...."

Dear Reader,

They say all good things must end someday, and this month we bid a reluctant farewell to Nora Roberts' STARS OF MITHRA trilogy. *Secret Star* is a fitting windup to one of this *New York Times* bestselling author's most captivating miniseries ever. I don't want to give anything away, but I will say this: You're in for the ride of your life—and that's after one of the best openings ever. Enjoy!

Marilyn Pappano also wraps up a trilogy this month. *Knight Errant* is the last of her SOUTHERN KNIGHTS miniseries, the story of Nick Carlucci and the bodyguard he reluctantly accepts, then falls for—hook, line and sinker. Then say goodbye to MAXIMILLIAN'S CHILDREN, as reader favorite Alicia Scott offers *Brandon's Bride,* the book in which secrets are revealed and the last of the Ferringers finds love. Award-winning Maggie Price is back with her second book, *The Man She Almost Married,* and Christa Conan checks in with *One Night at a Time,* a sequel to *All I Need.* Finally, welcome new author Lauren Nichols, whose *Accidental Heiress* is a wonderful debut.

And then come back next month for more of the best romantic reading around—right here at Silhouette Intimate Moments.

Yours,

Leslie Wainger
Senior Editor and Editorial Coordinator

Please address questions and book requests to:
Silhouette Reader Service
U.S.: 3010 Walden Ave., P.O. Box 1325, Buffalo, NY 14269
Canadian: P.O. Box 609, Fort Erie, Ont. L2A 5X3

ONE NIGHT AT A TIME

CHRISTA CONAN

Silhouette
INTIMATE MOMENTS

Published by Silhouette Books
America's Publisher of Contemporary Romance

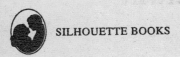

SILHOUETTE BOOKS

ISBN 0-373-07839-0

ONE NIGHT AT A TIME

Copyright © 1998 by Vickie Conan & Christine Pacheco

This edition published by arrangement with Harlequin Books S.A.

® and TM are trademarks of Harlequin Books S.A., used under license. Trademarks indicated with ® are registered in the United States Patent and Trademark Office, the Canadian Trade Marks Office and in other countries.

Printed in U.S.A.

CHRISTA CONAN

is the writing team of Vickie Conan and Christine Pacheco. Vickie states that writing has always been her favorite mode of expression. The magical power of words, how they create images that excite the mind and imagination, never ceases to fascinate her. More than anything, she loves romances and happy endings.

Christine doesn't remember a time when she didn't write, and was thrilled when she finally sold a book, believing that reading is a universal link that can bring our dreams and hopes together.

Both writers live in the Denver area.

With thanks to Cathy Forsythe and Kathy Williams for all your wonderful support! And to Tina Novinski, for all the research assistance. Couldn't have done it without you guys.

Chapter 1

"**I** sent a client your way."

Doug Masterson leaned back in his chair and propped his feet on the desk. Already detached from his responsibilities, he studied the framed picture in front of him. *Destiny*. His yacht. She was a beauty, polished mahogany, fresh paint, a fully stocked galley, and a bed big enough for him to stretch out on.

The boat represented his chance to escape from it all, recover from the burnout that had washed over him like a tidal wave. "Sorry. Not interested." Right now, seven seas of possibilities lay ahead of him.

Rhone obviously didn't take a hint. "Arielle Hale is a schoolteacher and a friend of my wife's. She's in some sort of trouble."

"Who? Shannen?"

His ex-partner's sigh came through the telephone line loud and clear. "Shannen was hoping you'd handle it personally."

"The only handle I'm interested in is the door handle."

His bare legs, now chilled from the unforgiving bite of the building's air-conditioning, would be bronzed in only a few days. A cold beer, a warm trade wind, the tropical sun on his back…a date with *Destiny*. What could be better?

"Hear me out."

"Sorry, the sound of your voice doesn't begin to compete with the seductive whisper of wind in canvas. You ever heard it? It can be sweeter than a woman's sigh. Softer, too." Reaching forward, Doug retied the laces of his deck shoes and let out a ragged exhalation.

"She's drop-dead gorgeous. Tall. Long hair. Thin, but with curves in all the right places. And her eyes…" Rhone whistled softly into the phone. "Man, her eyes are enough to make a man think of spending the night at home."

"Not this man."

Doug reached to drop the phone into its cradle, but was stopped by the restrained urgency in Rhone's voice as he asked, "As a personal favor?"

That was low. A soft knock on Doug's door saved him from an immediate reply. Placing his hand over the receiver, he called out, "Door's open."

Miss tall, long hair, thin, but with curves in all the right places walked into his office.

Only one thought ran through Doug's mind: Rhone's description hadn't done her justice. "Gotta go," Doug said, then hung up.

Dropping his feet onto the floor, he stood. She could stop a man's heart at fifty paces. And her eyes… Wide, fringed by impossibly long lashes and unshaded, containing raw honesty. Bedroom eyes.

Rhone Mitchell had been right, Doug realized. He could imagine wanting to find her at home every night—naked beneath the covers.

Problem was, Doug rarely went home. And when he did, he wasn't fit company for man or beast—a fact made obvious when his cat had refused to stick around.

"Doug Masterson." He extended his hand. She closed the door behind her, then double-checked to make sure it latched tightly. Odd. But the people who crossed his threshold usually had good reason to be wary.

She glanced to the left and then the right as she moved toward him. The smile that touched her full lips was hesitant. Shy. A ghost. And maybe, just maybe, an impostor.

He closed his hand around her much smaller one. The icy chill of her fingertips nestled in his palm. New York was experiencing a heat wave unusual for late September, and her face bore the mark of a faint blush. She wasn't cold. That left fear.

Their eyes met. Hers were blue, maybe a notch darker than they usually were. Bedroom eyes, sure, but with a haunted expression that he recognized all too well.

Damn it to Cozumel and back.

Doug despised the sight of fear. He hated the subtle aroma of it. Detested the way it affected a person's body, made him seem smaller, more pulled into himself. Made him vulnerable.

He experienced a moment's worth of regret. Too bad he hadn't just returned from the Bahamas, rested, recharged—with burnout a relic of the past. But he hadn't and it wasn't. He wasn't sharp enough to take on a new case.

The edge was gone.

Without that, he was a liability to himself, a danger to anyone he might try to help. He had to turn the woman over to Brian—the lucky S.O.B. Still, maybe when he got back and the trouble was over....

"I'm—"

"Arielle Hale," he finished for her. He glanced at the phone. "I was talking to Rhone." Doug released her hand. Shrugging off the unwelcome feeling of regret, he waved his hand, indicating she should take a seat across the desk from him.

She smoothed her skirt over the feminine curve of her hips.

Doug all but slid into his chair.

He fought for and found professionalism. He folded his hands on top of his desk and appraised her in silence for a full minute—well, appraised her in as much silence as one ever found in New York City.

He waited while she fidgeted. He imagined that her unease was made worse by his lack of response or encouragement, but he was enjoying the scenery. Although, he admitted, he could have done without seeing her fright.

"I appreciate your taking the time to see me, Mr. Masterson."

Seeing her was no hardship. In fact, he could easily picture her image taunting him as he lay on that bed all alone.

She blinked, but the dark shade of dread still colored her eyes. "Rhone says you're the best."

He shrugged. "He tells everyone that. Not true." He paused, then added, "He is. But since he's not in this business anymore, that leaves me."

Arielle didn't smile. She finally stopped fidgeting and laced her fingers together. Casting her eyes downward, she stared at her lap.

Doug performed a quick inventory. She was trembling. Her shoulders were bunched, and several strands of her hair had tugged loose from its ponytail, hanging in glorious disarray around her face, making him think of lovemaking's aftermath.

Forcing himself to focus on the facts, he mentally took note of the things that didn't make sense. She was a schoolteacher. Fairly young. Tremendously attractive. So what the hell had her so scared that she needed protective services, especially his, which were so highly specialized?

And then he reminded himself that it wasn't his problem.

"I apologize in advance, Miss Hale, but I was just leaving. A long-overdue vacation."

With a nervous motion, so quick he nearly missed it, Arielle licked her bottom lip. His gut constricted.

"I need help, Mr. Masterson."

He regretted that he wouldn't be the one to give it.

"I can't afford to pay a lot, but—"

"No one's asked for your money. We haven't discussed your case." He allowed the quiet to stretch and grow. The tension mounted along with it. Honking horns were the only sounds other than their combined breathing, his slow and measured, hers rapid and shallow.

He drummed his thumb on the glossy desktop, and then, against his own better judgment, aware that he was offering hope where he shouldn't, Doug stated, "You haven't said what kind of trouble you're in."

He waited, observing the way she schooled her face into relaxation, repressing emotion. She forced her shoulders back and met his gaze directly. Now, if she could only manage to void her eyes of emotion... Obviously, she hadn't mastered control of her most expressive feature. They were wide, unblinking.

Terrified as hell.

She was here, Brian Yarrow was still at lunch, and it appeared the agency would be handling her case, sans Doug. It wouldn't take a lot of effort from him to make Yarrow's job easier.

Doug grabbed a yellow legal pad from a drawer and scrawled her name across the top. Next to it, with a few quick strokes of his pen, he drew her likeness. It wasn't really realistic, though. Ink didn't come in a bright enough color for her eyes.

With a sigh, he poised the pen. "Okay," Doug said, glancing at her ring finger. Bare. Which translated into alone. Alone and scared. A double whammy to his protective instincts.

To distract himself, he wrote down the fact that she had

been referred to them by Rhone Mitchell, affording her priority status with his agency. "You're single?"

When she confirmed that detail, he added that information for the record.

He realized it was a good thing he was leaving. This woman appealed to him, too much. He wouldn't be objective and he suspected things would become far too personal. A lethal combination.

"Miss Hale, what seems to be the problem?"

She twisted her hands together again, not looking at him for long moments. That didn't matter. He'd resolved to handle this much of the case, and Doug Masterson was nothing if not a patient man. He'd learned the art early, relied on it for his survival more than once.

Finally, she met his stare with one of her own...intense and frank.

"Someone's trying to kill me."

The pen dropped. "Kill you?"

"It's a long story."

Her words were delivered in a flat monotone, an interesting contrast to her exotically beautiful appearance. Her statement shouldn't have surprised him—after all, that wasn't an unusual predicament in his office—but coming from her, it sounded obscene.

Arielle swept stray strands of long hair back from her face, tucking them into the loose ponytail at her nape. A few errant wisps escaped, teasing her eyebrows, toying with her high cheekbones.

"Give me the short version."

"But if you have to leave..."

"I do," he agreed. Her expression, which had been so hopeful, plummeted. His gut took a corresponding nosedive. Oh, Lord, if he was just rested, still had the edge. "My colleague, Brian Yarrow, is more than competent." Yarrow was one of the best, had proved his worth over and over. Excluding Rhone, there was no one Doug would rather have at his back. "I'll give your information to him." Along with a "Don't touch" notation.

She'd be in safe hands. His agency would do everything possible to keep her safe—even without Doug at the helm. His conscience should be clear.

So why the hell did he instinctively know her eyes would haunt him as he filled the sails and headed south?

Her expression betrayed, for the first time, the depth of her inner feelings. Her eyebrows dropped, her mouth turned down slightly. Disappointment.

Her look accused him of destroying her faith, made him feel like a failure. And he'd sworn no woman would ever do that to him again. Yet there it was. No matter what, Doug couldn't politely excuse himself now, especially after Rhone had sent her.

"Look…" The siren song of the sea sailed slowly away. "I'll introduce you to Brian. Hold off on your decision until that time." He lowered his pitch, laced his tone with reassurance. "What have you got to lose?" Besides her life?

With obvious reluctance, she nodded.

He asked routine questions, completing a file on her. She supplied her age—late twenties—her address, along with her phone number. He mentally filed away the series of numbers, despite the fact that he couldn't get involved.

Wouldn't.

No matter how tempting it was.

And when he factored in his mental state, Yarrow's hands were safer for Arielle.

Doug looked up after jotting her personal information. Her lower lip was nestled between her teeth, and a more provocative punch he couldn't imagine.

Drop-dead gorgeous?

An understatement.

"Occupation?" he asked, even though he knew the answer. He had to do something to divert his attention from where it had inadvertently wandered.

"Schoolteacher," she supplied. "Seventh grade, gifted and talented students."

"Isn't that an oxymoron?"

She scowled and her eyes drew together. Protective. Like a mother hen.

After threading the pen between his fingers, he rested against the back of his chair. Down to business. Keeping his gaze trained and steady, intent on not missing a single detail, he asked, "Okay, Miss Hale, any known enemies?"

"No." She'd been fidgeting with her fingers again, but under his studied scrutiny, she stilled.

"None?"

"No."

The case was getting more interesting by the second. A part of him thought of dismissing her claim as nonsense. Except for Rhone. Rhone wouldn't be fooled by a pretty face. "Did you go to the police?"

"The police wouldn't be interested in my case."

He allowed his shoulders to drop slightly, as if in relaxation. Truth to tell, he was nowhere near relaxed. His mind was racing over every piece of information she'd shared. But it was her omissions that gridlocked his interest.

So far, nothing she had shared with him added up to murder. "Regardless, you believe someone is trying to kill you."

She'd formed her expression into careful neutrality again. "Yes."

"And have there been any attempts?"

Arielle blinked once, momentarily shutting out the flare of fire in her eyes. "Not yet."

"Let me see if I have this straight."

She inclined her head slightly.

"You're a teacher, you have no enemies, and you believe your life is at risk."

"My life is at risk, and there's no 'believe' involved, Mr. Masterson."

He continued, "Yet there has been no attempt on your life."

She nibbled on her lower lip. Then, bravely, she met his gaze. "That's correct."

Hell. Rhone had been taken in by a pretty face. And she'd kept Doug from *Destiny*. He leaned forward. "What's your crime, Miss Hale? Failing a student? Not putting a notice of the PTA meeting in the teachers' lounge? Or maybe you skipped out on cafeteria duty?"

Arielle grabbed for the purse she'd placed on the floor. "Good day," she said in a clipped tone. As she stood, he noted a betrayal of emotions—heightened color stained her cheeks. "I can see you're very busy."

She swept her gaze over him, and he was suddenly conscious of his attire: cutoff shorts, faded T-shirt, deck shoes and a nine-millimeter automatic comfortably nestled in a shoulder holster.

She'd placed her purse strap over her shoulder and ran from the room before he had a chance to apologize for his thoughtless comment.

Whatever her trouble was, it was real to her.

With a soft curse, he followed, several precious seconds lost when he stopped to pull on a sweatshirt, with large holes cut where sleeves used to be. Guns might be a common enough sight these days, but he didn't like attracting undue attention.

He turned his key in the lock and ran down the hallway and across the lobby.

Doug caught a glimpse of her gleaming ponytail as she pushed through the revolving glass door.

He vaulted over a Wet Floor sign and headed to the side door. He'd apologize, once he caught her—and he would catch her—and then he'd make arrangements for Yarrow to check out the situation and provide a guard and surveillance, if necessary. Doug would be on his way, beneath sunny and cloudless skies, before the hour was out.

"Miss Hale!" He pushed through the door and lengthened his stride to a virtual jog. He didn't intend to lose her
on the crowded lunchtime sidewalk. "Arielle, wait!"

She didn't pause.

He pursued.

Several seconds later, he clamped his hand around her
upper arm, swinging her back slightly into a halt.

"No!"

Her eyes were terrified, and her whole body convulsed
with silent sobs. "Arielle," he said in a controlled tone,
the pitch low, calm.

She gulped in a breath of hot, humid air. Doug moved
them closer to a nearby building, out of the way of pedes-
trian traffic, backing her toward a plate-glass window.

He cursed himself for a thousand kinds of fool. He'd
been an insensitive idiot. "That crack, about the cafeteria—"

Brilliant light flashed, halting his words.

He looked again in the window.

Sunshine. On metal.

Adrenaline slammed reaction into instinct.

Doug pivoted. He shoved Arielle down, placed his body
between her and the barrel of the unseen gun, reached for
his automatic and drew it with deadly speed and controlled
accuracy.

"Clear the area. Now!" he yelled.

Glass shattered. Arielle's scream was accompanied by
others.

Chaos reined. He shouted the order again. Pedestrians
pushed, shoved, and scattered.

Noise and panic surrounded them, then faded into the
distance as the crowd responded to his commands, clearing
the sidewalk.

He cursed, chasing away emotion and acting solely from
years of training.

He smelled something.

Fear. Intent.

Desperation.

The second bullet missed his skull by a fraction of an inch.

Getting Arielle to safety was paramount.

Seeing a passenger lean over to pay a taxi driver, Doug crouched, reached behind him to find her arm. "Let's go for a spin."

Gun ready in one hand, he darted his gaze from side to side, not relaxing, although he'd calculated the odds and decided the would-be assassin wouldn't risk a third shot. Wouldn't have enough time to get away.

He pushed the disembarking man aside and shoved the shaking Arielle into the cab.

"Where to?" the driver asked.

Doug slammed the door. "The docks!"

His gaze on Doug's gun, the man nodded and followed the command.

"Jeez," Doug said as they pulled into traffic, cutting off a car. The cabdriver sped through a yellow light, buying them a few seconds of comfort. "Wasn't ready to play cops and robbers."

Arielle had huddled against the far door. Loosened hairs fanned her face. The soft curtain couldn't hide her abject misery. Holstering his gun, he pulled her close to him. Safer that way, he told himself. But for whom?

"Arielle?"

Her teeth chattered, and goose bumps prickled her arms.

"If I'm going to be putting my butt on the line for yours, you better tell me why someone wants a piece of it."

The driver gestured wildly and shouted in a language Doug couldn't decipher. He turned to look out the back window. Cargo van. White. No license plate.

Just his luck.

He had a beautiful woman beside him, he was heading for open water, and someone wanted to have a tea party.

Through the van's dark tinted glass, Doug could see only the silhouette of the driver and a passenger. And the distinctive outline of a gun. "Step on it!"

The man responded, and the taxi lurched forward. Shoving Arielle low, Doug swiped his nine-millimeter from its holster again, keeping one eye carefully focused on the van.

It moved into the right lane. Accelerated.

"Hold on!" Doug braced against the back of the seat, steadying his shooting arm. The street was thick with traffic. Which meant he couldn't get off a clean round. He cursed. Endangering civilians was something he'd been taught not to do. And if he fired, he'd do exactly that. Swearing again, he kept his aim trained between the driver's eyes.

The van kept coming, crashing into the right rear bumper, shoving them sideways.

"Oh, God! Oh, God!" Arielle's cries seemed to come from a great distance. Her fervent prayer mixed with the cabdriver's curses, the sickening scent of burning rubber, and the crunch of metal against metal.

The van attacked again, colliding with the taxi on Doug's side, knocking him backward. The taxi spun out of control.

Doug ground his back teeth together as they headed into an intersection and oncoming traffic.

As he regained his balance—wrapping a protective arm around Arielle and bracing—he had one thought.

Now it was personal.

Chapter 2

Terror choked off the scream that rose in Arielle's throat. Grabbing a fistful of cotton fleece, she squeezed, burying her face into the taut muscle that lay beneath the fabric.

The faint scent of woodlands and spice penetrated her numbed senses, her shocked mind.

Memories and images flashed, in no particular order.

The house in Vermont where she'd grown up...where her parents still lived. Danny. Her dear brother, Danny! Exorbitant medical bills. Her childhood. The mortgage on a house that had been paid for in full once. Retirement that was now, for her parents, only a dream.

Dear Lord, she had to survive this. She had to. She couldn't bear to see her parents' hearts broken. Not a second time.

Horns blasted and tires screeched as their driver gunned the engine. The battered taxi lurched forward. Arielle winced, fully expecting to feel another impact.

Doug's curse, immediately followed by a sarcastic comment, had her struggling to sit up, but his arm, like a band of steel, forbade the motion.

"Pull over. Right here," Doug ordered the driver a couple of minutes later.

Only when he shifted to reach for his wallet did Arielle dare move. Extracting a couple of large bills, he shoved them into the driver's hand and opened the door.

"Hardly enough to cover damage to the poor man's car, not to mention the near miss on his life," Arielle remarked as she scooted across the seat after Doug.

"Well, now, sweetheart, that's not my fault. Is it? Did you want to hang around and discuss insurance coverage, or would you prefer to make tracks in an attempt to save your hide?"

Arielle glared up into sparkling sea green eyes as she alighted. Defensive, knowing she had no right to be and at the same time knowing she'd had more than enough of his sarcasm, she couldn't help adding, "Are you always this charming to potential clients?"

"Only when a pro tries to scalp me."

"Professional?" She swallowed hard, struggling to maintain her fragile hold on her composure. Somehow, in that moment, she realized that it was Doug's wise-guy act—irritating as it was—that strengthened her nerves. If he showed sympathy, she might crumble under the stress. "How can you tell he's a professional?"

Doug's eyes darkened, and Arielle wasn't at all sure she was ready for his answer. She was living a nightmare. None of this could possibly be real.

"Determination. This guy has something to prove."

A shiver chased along Arielle's spine at his matter-of-fact tone. His words provided an eye-opener to a side of life she'd managed to ignore. And now she was smack in the middle of it. She, a seventh-grade schoolteacher whose life, by comparison to Doug's, had been comfortably dull. Terminally safe.

"Don't suppose you've got jogging shoes in that suitcase you're carrying?"

She shook her head, envying him his deck shoes and shorts.

In the stifling heat, her stockings stuck to her legs like a second skin. She reached up, releasing the button at her throat. Silk wasn't much better.

Doug grabbed her hand. "Let's move."

His touch was impersonal. Her reaction, anything but. Hastily Arielle denied the tingling warmth that raced up her arm. Denied that her inability to catch her breath had anything to do with him, that it had since the moment she walked into his office.

Denied that she was even remotely attracted to a man who obviously couldn't wait to pawn her off on his associate.

Determined to keep up, she paced herself to Doug's long strides. No easy task, when the straight skirt she wore confined her legs. And her new high-heeled pumps were already a painful reminder of why she rarely made the investment.

She grimaced when he led her down a narrow, semidark alley, the scent of rotting trash permeating the air. Hugging the wall, Doug urged her along with a none-too-gentle tug on her hand.

"Where are we going?"

He answered without turning, making it difficult to hear. Something about destiny. Well, she certainly hoped his was more promising than her own.

Struggling for breath, she grimaced when he tugged on her hand. Not wanting to irritate him further, she kept her silence and did her best to keep his pace.

Arielle couldn't have said that Shannen hadn't warned her. Doug's tactics might be a bit rough around the edges at times, but he was definitely Arielle's man, Shannen had said. And the only one, besides her husband, Rhone, that she would entrust with her life.

Shannen hadn't minced words, either, in her description of the man who, at the moment, was casting an impatient glance over his shoulder because the heel of Arielle's shoe had caught in an iron grate.

"Sorry," she mumbled, pulling it free.

She saw his glance track over her head.

"Aw, hell."

Before she could turn to see what had caught his attention, Doug shoved her into a doorway. Straight ahead, on painted gray steel, were the words *Freight Only*.

Her back against the wall, Doug's hands rested against the concrete on either side of her head. Green eyes met blue, defying her to look away.

Determinedly Doug clipped out, "I don't know who the hell wants you dead, or why. Before this day ends, I will know every gory detail. I'll have answers, Arielle. In the meantime, you're a mark he's determined to hit."

Arielle gulped, tried to swallow and couldn't. "You saw the van again?" she croaked.

Doug peered around the corner. "Yeah. It looked real similar to the one that just backed up and is turning in."

Without ceremony, Doug forced her into a crouching position, pushed her around the corner and shoved her into the narrow space between a huge, overflowing Dumpster and the wall.

"Lay down," he commanded. His expression devoid of any emotion, he withdrew his gun.

"Are you kidding? The ground is filthy." Even as she protested, she did as she was told, gagging on the pungent odor.

"Next time you want me to save you, I'll make sure the Trump Tower isn't booked."

Closing her eyes, she fought a wave of nausea, determined not to lose the tiny bit of lunch she'd been able to force past her fear.

"Dirt washes out easier than blood," he offered. Too big to join her in the narrow space, Doug stacked a couple of smaller trash cans in front of him and jerked empty boxes closer to block the gap.

The van approached, and Arielle held her breath. She held it consciously, as if the driver might hear her breathe.

When it slowly passed, she started to give a sigh of relief. Suddenly, the van stopped.

In the silence of the alley, she heard a door open. Clapping both hands over her mouth, she turned her face toward the wall. She drew her knees up when she felt Doug's weight push against her feet.

Eyes closed, Arielle fought to hold back the panic demanding to be let loose.

A spray of gunfire ripped metal with deafening persistence. Her body jerked violently, as though she'd been hit. Horrified, she knew she'd never forget that sound of cold-blooded intent.

After what seemed an eternity, sirens screamed across the sky. Seconds later, she heard rushing footsteps and the slam of a door.

Tires squealing, the van took off.

Doug. Oh, God, was he hurt? Or, worse, was he—?

"I'm going to get that bastard."

The sheer venom in his voice was music to her ears. With a shaky laugh that caught on a sob, she managed to rise to a semisitting position. She took Doug's hand when he held it out to her.

On legs that felt like rubber, Arielle collapsed against him. She wrapped her arms around his waist. Relief flooded her, and she hugged him tightly, unable to stop the flow of tears.

"I don't carry hankies."

Despite that, he wrapped his arms around her. Terror and

guilt choked her—because of her, he could have been killed—blocking off rational thought.

"Arielle?"

Hearing the impatience in his tone, she tried to tamp down the tears, tried and failed.

"Shh, it's okay."

Despite his reassurance, her sobs still racked her body. Her palm rested on his chest, and she felt him sigh. Doug, his touch tender, traced the outline of her cheek, stopping when his finger was beneath her chin. He tipped back her head, and she saw that the cool distance had faded from his eyes, replaced by something she couldn't have named.

Then she couldn't think at all, as he lowered his head toward her.

She sucked in a breath.

His lips claimed hers in a hard kiss.

Under his commanding assault—one that flooded her senses—clawing fear gently subsided.

When he finally released her, she was able to drag in a drink of air.

"You okay?" he asked, his tone gentler than she could have imagined possible. This wasn't the same man whose office she'd entered. He was so much more real, powerful, tender.

She told herself he'd kissed her to calm her, nothing more. Why, then, did her heart keep thudding? She was a logical person, conservative. Not one given to flights of fancy. Certainly not one to let a man she barely knew kiss her. And like it.

But then, logical and conservative people didn't have professional gunmen trying to kill them.

Dear Lord, what had she done?

Doug slid his thumb lightly down her cheeks, wiping away the tears. Continuing lower, he outlined her lips, which were swollen from his touch. The corner of his mouth tilted slightly. "Feeling stronger? We still have a couple blocks to go. Or do I need to kiss you again?"

A wave of emotion crashing over her, leaving her adrift on feelings she couldn't have begun to name, she nodded.

"Is that a yes to the kiss?"

Good God, not that. "No," she said quickly. Too quickly. "I'm ready."

Taking his hand once again, she ignored the tremor in her knees and followed close behind.

Obviously, he'd meant the kiss as nothing more than a means for her to regain control, to shock her back to the present. She shot a glare toward the broad shoulders that filled her line of vision, berating herself for imagining—secretly wishing—that it could have meant something else.

With each step, Arielle winced in pain. The balls of her feet throbbed and burned, and her arches ached. Friction had long since rubbed tender skin raw. Worse, though, was the stench that wafted around them, and she knew it clung to her.

To keep her mind off what she hoped was temporary misery—though thinking about that was better than facing the reality of her situation—Arielle switched her thoughts to another topic, and was not surprised when her focus returned to Doug and a conversation she'd had about him with Shannen.

Her friend had described Doug as a private person, not one to openly or willingly share his innermost feelings. Shannen had laughed, saying that, like Rhone, Doug could be stubborn, a hard man to read. And, too, like Rhone, Doug was loyal, totally trustworthy and completely capable.

Already, Arielle could see the likenesses, could see how Doug and Rhone had once worked together in perfect tandem.

Shannen had volunteered more, her tone carrying a thread of warning. Unlike Rhone's, Doug's softer side lay much deeper, residing beneath layers of his life experiences, protected against discovery and exploitation by a sometimes cynical attitude.

Don't let that bother you, Shannen had said, before going on to add with a smile that behind every good man was his female equal. It was high time Doug found his. Shannen's meaning had been clearly evident in the pointed look she bestowed on Arielle.

Not for one minute would Arielle fool herself into believing she could be Doug's equal in a relationship. Their backgrounds were opposite in the extreme.

Undoubtedly, their views on life and their thoughts about how they wanted to fulfill it were different, too.

Arielle wanted a home, a family. The works. She wanted to trade in the white picket fence for split-rail and live in the country. Wanted to provide a wholesome environment for the babies she'd dreamed of having for so long.

Somehow, Arielle couldn't picture Doug fitting into that scenario. Least of all with her. It saddened her to think that, to date, no man had. She should have been married ages ago, with kids of her own. But no, she always managed to date the guys who ran to the nearest exit at the slightest hint of commitment.

So, if only in her own mind, she had adopted the kids she taught, considering them the family she'd basically given up on having.

A streak of panic raced through her at the thought of her kids.

She squeezed Doug's hand, wanting his attention. "I need to call the principal and tell him to line up a substitute teacher for a couple days—"

"There she is," Doug said, interrupting her. There was no mistaking the pride that lined his voice.

Lost in her thoughts, Arielle had paid little attention to where they were headed. Peering around him, she saw the wharf. Yachts in various sizes and huge catamarans lined the pier on both sides.

Arielle frowned. "There who is?"

"*Destiny*. Hope you like sailing."

Doug pulled her forward, not giving her a chance to respond. Obviously, it didn't much matter whether she liked sailing or not. Truth was, she'd never tried it.

"There's a shortwave radio on board. We can patch your call from there. As for your sub, better tell your boss to find one that can fill in indefinitely."

"Indefinitely? But I have..." Meetings she'd already canceled, she finished silently. Furthermore, on the pretense of an impending family emergency, she'd also already given the principal a list of willing substitutes.

Standing on the pier beside *Destiny*, Doug sent her a cursory glance. "Sweetheart, whoever is trying to kill you doesn't give a damn about what's on your calendar. And neither do I." He released her hand to take her elbow. "After you," he added.

He assisted her from the pier into the craft as it rocked gently against its moorings. Jumping down behind her, Arielle thought him amazingly light on his feet, his entrance causing less of a ripple than her own had.

"The navigation station where the radio is located is down the stairs near the galley, or the—"

"Kitchen. That's the extent of my knowledge." She smiled.

"Does that mean you've never sailed before?" His tone held a note of incredulity.

"First time to sail. First time I've been shot at."

Doug reached out, lightly running the back of his finger over her cheek. While the expression in his eyes revealed nothing of his thoughts, a measure of comfort communicated itself in his light touch.

"I'm thinking," she half whispered, more to herself than to him, "this could be a trip for many firsts."

His eyes narrowed, and his lips tightened. Abruptly he stepped back, dropping his hand to his side.

"Give me the phone number, and I'll patch through the call," he said as he swung away from her.

In the close quarters belowdecks the heat of his body surrounded her, embraced her. A muscle twitched along his jaw as he flipped a switch and punched buttons with impatient accuracy.

He handed her the mike and, in a clipped tone, told her how to use it.

She hesitated, then took it from him. "Look, I'm sorry to be the problem that messed up your vacation. If I've said or done something to anger you—"

"You're an inconvenience that has delayed my vacation. That's all. As for being angry with you, don't jump to conclusions. It has nothing to do with you."

She winced, the sting of his words pricking raw feelings. "Gee, thanks. I feel better already."

Cursing softly under his breath, Doug opened his mouth to speak. Before he could utter the apology that was reflected in his eyes, Arielle turned her back to him and found a tiny victory in his exasperated sigh.

The sound of a ringing phone via shortwave radio seemed strange. Hearing a familiar voice at the other end, even stranger. When Arielle learned that Jack was out of the office, she explained the reason for her call to the school's secretary, leaving out pertinent details, adding that she would be in touch.

Arielle handed the mike back to Doug. Following her mental list of priorities, she eased swollen, sore feet from shoes she swore she never wanted to see again. Then, giving Doug her undivided attention, she listened while he demonstrated how to use the radio. A twinge of alarm skipped through her when he told her it couldn't hurt for her to know.

Her imagination filled in the blanks. The idea that she

should know in the event that he was incapacitated did nothing to buoy her confidence. Casting a quick glance through the small windows, she decided he must have meant if he was otherwise occupied. Ropes, sails, wheels and pulleys all looked terribly foreign, and each, she was sure, had a specific purpose. She certainly hoped he didn't expect her to...

"We need to get under way. You can help."

She wasn't certain, but thought she heard him mutter something about being an anchor.

Arielle drew in a deep breath, immediately reminded that more than the scent of salt water drifted in the air. "Don't suppose there's a shower on board?"

Doug grinned.

Arielle's breath caught at the unexpected transformation. It was the first real smile she'd seen since meeting him, and she heartily approved. He looked boyish. Devil-may-care.

Cancel boyish, she thought, watching as the wind ran its invisible fingers through dark blond hair, carelessly rearranging it across his forehead. Sexy. Plain and simple. And way out of her league.

"Wait until we've made a getaway. In the movies, the girl never showers when she might be shot at."

Unable to help herself, Arielle grinned back at him, finding in it a measure of relief from the tension that held her snug in its grip. "If you can stand me that long, I guess I can, too."

"Grab those rope ties over there," he said when they were on deck, "and undo them."

She watched as he loosened one of the ties that moored the yacht to the dock. She couldn't help but notice his motions. They were controlled, methodical. Confident. She was in good hands...at least for now.

She set to work, the rope abrading her already raw skin.

"Good girl," he said. Obviously conscious of a need for

haste, Doug fired the diesel engines. He cursed during the few seconds of preheat lag time.

Then, the boat free, she followed the instructions he called out to her, and removed the sail covers as he eased *Destiny* from her slip.

His gaze checked and rechecked his position while alternating glances toward the shore. A ripple of tension spiked through her. Was he concerned that they had been followed?

Arielle's glance followed Doug's. Breathing easier, she noted nothing out of the ordinary.

Sunlight glinted from the polished railings that Arielle clung to for balance. No more words were spoken as they headed from the harbor, Doug pointing the sleek prow toward the ocean.

Arielle watched as the distance between the shoreline and the yacht grew with surprising speed. In her mind's eye, she saw the image of her parents, of her home. And she wondered when she would see them again.

Wondered if...

Not caring for the track her thoughts were taking, Arielle shook her head in firm denial. Closing her eyes, she filled her lungs with the unmistakable scent of a sunbathed sea and tried to assimilate all that had happened.

Like a living and breathing thing, dark shadows of fear lurked in her mind and played a relentless game of hide-and-seek with logic and reality.

Being protected—having the need to be—seemed so unreal. Any minute, she told herself, she would wake up, and when she did, she'd be alone, safe and secure in her own bed, in her own condo.

Alone.

She turned, her gaze seeking the rugged blonde who moved about the rolling deck with ease. She wanted to believe that Doug, and the terrifying events of the afternoon, were only vague memories from a bad dream.

Arielle inhaled a shaky breath, her eyes skimming his broad shoulders and back. Toned muscle bunched and relaxed, stretching the well-worn cotton fabric with each movement, leaving nothing to her imagination.

Not that she needed to rely on fantasy. She'd already experienced the steely strength of his arms, felt the solid wall of his chest. Had heard the soft-spoken and yet gruff tone of his voice. All too well, she remembered the touch of firm lips that, for fleeting seconds, had softened against her own.

In the span of a pulse beat, Arielle knew that Doug Masterson could never be categorized as a vague memory. Furthermore, he was anything but a bad dream. She sighed, because the thought that she was in over her head was undeniable. In more ways than one.

When *Destiny* cleared the harbor, wind and current tugging her across the threshold to the open water, Doug stood, braced his legs and started to hoist the mainsail, grunting at the effort. His arms flexed and his biceps bulged with each measured pull.

The sail began to billow and fill. Doug kept a constant check on the sky, the sails, the rigging.

Finally, apparently satisfied that all was as it should be, he gave Arielle the promised tour, ending it in the head—a very real term, she learned, for the bathroom.

"Water's in short supply, so conserve," he told her, taking a towel from a drawer. From a narrow closet, he pulled out a clean T-shirt. Faded lettering across the chest spelled out SWAT.

"There's a bathrobe hanging on the back of the door. Feel free. Of course, feel free not to, as well." He eyed her soiled clothing with a small grimace and laughed outright when she made a face at him.

"We should reach our destination by dawn. I'll call ahead and have Brian pick up something more suitable for you to wear than terry cloth," Doug added.

His glance swept over her from head to toe, and his eyes were a distinctive shade darker when they returned to meet hers. "Silk suits you better."

Arielle swallowed, momentarily at a loss for words. An ornery gleam in his eyes contradicted his serious tone, making her unsure whether he teased or not. No longer certain of anything—and heaven forbid she should jump to conclusions—she opted to let his comment slide.

"Jeans, a T-shirt and tennis shoes would be great." An appreciative smile tilting her lips, Arielle supplied him with the sizes.

When the door closed behind him, she quickly stripped and stepped inside the tiny cubicle. Adjusting the temperature of the water, she lifted the handheld showerhead.

She sighed out loud as warm water sluiced over her face and down her body. Turning off the water as Doug had instructed her to do, she soaped the washcloth, scrubbing her skin vigorously, ridding herself of the stench that she was disgusted to realize she'd grown accustomed to.

After she rinsed, she reached for a miniature bottle of shampoo. With her fingertips, she worked the lather into her scalp, then through to the ends of her hair. She took her time, longer than usual, delaying the inevitable.

The sigh she released this time was filled with dread. He would know every gory detail, Doug had said. Heaven knew, if the man was risking his life for her, he darned well had a valid reason for wanting to know why.

Without a doubt, he would think her insane. She couldn't blame him. She'd even go so far as to agree that, temporarily, maybe she had been.

Would he, could he, understand a desperation so great that it reached far beyond the realm of reason? Had he ever experienced bone-chilling fear, so complete that it robbed him of rational thought and response?

Somehow, she doubted his experiences had left anything

to his imagination. He could probably tell horror stories that made hers seem tame by comparison.

When she was finished rinsing her hair, Arielle turned off the water. Opening the door, she stepped out, reaching for the towel Doug had set out for her.

Clean and dry, she felt like a new person. Or would have, under different circumstances. Arielle folded the towel and hung it over the brass bar. Turning, she reached for the borrowed T-shirt and pulled it on over her head. The hem skimmed her upper thighs, barely covering all the right places. Had she been shorter, it would have been a perfect nightshirt. As it was, it would have to do.

After locating a brush and smoothing the tangles from her hair, Arielle took the navy robe from the hook on the back of the door. The spicy, outdoorsy scent that clung to the fabric prompted a picture in her mind of the man who wore it.

She breathed deeply, burying her face in the nubby material. If only it didn't matter so much what Doug thought of her. Selfishly, she wanted him to stick by her side until she was safe again. She was afraid to trust anyone else. But then, if anything happened to him, when she'd known he wanted to bail, she'd never forgive herself.

Energy sapped, she gave a weary sigh as she slipped her arms into sleeves that extended well past her hands. Arielle rolled them up to a manageable length, and tied the belt snug around her waist.

With a final glance in the mirror, she decided against bothering with the cosmetics in her handbag. Clean was a definite improvement, and that, too, would just have to do.

With a deep breath that reached to her soul, she opened the door and headed up the stairs to the main deck.

The sight that met her was like nothing she'd ever seen. Never in her wildest dreams had she thought a sunset on open water could be so incredibly beautiful.

Brilliant hues of orange, red and yellow stained the sky,

surrounding a sun that looked like a ball of fire as it paused on the horizon.

Arielle felt, rather than heard, Doug's approach as he stepped up behind her.

"I hoped you would get out of the shower in time to see your first sunset from this vantage point." He rested his hands lightly on her shoulders. "What do you think?"

Unable to resist, she leaned her back against the rock-hard expanse of his chest, hoping he'd blame the movement on the gentle sway of the yacht and the fact that she had yet to get her sea legs. "Breathtaking," she whispered. "I've never seen anything like it."

In silence, they watched the colors change and slowly fade as the sun began to sink, seemingly, into the water. Arielle could have sworn she felt Doug's lips against the damp hair at her crown. Vaguely she wondered what he would do if she turned in his arms to face him. Would he kiss her? Could she ask him to? Silently she cursed her shyness, and the fact that she wasn't aggressive enough to find out.

All too soon, the sun disappeared completely, leaving in its wake muted colors and a memory she would never forget.

Doug's return to business accompanied the shroud of darkness, and it seemed equally threatening.

"Arielle, enough fun stuff. Time for answers."

She shivered, even though she wasn't cold. "I know." Arielle moved away from him, needing the distance.

At the railing, she curled her fingers around the cool brass, unconsciously tightening her grip.

"Who wants you dead?"

Her body tensed and she closed her eyes as the impact of the cold question sliced through her. She tried to speak, but the words wouldn't come. From behind her, she heard Doug's irritated sigh.

"Damn it, Arielle, toss me some crumbs. Something I

can gnaw on. Considering the fact I dodged a few bullets this afternoon and have a companion on a solo sail, I damned well have a right to know what's going on.

"If Brian is going to risk his life for your pretty little neck, he'll sure as hell want to know why. And I want to know who, exactly, we're up against."

She dropped her chin to her chest and took several deep breaths. Letting the last one out slowly, she looked up, unknowingly raising her chin to a defiant angle.

"You're right," she said. "You have a right to know." Before she could lose her nerve, Arielle swung around to face him. She continued to grip the rail, now at her back, for reinforcement.

Focused directly on her, Doug's eyes glittered in the soft glow of the lanterns, challenging her, reminding her of a panther ready to spring.

Bravely she took one breath, then another. "There was a hit hired on my life."

He didn't blink, didn't react. Was he truly as superhuman as he seemed?

"How do you know this?" he finally asked.

"I know it for a fact," she whispered.

"Go on."

She dug deep for a serving of courage and laid it all bare before him. "I know because..." She paused, swallowed, then swallowed again. "Because I...I hired the hit myself."

Chapter 3

Doug sucked in a breath, then released it through clenched teeth.

The flatness, bleakness, in her tone stunned him, momentarily distracted him from the impact of her words. He looked into her eyes, trying to read the guarded expression. Couldn't. The dim light hooded her gaze, and so did her intentionally blank stare.

"You...?" Doug trailed off, unable to believe he'd heard what she said, and just as certain he hadn't misunderstood. "You hired a hit on your own life? Good God, woman, wouldn't it have been easier to kill yourself?"

She looked up at him, the drape of her hair partially hiding her face, but not the deadly despair and fear in her eyes. And the sting of his remark. "It's..." She paused and swallowed, though she bravely continued to meet his gaze. "Like I said before, it's a long story."

"And we've got all night." Wanting to give her his full attention, he'd switched on the automatic pilot. Doug folded his arms across his chest and regarded her. He admired her guts in not looking away. This wasn't a game to her, nor was it a game to him. He knew his own stare sparked with intent. He'd know her story. Intimately. Oh, yeah, every single sordid detail. And he'd know them now. "Sit down, Arielle."

She did. Without saying a word, she twisted her hands in her lap, a repeat of her nervous gestures in his office.

Doug stood with his legs apart, body braced for the natural roll and pitch as the yacht rode the swells. For minutes, the silence stretched between them, broken only by the sounds of a living, breathing ocean.

"You're making me nervous," she said softly, her voice nearly inaudible.

He arched an eyebrow, but made no move to offer her comfort. Because of her, some professional marksman had taken a shot at him. Not the ideal way to begin his long-awaited vacation. "Spill it, Arielle. Everything."

"I don't exactly know where to start."

"The beginning generally works."

She gave a slight, nearly imperceptible nod.

He drummed his fingers on a metal rail.

"I know," she admitted. "I have a hard time believing it myself."

"Rhone knew?"

"Yes."

Doug silently cursed his friend. Rhone had dozens of competent, trustworthy contacts in the area. He had chosen Doug, even though he knew Doug's intention of sailing away. This northerly course was definitely not the one he'd charted. And Rhone had known that, too. It spoke volumes about the kind of person Arielle was, the kind of regard in which the Mitchells obviously held her.

But none of that mattered to him.

"A couple of years ago, my brother, Danny, was in a motorcycle accident."

A grainy undercurrent of pain textured her voice, sending

a shiver down Doug's spine. He nodded, waiting with customary patience for her to continue.

"And he didn't die right away."

The lack of emotion in her tone bothered him more than the lacing of anguish had. She was reciting from memory, but shutting off the memories she drew from.

"He lingered for months." She twisted her hands. After letting a small breath out her pursed lips, she continued, "Respirators, IVs, monitors. He never regained consciousness. The worst part was watching how helpless he was, you know?"

For a moment, through Arielle's expression of despair, Doug did know. Better, he knew the pain of losing a loved one. With an effort that time had made easier, he shoved away his own memories and concentrated on Arielle's words.

"It was hard on my parents, watching their son lie there, never moving, never opening his eyes. We…" Her voice cracked, her words wavered. "We prayed. Begged. Pleaded."

"But he never got better?"

She gulped, didn't answer. Luminescent tears, evident in the moon's glow and the yacht's artificial light, pooled in her eyes. She needed to gather herself. Doug needed to escape. A woman's tears were the one thing that struck raw terror in him.

He jogged down the few stairs that led to the galley, grabbed a couple cans of sodas and returned to the deck. He popped the top on one, and offered it to her.

"Thanks."

Her hand shook as she accepted it, her unnaturally cold fingers brushing his.

Throughout his career, Doug had played the cat-and-mouse game of survival, cheating death, teasing it, testing it. And he'd played the game far too many times to count. He was intimately acquainted with adrenaline flow, along with its inevitable and often unwelcome ebb. The crash was the worst. But he knew how to deal with it. From the looks of his lovely passenger, though, she didn't.

She needed company, and his was the only available, much as he wished it otherwise.

He drank from his own can and tried not to notice the way the scent of her just-showered freshness teased his long-neglected senses. The robe cinched at her small waist hung on her, too big, yet comforting. It was the same comfort he wanted to, but dared not, offer.

Her blue eyes were open wide, exposing her inner emotions. She raised the aluminum to her lips and sipped.

She looked delicate, fragile. Her complexion was milky white, her eyes appeared too big, too bright for her pale features. But he'd already learned what resided beneath that false surface. And it didn't have a thing to do with delicate. Or fragile.

Arielle Hale possessed an inner source of strength that he admired. She'd kept going after the attempt on her life, even finding a wry sense of humor. And the elementally male part of him couldn't help but note the way she'd responded to his unplanned kiss. She'd remained calm, unblinking.

A courage to match Rhone's wife, Shannen's, and a quality Doug had always said he wanted in a woman.

Trouble was, he wasn't in the market for a woman. Any woman. The only company he wanted was *Destiny*. She heeded his calls, responded to his whims. She went where he wanted, when he wanted. She was a caring mistress, an undemanding lover. What more could he want? Sure as hell not a wife.

Still, he had Arielle aboard. And while she struggled to combat shock, he had an obligation to care for her, at least until he made the transfer already arranged with Brian. "You need to eat something."

She shook her head. "I couldn't."

With a shrug, he went belowdecks again and returned a little later with grapes, and sandwiches. Without a word, he offered one to her. Again she shook her head.

"Eat, Arielle," he instructed, the tone leaving no room for argument. "This interrogation isn't over. I'm far from finished with you."

She placed her cola can in a recessed holder and wrapped her hands across her upper body, absently massaging her shoulders.

"You need your strength, if you're going to be any good to me or yourself." He took a couple of bites, then nodded toward the other sandwich.

With obvious reluctance, she unfolded her arms, reached for the food and took several small, unenthusiastic bites. "You live like this," she stated flatly.

He popped a couple of grapes into his mouth. Then he met her intense gaze. She wasn't talking about the boat or the impromptu meal. She was talking about the events that had transpired, the way he kept a wary eye on the coast, the sky, the water. "Yeah," he said. "It pays my bills."

"Does it ever get to you?"

Doug gave a wry smile. How long had she been with him? A few hours? And she was already asking questions he'd spent years dodging. He nodded, then responded honestly, "Not enough to quit."

She placed the remains of her dinner on a paper plate and shook her head at his offer of fruit. "I guess I'm grateful."

He hadn't told her he'd already planned a rendezvous with Brian, plotted it while she freshened up in the shower. Doug sensed that she wouldn't like to know that fact, so he kept it to himself for now. Later was soon enough to see that wild panic fill her gaze again.

"You were telling me about your brother," he prompted, when she allowed time to drift between them and his questions.

A detached expression flirted, then settled on her features. He recognized the tactic. Distance yourself from the pain. That way it didn't catch you, haunt you.

Right.

Didn't work that way. When you least expected it, it returned tenfold, crept up, stole over you. Doug shook his head. It wasn't his own pain he was interested in, it was hers.

"Danny stayed alive for about nine months."

Silence dragged.

"It was devastating." Her voice was hollow and soft, making him strain to hear. "Emotionally, as well as financially."

He nodded and waited.

"My parents have never quite recovered."

From the looks of her, neither had Arielle. "He was your only sibling?"

That brought a ghost of a smile. But it didn't linger, and he experienced a frisson of gratitude. Her smile had the power to undo him. Doug definitely didn't care for that.

"Danny was two years older than me. And he made no bones about the fact he wanted a brother, not a sissy girl, around the house."

Doug would have been grateful for any company, anyone to share the burden of being an only child who just couldn't heal the hole in his parents' relationship.

"Around the time he was fifteen, he decided having a kid sister wasn't so awful after all. When I was sixteen, he taught me to drive, how to drag race. Chaperoned my dates, and asked to be introduced to the women in my college classes." She paused. Her tone took on the subtle, grating nuances of the pain she no longer attempted to tamp down. "He was always a little reckless. Boys will be boys, as my dad used to say. But Danny couldn't argue with the wheels of a tractor-trailer."

Doug winced. He'd seen enough destruction to clearly picture what it had looked like.

"In the end, he lost the battle."

Waves slapped against the hull, and he saw her shiver. Doug opened a storage compartment and grabbed a blanket. He shook it out, then closed the distance to his companion and draped it around her hunched shoulders. The breeze from the ocean fanned upward in cool crests, but he'd have bet her chill came from the inside. From the adrenaline crash, from her memories, from her loss.

She whispered her thanks, and he experienced a pang of remorse for being the one to force her to remember the pain. But what had to be done, had to be done. Lives depended on it, including her own.

"My parents had mortgaged their home to the hilt, praying for a miracle that never happened. I took out a loan to pay for his casket." A wayward tear slipped down her cheek.

Doug fought to suppress the urge to wipe the moisture away. Oddly, though, he had no desire to turn his back on her.

"A loan, if you can believe that."

She gulped. No matter how hard he tried, Doug was unable to completely distance himself from the effects of her heart-wrenchingly real words. He'd thought himself past such mundane thoughts, but he wasn't. Doug wasn't sure he liked the realization. To occupy his hands, resisting the urge to reach for her, to give her the comfort she so desperately cried out for, he took a long drag from his soda, draining the bottom.

He crushed the can in one hand.

Arielle Hale was a client. And technically she wasn't even his client. Emotional detachment was a necessity—especially since he wouldn't see her after tomorrow.

"As Danny wasted away, so did Mom and Dad. I watched their decline. In a different way, it…it matched his." She drew a shallow breath. "They're not the same people anymore. Mom takes medication for her heart and high blood pressure. Dad seems to be stuck somewhere in the past. And the darnedest thing, these should be their golden years."

Her expression took on a faraway air. Doug realized she was no longer looking at him, but somewhere in the future.

"They dreamed of taking a Caribbean cruise. They saved for twenty years for their second honeymoon.

"They're both still working, Mom part-time at the grocery store, and Dad's struggling to put tiny metal pieces together on an assembly line he should have left years ago."

She leveled a compassionate stare on Doug. For a moment, for a brief, foolish moment, he wondered what it might be like to be the recipient of that depth of emotion. Before allowing the image to shape and form, he shook his head, scattering the teasing thought to the chilly breeze.

"They have nothing, nothing to call their own. Not even dreams. Can you imagine, all those years of marriage and nothing to show for it?

"I swore I'd never put my parents through that kind of pain. I vowed I'd do anything—anything—to avoid it."

"So why...?"

To her credit, Arielle tipped back her chin, didn't flinch from the inevitable. "Why did I hire someone to murder me?"

He was glad she'd said it. Suddenly he didn't think he could have. The question seemed to burn a metallic taste into his mouth.

"I've watched my parents be destroyed by a medical crisis." Her lips twisted in a way that didn't reflect amusement.

Doug nodded encouragement. She had his total, undivided attention. No other woman had ever so completely captivated him. Her voice was rich in texture and substance, reminding him of a trade wind, carrying him to paradise.

She fingered back strands of now dry hair errantly tossed by the breeze. "I decided to take out an insurance policy."

Doug recoiled.

Seemingly sensing his instant distance, she shook her head. "It's not what you're thinking."

He arched a brow.

"I wouldn't, couldn't, hire a hit just for the money. I wanted an insurance policy so my parents wouldn't be burdened a second time if something horrible happened to me."

He forced himself to draw from the well of patience he'd filled through the years.

"Before they would issue a policy, the insurance company required a complete physical examination, lab work, everything. They needed to rule out preexisting conditions."

Somehow, he liked this direction of conversation even less.

With determination, if not volume, she continued, "They ran all kinds of tests, asked every conceivable question. I admitted I'd been having headaches. I thought they were stress-related, but the doctor ordered an MRI...."

She trailed off, stared out to sea, then went on once more. "My doctor's office informed me they believed I had glioblastoma multiforma."

Doug frowned. "Had what?"

"It's a kind of brain tumor. Very distinctive on an MRI, not much chance of the radiologist missing the diagnosis. I went to the library at the medical school."

He had no trouble believing that.

"It was inoperable, they'd told me. There has been some minimal success with chemotherapy, but..." Her voice had dropped to a tortured whisper. "I couldn't bear to think of my parents being forced to watch me go through that, only to have me eventually die.''

"So you took matters into your own hands?"

"No, not initially. I went through denial. Couldn't believe I was living on borrowed time. But even as I tried to convince myself, I knew the headaches were real. Still, though, I triple-checked with the doctor's office, hoping against hope that the results would change overnight.''

"They didn't.''

"I didn't want to believe life was so cruel as to do that to our family a second time." She sipped again from the can, seeming to find strength somewhere at the bottom. "Yet results were results. I called three times. And I received the same answer each time. They would be scheduling me for more tests. Dr. Hatcher said we'd talk about treatment options at that time, too. And she said I'd probably be referred to the Brain Tumor Center in Massachusetts. Away from my family. With history repeating itself.''

A picture started to form in Doug's eye, that of a terrified schoolteacher, lonely and wanting to protect others from pain, fighting for her survival. He didn't like the image.

Not one damn bit.

"Dr. Hatcher calmly assured me she'd do everything possible...."

"You panicked."

"That's the best way to put it." She snuggled deeper into the blanket and drew her knees to her chest. "I thought about my parents, their financial situation, their mental state. They'd crumble.''

He wondered why she hadn't.

"I took the afternoon off from school, wandered around, numb. All the awful feelings that surrounded Danny's death seemed to be clawing at me. I felt helpless. Confused.''

There was something about her, something that compelled Doug to want to fold her in the protective circle of his arms and keep her there, keep her safe.

And that was the only course of action not possible.

The idea of her vitality, her loveliness, eaten away by some horrible thing he'd never heard of sent a spike of heated, angry disbelief through him.

"I..." She stopped, swallowed, fidgeted. Stalled. "I bought a magazine, one of the military ones. But not one about our armed services."

Doug's jaw tightened. He knew the type of publication. On the fringes, they pedaled destruction, distrust, and even death.

"I'm not proud of it," she said softly. "But I wrote to a post office box and received instructions two days later."

Arielle shuddered and he inhaled the fear she felt.

"I had to take money to a hotel. It was horrible. Dirty and dingy. I could feel him staring at me through that hole in the door.

"Dr. Hatcher called a couple of days ago. Said she had wonderful news, though she deeply regretted the horrible anxiety she'd put me through."

He waited.

"Seems there was a mix-up."

"But how...what?"

"Human error. Apparently the slides were mislabeled. However unforgivable, it happens."

"And the headaches?"

"Stress."

Big surprise.

Doug cursed again—a single, succinct word.

She was struggling for her survival.

Arielle faced a bright future, she was going to live, have a long, healthy life, maybe have a few kids of her own...if Doug could get her into safe hands.

"When I realized I was no longer going to die, I went back to the hotel. I knocked and knocked. There was no answer. I checked with the manager, he said no one had been in that room for weeks."

"He lied?"

She shrugged, strands of hair flirting with her face, framing the features with filtered moonlight.

"We have to find him." Doug's hand curled into a fist as he silently cursed the inaction, the fact that he was running instead of fighting. "Stop him."

"That's why I came to you."

Doug stood, impatience and frustration lancing through him. With a few quick strides, he dwarfed the distance between them, curling his fingers into her shoulders. "Can you describe anything about him?"

"Describe…?"

"The man you contacted. Height, weight, hair, any distinguishing marks that will help us find him."

He saw her hand tighten on the can. As he held her firmly, his mind raced.

"How tall was he?"

He heard the shallowness of her breaths. "I don't know," she began, then blinked when he glared. "He only opened the door as far as the safety chain allowed. All I really saw was his arm. It was tanned, with dark hair." She shook her head. "I'm sorry."

"Did he say anything?"

"He promised he'd do the job right, that I was to be alone as much as possible. I gave him my schedule, but he swore he wouldn't harm me at school, that he'd leave all the students alone. And he said he'd do it quickly, that he'd do what it took."

"Did you specify the caliber of the weapon, too?" Abruptly he released her. Her shoulders sagged. Doug pivoted and strode away, gripping the railing and staring out at the vast velvet night.

Doug dragged spread fingers through his hair. Why in God's seven seas was he involved in this mess? And why was he allowing winsome eyes and a desperate tone to travel through his resolve?

He wasn't.

Definitely wasn't.

She was Brian's concern—or would be in less than twenty-four hours.

"Doug?"

The sound of his name, whispered in the darkness, with uncertainty and a trace of fear, started to unravel him. The touch of tentative fingers on his back undid him. And when the scent of her swirled into his hungry senses, his remaining resolve pooled into the ocean, drowning in unfathomable depths.

She wanted reassurance. And he was the one she sought it from.

Turning, he recaptured her shoulders between his fingers. Again, he noticed how feminine she was, how utterly sexy she looked in his robe, the soft cotton of his T-shirt snuggling her beneath the lapels.

Her palm pressed against his chest, the heat of human contact burning his skin. Her head tipped back, hair fanning behind her. The dim light made her appear ethereal, tantalizing.

He'd never had a case like this, never met a woman like her.

He recalled the coldly impersonal kiss in New York. It had been a means to an end, a way to make her get a grasp on the situation, help her find calm.

But he knew this one wouldn't be cold. Or remotely impersonal.

The first had meant nothing.

This, this, meant something.

Just what, he didn't know. But he knew it would mark a changing point. For both of them.

He wanted this, maybe as much as she did.

She sucked a breath deep into her lungs as he pulled her gently but inexorably closer. He lowered his head in perfect time with her rise to her bare tiptoes.

They were nearly one, separated by only a scant few inches. And then they were one—she opened her mouth, and he accepted the unspoken gift.

He was gentle at first, then her fingers tangled with the hair at his nape. A primitive urge to protect and dominate surged, and he instinctively responded, deepening the kiss, drawing deep on his own desire and demanding her surrender.

She moaned softly, the sound swallowed between them. It urged him on, farther, farther than he'd been in years. Her tongue was warm and tender, then passionate and seeking in equal measure.

Doug was in trouble, and he knew it.

The roll of the yacht forced them closer, and the kiss deepened. Their breath blended, and for a moment, just that moment, it was meant to be.

The shortwave radio squawked, shattering the thundering tension. With a silent curse, Doug ended the kiss. Reality and reason returned.

And he was left with a hell of a question: What in the name of creation was he supposed to do now?

Chapter 4

Cold crept around Arielle when Doug stepped away, the chill seeping in to replace the warmth his body had provided.

"I'll be back," he said, voice ragged, as if the words had been torn from his throat. "Don't go anywhere."

As if she could.

When he pivoted and left, she pressed her fingers against her swollen lips. Like waves slapping the shore, sanity returned, flooding her with conscience and remorse.

What had she gotten herself into?

In the past three years, since the disastrous end of her engagement, she'd been kissed only once, a gentle peck on the cheek from a man who never called again. And now, in the space of several hours, Doug had claimed two kisses—two devastating kisses that reached deep inside, to a place no man had ever reached.

The first she could excuse. She'd been frightened witless, unable to think. The kiss had shocked her back to reality.

But the second? The second kiss she'd responded to,

melded into, wanted. Insanity. It had to be. Insanity blended of fright and hope.

Until Rhone suggested she call Doug, Arielle hadn't believed she had a chance of survival. She'd given up hope, been living in shadows and fear.

And in a single day, she'd sought protection from a man who didn't want to offer it and been the target of an assassination attempt.

The first attempt, she painfully reminded herself, but not the last. The man she'd hired wouldn't stop until he'd succeeded. Or until they put a stop to the hit.

At that very moment, she knew how very much she wanted to live.

Suddenly the wash of emotions proved too much.

Her knees buckled, and she sank onto one of the cushions, drawing the robe across her chest and holding it closed with numb fingers. She shivered, goose bumps chasing up her arms.

Arielle Hale, schoolteacher, had been shot at. Worse, she'd been kissed nearly senseless by a man so masculine that her feminine instincts swam with recognition.

And he wanted to get rid of her.

Not that she could blame him.

Thanks to her, he'd nearly been scalped. Thanks to her, his long-awaited vacation was going to be even longer-awaited.

Still, no matter how hard she tried, she couldn't erase the image in her mind of his eyes darkening as she rose—without any plan or conscious thought—onto her tiptoes.

For a moment, it had been as though nothing else mattered.

She'd been scared, desperate for human contact, for reassurance. Reliving Danny's death took a toll on her heart, the pain of the memory worse than the fear of losing her own life.

Gazing sightlessly out to sea, she dragged the robe tighter, in the hope of keeping warm. A futile effort, she belatedly realized. The cold came from inside, not outside.

The drone of Doug's voice surrounded her, reaching out and offering a lifeline of support in a world gone crazy.

She heard her sizes repeated into the mike, the words followed by a long pause. Looking toward the navigation station, she noticed Doug staring at her. His gaze traced her body, from bare feet to damp hair.

Self-consciousness claimed her, making her swallow, even though her mouth had gone dry.

Arielle struggled for a calm and casual air, as if getting shot at and kissed happened every day. But the thundering of her heart, much like the swells of a restless sea, proved otherwise.

She turned her head, breaking eye contact, as needles of sharp awareness pricked her insides, injecting desire, wants and needs long denied.

He continued his conversation, clipping out instructions with laser-sight precision.

Less than five minutes later, Doug returned, bringing with him an aura of power and the scent of windswept danger. He stood near her, legs braced, the muscles in his arms shaped and defined as he crossed them over his chest. He resembled a pirate. But instead of a sword glinting in the moonlight, the cool threat of firepower nestled between his shirt and his shorts.

This was no ordinary man.

But she was an ordinary woman.

"There are no leads on the van." He paused, holding her attention. Then he finished, "Yet."

Lead seemed to sink in her stomach. "Thanks for trying."

"Would have helped if I got the entire license plate number."

"How much did you get?"

"Last three numbers."

"I got the whole thing."

Animation raced into his eyes. "Go ahead."

She recited the numbers, and he smiled. "I like a woman with brains."

He excused himself and returned a couple of minutes later. The wind whispered, along with doubts in her heart.

"Brian's running another trace. He'll meet us at the house late tomorrow morning."

"The house?" Arielle had always prided herself on the way she took charge of her life, organizing everything and leaving nothing to chance. But ever since the phone call from the doctor's office, nothing had been the same. Now, each and every detail of her life was being handled, directed, by someone else.

She hated inactivity, the fact she was dependent on Doug for so many things. Being in this position went against the grain. And she vowed to do anything possible to get herself out of this situation and return to her ordinary life.

"My house. You'll be safe there."

She reached for the can of soda, dragging the robe's lapels back together when they gaped. After taking a steadying sip, she said, "I'm sure you'll be relieved to get rid of me."

His jaw clenched, and his back teeth obviously ground together. "Listen, Miss Hale, this has nothing to do with getting rid of you. It's not personal."

"I know," she murmured.

The tension eased from his face, leaving behind a man who looked half a dozen years younger.

"It's been a hell of a day," he said. "You probably don't dodge bullets on a regular basis."

Unlike him, who probably leaped tall buildings in a single bound.

"You need sleep," he said.

On her brief tour, she'd seen only one bedroom. One bed. She gulped a swig of the soda.

"It's big enough for two," he said, as if reading her mind.

When she looked at him, she saw a devilish smile dancing at the corner of his lips. "Where...?"

"Will I sleep?" he finished. "*If* I sleep, it'll be in my bed. Share and share alike. I don't snore, and I don't steal the covers."

The thought of Doug's body pressed against hers made her pulse roar in her ears.

With a single step, he'd dwarfed the distance between them. She tipped back her head in order to see him.

"Look, you came to me for protection. Until you're in Brian's custody, you're my responsibility." He strung several seconds of silence into a thunderous anticipation. "I don't have sex with women I'm taking care of."

The darkness that had earlier painted his features with pain returned. Shannen had hinted that something terrible had happened in Doug's past but, out of respect for him, hadn't told Arielle what the tragedy was.

A foreign, never-before-explored part of Arielle made her want to reach out, to erase the lines at the corners of his eyes.

She reminded herself that after tomorrow she'd never see him again, told herself that whatever feelings she might have were a result of what they'd shared...nothing more.

But that didn't stop her heartbeat from racing wildly.

"Bed," he ordered.

He offered his hand. Hesitantly, she accepted, her fingers disappearing in his grasp. As he eased her upward, their gazes remained fixed on one another. His warmth surrounded her, chasing away cold, but leaving her with a terrifying sensation of want.

Before she could succumb to the dangerous impulses charging through her, Arielle managed a weak "Good night.'' When he didn't instantly release her, she pulled free and hurried toward the steps.

She didn't slow until she reached the small bedroom.

Her insides still adrift, she shut the door and drew a deep breath. Then another. Finally, she counted to ten. The techniques that had always been so successful before didn't settle her, though, not when Doug's indomitable presence pervaded the room, stamping the atmosphere.

The bed loomed in the center of the small space, a hunter green comforter fluffed on top. The decorations were sparse to the point of being nonexistent, everything functional, nothing frivolous.

A single book sat on a small table, next to a lamp and clock. Trying—and failing—to resist temptation, she moved toward the book, tracing her finger down its spine. A bookmark peeked from the pages, marking his spot in a psychological case study of a notorious criminal. Even in his free time, Doug didn't rest.

It was wrong, she reminded herself again, to wish he'd stay with her until the hit had been canceled. But hope was the only thing she had to cling to.

Sighing, she crossed to the bed, pulling back the comforter to slide between the crisp sheets. She plumped a pillow, wondering which side of the bed he preferred to sleep on.

Knowing she was totally out of her element, Arielle offered a prayer for strength, instinctively realizing that she'd need it. He'd said he didn't sleep with the women he protected—and she wondered...did he even want to?

Doug drained the dregs of the coffee cup. Barely warm, thick-as-tar caffeine landed in his gut.

Night watch stank.

He was getting too damn old for this. Surveillance was for kids, rookies and screwups. Screwups. The reason he stood on deck, looking into the darkness, while a desirable woman curled beneath the covers of his bed.

His bed.

Tall, long hair, thin, with curves in all the right places was snuggled in his sheets, without a bra or probably even panties, while he watched the curve of the horizon instead of the curve of her derriere.

He slammed down the mug.

He'd known better than to allow winsome eyes to distract him. But what choice had he had?

If he hadn't followed her, she'd be dead now.

And that wouldn't happen—not on his shift.

While he watched, the first splashes of dawn inked the sky. Despite the gravel in his eyes, he hadn't been able to force himself to crawl into bed next to her. The soft sounds she made while readying herself for bed had haunted him all night.

Fantasies didn't make good companions, he realized, but they sure beat the alternative. Memories. With memories, it didn't matter how fast you ran, they always seemed a step ahead of you, waiting with open arms. And if you stumbled, they'd catch you, suck you in.

The sky brightened, chasing the demons back to the dark spot reserved for them in his soul. After stretching the knots from his muscles, he dropped down the few steps to the galley and searched out filters. Fresh coffee for the new day.

The first satisfying drop hissed into the glass carafe. Doug needed a shower and a shave. He also needed a white, sandy beach. Two out of three wasn't bad—better than his normal average.

He paused in front of his bedroom door. She'd still be asleep, long hair scattered across the pillow. The pillow on his side? Or the side that had never seen company?

Would she have kicked off the covers, or would they be bundled beneath her chin?

Redirecting his thoughts, he continued down the passageway to the head.

Ten minutes later, razor blade poised perilously close to his Adam's apple, he heard the door slowly open.

Instantly alert, Doug dropped the razor—and, unfortunately, his towel—when he reached for his gun. He aborted the reaction quickly when he saw Arielle.

"Sorry," she said, swallowing deeply, gaze fixated on the weapon. "I knocked, but..."

She was going to be the death of him yet.

"Brian's on the radio." She blinked and looked up. A shade of pink matching last night's sunset slid up her face, stopping on her cheekbones. "I'll, er, meet you on deck," she said, turning her head.

The door clicked behind her before he had a chance to respond.

After pulling on his cutoff jeans, Doug answered the call.

"She has a nice voice," Brian commented, sounding disgustingly fresh and rested. "Competent, too—answered right away and didn't send a squall down the line."

Just what Doug needed, an outline of her positive attributes. As if he hadn't spent the night enumerating them.

"She as gorgeous as Rhone says?" Brian asked.

Doug's voice slid rawly past a sleepless night. "More."

"Didn't get much sleep, huh?"

"She did."

"Having clients is hell."

"Yeah." He glanced at Arielle's profile as she stood out of hearing range on the foredeck, hip propped against the railing. She was endlessly stirring a spoon of sugar into a mug. His shirt and robe still hung from her frame, and her hair had been cinched into a ponytail. A few errant wisps, caught by the breeze, moved across her forehead, not disguising the lines furrowed there. "Have you got something stronger than the coffee I made?"

"What I've got is strong enough to burn a hole in your gut."

Doug's spine stiffened.

"Someone paid Arielle's parents a little visit about an hour ago."

Doug's response came swiftly and succinctly. Arielle stopped stirring and looked at him.

"Gets worse."

Rule number one: Things *could* always get worse. And rule number two: They always did.

"The visitor slid a picture of Arielle under their doorway—a red *X* across her face. Her folks are panicked, according to Shannen. They called her when they couldn't reach Arielle...said something about filing a missing-persons report."

Doug drummed his fingers on teak, mind sifting through possibilities and probabilities. "What have you done to neutralize the situation?"

Arielle's face drained of color. Resolutely he turned away from her, needing to concentrate on the problem, not her emotional reaction. He knew he wouldn't much like that, either.

"Shannen handled the parents like a pro. She told them Arielle's staying with her. Then she called me."

"Get a team out there to sweep for bugs, put the house under twenty-four-hour surveillance. And keep them away from the cops."

"They want to talk to their daughter. If they don't get to soon..."

The rest of the sentence remained unspoken. After refining the details of their rendezvous, Doug signed off.

He sensed Arielle's approach and turned to face her. Briefly he considered telling her the conversation concerned another case. But the squared angle of her jaw told him she wouldn't buy it for a minute. How did women get to be so damn perceptive, anyway?

"That was about me," she stated, fingers curled around the spoon.

He nodded.

She peeled her fingers from the metal, then, trembling, slid the mug onto the countertop. "I can handle it."

"Someone shoved a picture of you under the door of your parents' house."

Her knees buckled beneath her. But before he could react, Arielle straightened.

He took a step toward her.

"I'm okay," she said, her voice shaky with unshed emotion. "I told you I could handle it."

Nodding brusquely, he said, "Shannen told them you're with her."

"I've got to call them."

Doug shook his head. "No can do."

Her hands formed a protective shield near her heart. Her chest rose and fell, in time with the strangled cadence of her words. "This is my family we're talking about, Doug. Please understand that I need to talk to them, tell them I'm okay."

He shook his head.

"You can't be serious."

"Serious as a heart attack." Doug steeled himself against the urge to give her anything she wanted. "We're not playing cops and robbers, Arielle. This is psychological warfare—and you're the trophy."

Her hands dropped, and she formed them into fists at her sides. She tilted her chin stubbornly, in a way he was coming to recognize. And intensely dislike.

"You can't prevent me from contacting them."

"I can. I will." Then he succumbed to temptation. In a few seconds, he had her shoulders captured in his hands. His fingers dug into the softness of her as he inhaled the seductive scent of sunshine. Some of his tension scattered, and with effort, he drew on patience. "It's my job to keep you safe."

Determination masked her vulnerability. "And that includes dictating my actions."

"When necessary."

She drew a shallow breath, then expelled it in a rush of frustration. "Just one call. I'll keep it under a minute."

"He's counting on you jumping. He could have tapped the phones, intercepted the mail. No doubt the house is being watched. He's not sure he got you in the alleyway. Figures your parents will know whether he did the job or not. The picture was a gamble to draw you out.

"He's dealing from the bottom of the deck, and we don't have a handful of cards. The only game we can play is one of intelligence, staying one step ahead of him."

In the silence, Doug played the one card he had. "Don't seal your parents' warrant along with your own."

He absorbed her weight as energy rushed from her.

Instantly he wanted the words back. Nothing was worth seeing that look of desperation flood back into her face.

"Oh, my God," she whispered brokenly. "What have I done?"

Doug wisely decided not to recite the events.

Tears glistened on her eyelashes, but she resolutely blinked them away. "Everything I did was to spare my parents from further hurt."

Self-recrimination drowned her tone. Guilt.

How well he knew the cost of *that* emotion.

"We'll protect them, Arielle," he insisted. "But you have to play by my rules. And that means staying away from them. And no contact."

He watched emotions war inside her. From the tears of regret, to the frown of frustration, to the eventual gulp of resignation.

"I want to call them the second it's safe."

He nodded.

"I've got to know that you'll do everything possible to protect my mom and dad. They should never have been a part of this. Please," she asked quietly, "promise me."

Promises meant nothing when you were dealing with a hired assassin. Arielle's disappearance had ticked the man off. The only thing worse than an assassin was an annoyed one.

"Doug?"

Years ago, Doug had made it a policy never to offer false hope. "I promise," he said, surprised to realize he meant it. Then again, what man blessed with a reasonable amount of hormones could resist bedroom eyes, especially at the distance of six inches? He was lucky his heart didn't forget its basic rhythm.

"Thank you."

She straightened her shoulders and tipped back her head. Strength flowed through her, and he marveled at it, at her.

He relaxed his hold, and she raised her hand, tracing her fingers down the side of his face. His earlier appointment with the razor had been worth the effort. He wouldn't have wanted her abraded by the roughness of an overnight shadow. Nor would he have wanted to miss the lightness of her touch against shaved skin.

Awareness sparked between them, their gazes locking. Abruptly, as if sensing the undercurrent that was as dangerous as a threat to her life, she turned, escaping from him. Smart woman.

Within seconds, he saw that she'd entered the galley and started pulling pans from a cabinet, seemingly without reason, other than a desire to distract herself.

"I'll make us some breakfast," Arielle said.

"Pancakes?" he asked hopefully, after clearing his throat. Having this woman aboard was more dangerous than the call of a siren's song.

"Eggs."

"Over easy?"

"Scrambled."

"My favorite," he lied. At least cooking would give her something to do, keep her away from him...from the radio. Doug didn't fool himself for a minute. She was resourceful, and had absorbed every lesson he'd given. If she decided to use the radio, she would, and nothing short of physical action would stop her...not that that idea was without merit.

Doug returned to his cabin and dragged fresh clothes from a drawer, trying not to notice the subtle differences she'd made in his space.

She'd made the bed—not with military precision—and halfheartedly plumped the pillow.

The pillow on *his* side of the bed. Which meant she'd slept there, between the sheets that usually conformed to his naked body.

Would the scent of her cling to the fabric and taunt him when he sailed south? Or would it saunter through his dreams on the rare occasions when he slept?

Shoving aside ridiculous thoughts of wanting to finish the assignment—protect her until she was safe—Doug stripped off his shorts.

When he returned to the galley, she was searching for plates. Seemed odd having her on board, the odd part being that he actually liked her presence...a fact he acknowledged with reluctance.

Thankfully, she'd brewed a new pot of coffee, this one as strong as the ocean was deep, and just as black.

He drank the first cup undoctored.

"What's the plan for today?" she asked when they were settled across from each other at the small table.

In her voice, he heard an underlay of fear, but she'd quashed it from her body. Yesterday, she'd been hunched into herself, more terrorized than hopeful. Today, though, he saw the spine of steel. She'd taken the news about her parents as well as could be expected—trying to deal with the situation at hand.

"We'll rendezvous at eleven. Give Brian a chance to secure the premises and take care of everything he needs to do."

"And you'll catch the next breeze out?"

Spearing a forkful of scrambled eggs, he nodded. They tasted a whole lot better than any he'd ever put together. Maybe Rhone was right—maybe he *should* start looking for a wife.

As quickly as the thought formed, he dismissed it. Loving was a hell of a risk. He wasn't that brave anymore. Maybe he could hire a cook.

He stopped eating, realizing she was looking at him.

Softly, Arielle said, "I owe you my thanks."

"Just doing my job."

"Does everyone fall for that line?"

"Line?" He put down the fork.

"You want people to think you don't care. But you couldn't do what you do without caring."

"Don't fool yourself."

Arielle placed her silverware at the side of her plate. She met his stare without blinking. "Then why did you follow me out of your office?"

"Because Rhone would have cut out my heart if something happened to you."

"But you want me to believe you don't have one."

Impatience swelled like a gathering tidal wave. "Are you an amateur shrink?"

"As a matter of fact—"

"I rescued a gifted and talented *shrink*?"

"I'm not licensed."

She wrapped her hands around her coffee mug, and he saw the goose bumps teasing the exposed flesh on her arms. She was cold—a bundle of nerves, he was certain—but still, she didn't complain. He couldn't have added many women to that list. "Listen, do us both a favor, leave the psychoanalyzing to someone else." He lowered his voice and finished, "I like my secrets where they are. Buried."

"I wasn't trying to psychoanalyze you."

"Then you'd be the first." He excused himself, checked his watch, then prepared to sail. The weather report looked good—clear skies for the rest of the day.

He was vaguely aware of her motions, clean and economical, as she straightened the galley and washed dishes. Ten minutes later, without so much as a glance in his direction, she disappeared down the passageway. Doug expelled a long breath, a breath he hadn't known was searing into his lungs.

Usually he treated women with the respect he inherently believed they deserved. But there was something about her, something that chased past his restraint. It was far more than physical beauty, it was that sense of a spirit he knew would never be broken.

When she returned to the deck, her purse swung from her shoulder. A hint of cosmetics lengthened her lashes and highlighted her cheeks. Her hair was still cinched in a ponytail and secured with a rubber band. A pair of his sweatpants sagged at her waist, barely disguised by his T-shirt. Ready for departure.

Pausing at the top of the stairs, she asked, "Permission to come aboard, Captain?"

"I don't bite," he said, maneuvering the wheel to compensate for a wave. "At least not after breakfast."

His comment passed without a response, and finally she tightened the sweatpants at the waist. "I hope you don't mind me borrowing these. I couldn't stand the thought of putting my old clothes back on."

"They never looked like that on me."

She settled on one of the cushioned seats, placing her shoes and purse beside her. Arielle tipped back her chin, offering herself to the fall sunlight, reminding him again of the sea goddesses he'd fantasized about as a boy.

Only years separated the boy from the man, he realized—not the dreams.

And one thing was certain—in his dreams, he'd never turned his back on a beautiful woman, delivering her into the care of another man.

"Right now, it's almost possible to believe it's all been a nightmare," she said, the wind carrying her words toward him. "I just wish it were. I wish my parents weren't scared, wish I could contact them, wish I could turn back the clock."

She sighed deeply, maybe from the soul, he thought.

"I wish none of this had ever happened."

How many times had he made that last wish, too? Too damn many to count.

She brought her head back into position and met his gaze. For a long moment, neither spoke.

"Ten more minutes," Doug said finally. Wanting to distract himself from the hypnotic power of her eyes, he added, "We'll be using those ropes when we dock."

"Let me guess. I get to help."

"No free rides."

"Aye, aye, Captain."

The sight of his house, a haven in a world often gone crazy, made Doug smile. He'd had it built to his specifications, large and airy, safe and secure, serene and comfortable. It had been his dream, and an architect's nightmare.

"Is this home?" Arielle asked.

"Vacation home."

"It's gorgeous."

Yeah, it was. And so was the vision of the Bahamas.

Doug eased *Destiny* into her slip as gently as he might slide satin from a woman's shoulder.

He and Arielle worked to secure the yacht, and he decided she made a good student…probably as good a student as she was a teacher. Too bad he wouldn't be around to show her a few more things.

When the yacht was bobbing securely against its lines, he checked his watch. Fifteen minutes early. By the time Brian arrived, Doug would be ready to head back out.

As he waited for Arielle to slip on her shoes and gather her meager belongings, the wind shifted direction. An acrid odor—something burning?—lingered on the air. One thing was certain: It wasn't a friendly neighborhood barbecue.

The small hairs at his nape stirred.

Trouble. He felt it.

As if they didn't already have enough.

Chapter 5

Doug exhaled in disgust. "Not again." No rest for the wicked. Maybe before he died he'd make it to the Bahamas. Vowing to mend his ways, Doug instantly reached for his gun and looked over his shoulder toward Arielle.

"Doug?" she asked on a short breath. "What's wrong?"

How did you explain a hunch to a woman who dealt in facts? "Stay close to me," he advised, wanting her within a couple of feet. "Got it?"

She nodded.

He stepped onto the dock, then turned and offered her his free hand. Her fingers, slender and chilled, met his touch. Although she was trying to radiate strength and courage, her body betrayed her. Doug offered a half smile, one that didn't quite communicate a belief that everything would be okay.

He released her and palmed his gun, narrowing his eyes as he turned toward the house. Everything appeared normal. But Doug knew how deceptive appearances could be.

If his guess was right, his second home had received

unexpected visitors. Sure wouldn't be Lady Luck paying her respects, he knew. She'd been pretty scarce lately.

Instead of a destination, the Bahamas were becoming a blurred vision. Maybe in his next life…

Doug debated his options. He needed to be certain their visitor was gone, but he didn't dare leave Arielle alone, on the off chance that they still had company. He could set sail again, but in the time it took to pull out, they'd run the risk of being sitting ducks.

And he'd never been much for quacking.

After sweeping his glance across the expanse of land, he quietly said to Arielle, "Follow my every order to the letter, no questions, no discussion. Understood?"

Arielle hugged herself. But, unlike yesterday, she didn't hunch forward. Unaccountably, he was proud of her. Trust, it seemed, had given her hope. Doug watched her swallow hard, waiting until she gave him the only answer he would accept. When she complied, he smiled, then motioned her forward.

A current of energy, the primal sense of anticipation that always accompanied the challenge of the chase, surged through him.

Like a bloodhound hot on the trail, Doug focused on his surroundings, tuned out distractions, listening for anything other than the surf, birds or wind. In the Middle East, he'd learned to hear someone approaching across the sand. In Central America, he'd learned to pick out the slither of a snake above whispered conversation. And in New York City, he'd learned to turn it all off occasionally and actually go to sleep.

Surveying the landscape, Doug noticed crushed blades of grass. The invasion of his sanctuary rankled. And the possibility loomed that the visitor wasn't random, which would mean they were being targeted, hunted.

And, more, that would mean Arielle's assassin knew

Doug was protecting her…and had done enough research to suspect he would be taking her to his home.

Fear for her stirring a sensation of awareness, he grabbed for her with his free hand. Her purse slung forward, bumping into him.

"Sorry," she said softly, the sound of her voice seeming to thunder in the stillness.

He should make her leave the small suitcase behind, but he had enough experience with women to know better.

She hitched the purse back onto her shoulder, and Doug looked at her squarely. "Don't let go of me."

She nodded.

Doug started toward the fencing. The feel of her, soft, feminine and trusting, seared into him. He'd betrayed another woman's trust before.

And the memory taunted him.

He didn't deserve blind trust. Not hers, not anyone's. But he was all that stood between her and death. He'd take a bullet himself before he let anything happen to her.

Determined to get her out of her situation alive, Doug blinked himself back to a clear focus. Distraction was a luxury he couldn't afford. But all of a sudden he had more sympathy for Rhone's plight when Rhone had thought his wife was dead. Women—life's biggest reward, life's biggest challenge.

Near the fence, charred grass surrounded unrecognizable metal. Releasing her, he bent and frowned. The scent of destruction from the semimelted silver was cloying.

He turned the flattened metal over, barely able to make out the remnants of a brand name he recognized.

"What is it?" Arielle asked.

"Spray paint."

"It looks like it was blown up."

"It was." A question gnawed at him: Why bother? "He's not subtle," Doug said. Taking her hand again, he continued toward the fence.

Five feet away, he rounded a corner, stopped and sucked in a breath.

Red oozed down the pickets, in stark contrast to virgin white.

Each letter was perfectly formed, as if the bloodlike streaks beneath had been intentionally drawn.

Tension gnawed in Doug's gut.

Semper fidelis.

The same words his ex-friend Samuel Pickins had screamed as he was led away, handcuffs blinking beneath fluorescent lighting. "*Semper fi*, and die!" he'd yelled.

Doug cursed. Pickins had promised revenge…sworn he'd live, if only for that.

Damn.

The visitor wasn't Arielle's assassin. Instead, Doug had blindly brought her into a trap laid for him.

In his desperation to save her, he'd committed a huge tactical error. Blindly, he had endangered Arielle's life… and history was replaying itself with sickening clarity.

He owed her an explanation, owed her so much.

"*Semper fidelis,*" Arielle said.

Her words shattered his thoughts.

"Isn't that the Marine Corps's motto?"

Doug dragged himself from the blur of memory, as well as from the debilitating cloud of guilt. He needed to be sharp—it was the only hope he had of saving her. He would no doubt play the mental game with himself later, but as for now, Pickins wouldn't win, because Doug wouldn't let him. Senses alert and honed, he said, "Always faithful." Then he straightened, glancing toward the house.

He smelled trouble, even above the stench of Pickins's chilling calling card, something, Doug realized belatedly, he should have recognized earlier.

Pickins's specialty was munitions. In their years together, Pickins had taught Doug a trick or two.

Obviously, Pickins still liked to mess around with explosives. And that was the thing that had gotten him in trouble in the first place.

"Are we supposed to be alone?"

The quiet urgency in Arielle's tone stirred his senses to greater awareness. Doug nodded.

"I...saw a shadow in the upstairs window."

Gunpowder cracked.

He yanked Arielle against the house, swearing.

The shot had come from the second story. Doug figured they had maybe half a minute to make a move before Pickins got down the stairs. *If* that was what Pickins intended to do.

And that was a huge uncertainty.

The only thing predictable about Pickins was his unpredictability.

Doug's mind raced through options, discarding several in the space of a few seconds. "I keep a car in the garage."

She nodded.

"You do drive, don't you?"

"Yes," she whispered brokenly. He saw her struggle for composure, gulping rapidly.

He dragged a set of keys from his front pocket. "This one will unlock the door to the garage." When she nodded woodenly, he added, "This button unlocks the vehicle and shuts off the alarm, and this is the ignition key. Garage-door opener is attached to the visor. Start the engine and wait for me."

"Are you going to cover me?"

"You watch too much TV," he said. "But yeah, that's the plan."

She swallowed deeply once more, then met his eyes. "Have you ever been scared, Doug?"

"Every day of my life."

She squeezed her eyes shut, and when she opened them again, he saw the glitter of determination that sparked azure eyes to deep blue.

"I'm ready," she said.

He barely submerged the impulse to kiss her.

Instead, he settled for a quick hug, offering that damnable reassurance again.

At a run, Doug moved away from the wall, kicking over a picnic table, a couple of chairs, then positioning himself behind a concrete planter.

He squeezed off a round, then another, smashing the glass of the special-ordered French doors. His insurance agent wasn't going to like this.

Nor was the housekeeper.

Pickins returned fire, a bullet whizzing from the guest bedroom window. Hell. Pickins had moved to another room.

Shards of glass rained down, large ones spiking into the earth around Doug.

After shooting off another round, he held his breath, knowing it wouldn't take Pickins long to return fire. As soon as he did, Doug let loose a volley of rounds.

In the deafening roar of the ensuing quiet, he heard the crank of a car engine. It sprang to life, settling into a well-maintained roar.

Sprinting toward the open back door, he felt the snap of a bullet blast past his ear. Pickins hadn't missed a beat, obviously anticipating their getaway plan.

If only the man had used that talent for good instead of evil.

Arielle was looking over her shoulder, eyes wide and mouth drawn in a tight grimace. When he reached the sport utility vehicle, Doug yanked open the rear door.

He met her gaze in the rearview mirror. Without looking, he dropped the ammo clip and slammed another into place. "Go!"

Rubber burned on pavement as she stomped on the accelerator. The vehicle jumped from the curb as the back window splintered, the safety glass barely holding together.

He was getting damn sick of being on the seeking end of a pistol. Gravel crunched and spewed as the rear end fishtailed. Doug had expected as much. The car wouldn't handle as well with a flat. The good news was, they were proving to be an unreliable target.

She took the corner too fast, slamming his head against the door frame.

"Sorry," she muttered, fighting with the steering wheel.

A couple of minutes later, there were no signs of pursuit. He knew better than to think it would be that easy, though. Pickins had never grasped the meaning of "You lose."

"Turn off here," he instructed Arielle.

"But there's no road," she protested.

"There's a barn we can hide behind," he said, hoping the farmer and the cows didn't mind.

She braked to a halt on the far side of the barn, out of view of the main road.

He climbed out. As he'd suspected, the tire and its rim were chewed up.

Figured. Those were brand-new tires, less than two hundred miles on them.

Arielle slowly emerged from behind the driver's seat. Her legs trembled, and he noticed her locking her knees. "You okay?" he asked.

"It's a little harrowing," she admitted, feathering her hair back from her face with shaky fingers.

He took in her pale features, and the way she wove her hands together in front of her. He'd seen the same kind of guts once before. In Shannen Mitchell. He'd never thought to see her equal, but in Arielle, he did.

"Can I do anything to help?"

He shook his head. She was something else, all right. She'd been shot at a number of times, pressed into service as a sailor and driver, dealt with the shock of having her parents targeted by her assassin. And she wanted to know if she could do anything to help.

Yeah, she was something else.

"You any good at being a lookout?"

"Does cafeteria duty count?"

"In spades." His respect for her nudged upward again. Even though she was shivering from fright, she kept an eye on their surroundings while Doug placed the jack beneath the frame.

Within a couple of minutes, he had the lug nuts broken loose and the wheels exchanged.

The drone of an engine clamored in Doug's ears.

"There's a car turning off the road," she stated, looking at him.

"Party's over."

"You're going to drive?" she asked, and he noted the quiet desperation in her tone.

Nodding, he tossed the shredded tire in the back, then climbed behind the wheel, adjusting the seat farther back. By the time he'd fired the engine, she'd secured her safety belt.

He stood on the accelerator, burning rubber off the new tire. At least he had four-wheel drive, while the other vehicle was a sedan. Made a dance through the farmer's field more interesting.

He hit a rut, jarring his spine. Stoically, she said nothing. When they hit pavement again, leaving behind a cloud of dust, he reached inside his jacket and pulled out a cellular phone. Handing it to Arielle, Doug recited a series of numbers and instructed, "Tell them to have the Masterson plane prepared for takeoff. I'll need a full crew."

Arielle's stomach pitched as Doug lowered his foot on the gas pedal and stared hard into the rearview mirror.

Since she met Doug, she'd discovered a reservoir of resolve she hadn't known existed. She wondered how deep it ran, though, and how long she'd be able to tap into it.

Her heart ached at the agony she'd heaped on her family.

Her body hurt from the pounding it had taken. And her emotions rolled, in constant upheaval.

Sleep had been scarce last night. She had tossed and turned, inhaling Doug's scent when she plumped the pillow, imagining that each whisper of wind was his footstep. How would she have reacted if he had walked into his cabin and claimed his bed?

She'd half feared he'd walk in...half hoped he would.

She looked at Doug, seeing that his gaze switched between the mirrors and the road ahead. As the speedometer needle edged higher and higher, Doug kept careful control of the vehicle.

As long as he was near, she held on to the illusion of safety. But when she was alone....

Her knees had knocked as she dashed to the car. With each awkward step, she offered a prayer that, in trusting Doug, she knew what she was doing. When he dashed toward the garage less than a minute after her, the blast of a bullet behind him, her fear had tripled.

But his cool veneer of calm hadn't faded, and they'd made another getaway. Thankfully.

She'd gotten herself, along with him, into this mess, and she had to deal with the repercussions. Dear heaven, though, she didn't know whether she possessed the resources to keep going. But she wanted so very desperately to live.

Doug took a corner too fast, sending her sideways. Arielle grabbed the door handle for support. The squeal of tires, the scent of rubber, renewed the fear she was struggling so hard to control.

Glancing her way, Doug offered a quick apology. Seconds later, he swore beneath his breath.

She glanced over her shoulder, seeing a blue car following in their tracks. Would there be no end to this nightmare? "He's still back there," Arielle whispered.

Doug nodded at her words. "He's starting to annoy me."

Waiting until the last possible second, Doug made another right turn. She grabbed for the dash as the shoulder belt sliced into the side of her neck.

They rounded a bend, rapidly approaching a set of railroad tracks. Arielle groaned out loud, seeing the lights blinking on the lowered gate that blocked their path to freedom. The echo of the warning bell vibrated through the interior of the car.

Doug slowed the vehicle, lining up behind the cars already stopped.

Desperately she looked toward Doug, knowing he had to have some sort of plan. He sat there, and only the sight of his drawn eyebrows indicated that he was remotely concerned.

Her heart hammered, in time with the intermittent ear-splitting blasts of the train's horn.

Doug glanced out the driver's window, and she followed suit. The locomotive blazed toward the crossing, thundering a promise of devastation to anyone who got in its way.

"Hold on," Doug said, jerking the steering wheel to the left and flooring the gas pedal.

No. He wouldn't. Couldn't possibly.

Horns honked and Arielle swallowed a scream when Doug crashed through the closed gates.

She looked out the window, her mind's eye filled with torn and twisted wreckage. Squeezing her eyes shut, she linked her hands in prayer.

Emotions derailed. Fear of dying consumed her, as it had since the day she spoke with the doctor. It wasn't death that disturbed her, as much as it was dying before she'd had the chance to...

Love. And be loved in return. To experience the passion she knew resided within her. Oh, God. She didn't want to die before she knew what it was like to be whole. To be one with another. To fill the lonely, empty void deep inside. She had so much to give.

The front end of the train clipped the rear end of the four-wheel drive. The scream she'd held back moments before broke free.

Metal crunched. Crazily they careened out of control. The vehicle spun, making her see stars, as Doug fought to yank their front end away from the stopped cars that lined the opposite side of the track.

The Blazer hit the gravel on the shoulder of the road, spewing dust and rocks, making traction difficult.

Doug steered into the spin, bringing them to a stop, faced, unbelievably, in the right direction. The engine coughed and died. Doug turned the key. "Next time maybe I'll rent a car."

She barely heard him over the crash of adrenaline and the squeal of metal on metal as the train's brakes ground and sparked.

Doug turned the ignition again and again. On the third attempt, the engine choked to life.

Turning in his seat, he looked at Arielle. When he spoke, his tone flowed mellow and easy, his smooth baritone soothing her as nothing else could.

"I keep asking if you're okay."

She pried apart her hands and tried for a quick smile. It died before she formed it. "I'm still alive."

"And we're going to keep you that way."

With her heart, she reached out to that promise and held it tight. The events she'd endured had been harrowing, yet she no longer fought the faceless enemy alone.

Arielle realized that if she was still alone, she wouldn't have survived this long. The killer had been closer than she ever imagined, following her, watching her. He knew her routine, where her parents lived....

She shivered anew, and Doug turned on the heater.

"Be back in a sec," he said, reaching for the door handle.

"Where—" When the word cracked, she tried again. "Where are you going?"

"To check for damage."

The minute or two that he was gone seemed like the longest of her life.

Finally, he took the wheel again. "It's drivable," he said, dropping the transmission into gear. "Train's almost stopped. And I don't want to give an explanation to the engineer."

They rode in silence for a few minutes. Finally, when she saw the sign for a small airport, she assumed their time together would soon end. Gathering her courage, she asked, "Doug...back there...at your house..."

Doug frowned into the mirror, his jaw clenched.

Thoughts spun through Arielle's mind. "You didn't seem shocked." She swallowed. "Did *Semper fidelis* mean something to you?"

Doug spared her a quick look. "Yeah."

"Then...?" She gripped the door handle until the blood flow to her hand seemed to be cut off.

Not looking at her, he stated with deadly calm, "You walked into a trap meant for me."

Her stomach knotted. She couldn't believe it. It wasn't possible. She was being hunted. And so was Doug? The possibilities crashed unbelievably into one another.

"I screwed up, Arielle. I had no business taking you to my home."

Despite the horror churning in her, Arielle heard the threads of guilt and self-disgust in his tone. And she had an insane urge to reach out to him, to offer comfort. The two things, she suspected, he wouldn't want from her.

Tension lay over the passenger compartment, as thick and palpable as a morning fog.

Flesh strained across Doug's knuckles where he gripped the steering wheel, a betrayal of raw emotion. She'd wondered, until now, whether he really experienced emotion, or whether he kept everything buried, tidy behind lock and key, like he'd said.

He was human, she realized, flesh and blood, like her. He felt pain, and that made them kindred spirits. Pain...a feeling she knew all too well.

"Pickins is his name," Doug said a minute or so later, after running a series of red lights. "Samuel Pickins. Expert in munitions. Destruction is his game. Recently released from prison, if my guess is right." Doug trailed off, then finished, "I'll have Brian pay him a little visit."

Arielle actually heard the anticipation that fired Doug's words. That brought as much of a chill to her as anything else had.

The man to whom she had entrusted her life didn't live the same way she did, didn't think the same way she did. He saw a life she'd never seriously imagined existed.

Within ten minutes, Doug entered the parking lot of a small airport and pulled into the first available spot.

Doug came around to her side, opening the door and offering her a hand.

Was this to be goodbye?

Oh, heaven above help her, she didn't think she possessed the power to turn and walk away from him.

Her pulse surged, and she wished she could read what he hid behind masked green eyes.

Doug released Arielle's hand, leaving her chilled...and afraid.

"Shall we?" Doug asked.

"Shall we what?"

"Go."

"Go?"

"To Colorado," he replied, as if it were the most natural assumption in the world. "You know, skiing, mountains."

Arielle had never been west of the Eastern Seaboard.

"Let me guess. You don't know if you're much of a flier."

"I've never—"

"Flown," he finished for her. "Well, Miss Hale, you're about to have the ride of your life."

Before she could form a response, he added, "Our chariot awaits."

"You're going with me?" she asked, drinking in and holding a breath full of hope.

Doug's response seemed a long time in coming. Afternoon sunshine beat down on them, warming her almost as much as what she dared to dream.

"Wouldn't miss your first flight."

She drew her lower lip between her teeth, her mind racing through what he'd just said. Surely she couldn't have misinterpreted, but just as surely he couldn't be serious. Since she met him, he'd been determined to get rid of her, every action moving toward that goal. "But you said you were burned-out, that you need a vacation, that Brian—"

"You wanted me, you've got me. You're my responsibility. And I won't fail you."

"But…"

"Anyone ever tell you that you talk too much?"

"No," she whispered.

He reached for her, and common sense warned her to resist. She'd been in his arms before, she knew exactly how much she responded to him. Inherently she recognized the danger to herself, to her sanity, and most of all, to her heart.

"Then allow me to be the first," he said, his voice huskier than usual. Gently he cupped her shoulders in the curve of his hands. "Arielle, you talk too much."

His eyes had darkened to a color she was becoming familiar with…that of purposeful intent.

He eased her toward him, folding his arms around her, offering the comfort she so desperately craved.

She'd been self-reliant through the past years, never having anyone to turn to, to lean on. She'd been the person others relied on. Her parents had called her their pillar of strength. But how difficult that had been. At times she didn't have the resources to hold herself up, let alone prop up others.

Being near him, close enough to hear the thumping of his heart, sent skitters through her. He was offering himself, his comfort. The saints save her, but she couldn't resist.

"I'm going to kiss you," he stated.

Her opportunity to protest passed without her speaking. She wanted this, wanted…him.

Doug lowered his head, and she tilted hers back, meeting him. His kiss was insistent, not soft and reassuring, but hard and demanding, like the man himself.

He tasted of power, of resolve. He tasted of man.

The pureness of Doug's masculinity coaxed a response and ignited passion she'd never imagined.

His tongue sought hers, demanding that she meet him in a dance. This wasn't a conquest, it was a joining of two people, each a mirror reflection of the other.

Her knees weakened and her blood thinned. A pulse of primeval power surged through her, and she wanted more, wanted something she didn't dare name.

A plane buzzed overhead, seeming to scatter the building energy. Slowly Doug released her and moved half a step back. His eyes were even darker than before, lines of deep teal spiking across his irises.

Where he'd touched, Arielle's lips felt warm and swollen.

But most of all, her soul felt comfort and peace…two things she'd thought she would never again feel.

When Doug spoke, his words sounded as if they'd been dragged across broken glass. "Consider me hired. You couldn't get rid of me now if you wanted. You're stuck. For better or worse."

Chapter 6

Doug dragged himself from the stupor of contemplation. He became aware, again, of the hum of the private jet's engines, the sensation of zipping through the sky, things he'd blocked from his mind.

He replaced the telephone and considered the few things Brian had told him. No news on Arielle's assassin. Her parents hadn't received any more presents, gift wrapped or otherwise. The bad news was that they were becoming more and more anxious to talk to Arielle.

Within the next twenty-four hours, he might have to authorize Shannen to share information with them. But he'd stall as long as possible. Compromised investigations gave him indigestion.

Brian had also learned that Pickins had been released from prison last month. The dirtbag hadn't been seen or heard from since prison bars clanged shut behind him, leaving him a free man to victimize the world.

There had been an explosion at a paint store in Boston, and a couple of dozen cans of paint and turpentine had been stolen. Not surprisingly, there hadn't been a single witness, not even the night watchman.

Every instinct screamed the explosion had been Pickins's work.

Now to find the slippery bastard.

But how the hell had Pickins known Doug was heading home? It'd been three months since he spent a weekend on the coast. His number didn't appear in any listing, and the house was registered in another name. He occasionally needed a safe haven. Until now, he'd believed he had it.

Doug despised puzzles. And now he had two of them.

Drumming his fingers on the table, he looked at the woman sleeping next to him.

She slept while guilt slithered around his insides, reminding him of the past. He hadn't saved Kerry. And he'd very nearly lost Arielle. His jaw clenched. Nearly lost her. Nearly. Now they were bound together, secured by his determination.

Arielle shifted, and he looked at her. She was curled up on the seat, feet tucked beneath her. Strands of long hair that had escaped their confines now feathered across the travel pillow, and wavy wisps of blond spilled over her forehead. A gray blanket snuggled across her shoulders, bundling her against the chill.

Her lips had parted slightly, reminding him of the way she'd tipped back her head, offering the sweetness of her kiss. He shouldn't have done it. Doug had made it a policy never to mix business with pleasure. With Arielle, though, it seemed the rule had been written on the wind.

He could no more resist her than he could sail against the tide.

The faint smudges beneath her closed blue eyes riveted his attention. She'd valiantly fought exhaustion, through their first landing and halfway through the second leg of the journey.

But the lulling motion had finally proved too much, and

she'd lost the battle. Now, long lashes fanned out, casting a shadow and making him ache to take away the pain that caused her hurt.

A wave of something another man might label compassion crested over him.

It wasn't compassion, though, not for her, not for anyone. Compassion was an emotion he never experienced. Kerry's death—especially his part in it—had destroyed his ability to feel, let alone sympathize.

At the airport, Arielle's determination to handle any circumstance had been reflected in the depths of her eyes. She'd stood before him, nonjudgmental, her face pale, her lower lip drawn between her teeth to hide the trembling. If he said he was walking away, she would have swallowed bravely.

And that was what had done him in.

Yeah, he'd hit the wall of burnout, but it had crumbled, brick by brick, beneath the assault of her strength.

In the afternoon sunshine, her eyes had communicated hope, trust and belief—the three things Doug needed to make himself whole again.

They'd already shared a lot, and he was learning to read her moods. For a reason he refused to consider, her safety mattered to him. He had that at stake.

Yarrow didn't.

Arielle had hesitantly walked into Doug's office, believing he'd offer her protection. And she'd been caught in the cross fire of an old friend wanting to serve revenge hot and fast. That was how Doug liked his cars and women, but he preferred revenge cold and calculated.

And that was exactly how he intended to dish it up.

She shouldn't have been there with him. Instead, she should have been standing at the head of a class, surrounded by students anxious to learn.

Doug finally met honesty head-on. It was guilt. A flash

of the past, a prayer that it wouldn't happen again. Yeah, guilt, burning a hole in his gut.

He'd keep her safe, because he had no other choice.

Failure wasn't part of this bargain.

A pocket of turbulence rocked the plane. He curled his hand around the cup of coffee and rescued it. He wasn't spilling it because a few clouds had a disagreement. He'd been through enough in the past twenty-four hours without sacrificing caffeine to the sky gods.

Arielle stirred, blinking several times before focusing on him. She offered a soft, hesitant smile, as if a constant threat were hovering. In the instant between sleep and consciousness, she appeared vulnerable and delicate. Yet she'd proved that was anything but the truth.

He'd worked with countless men, first in the military, then in covert operations for the government, finally in private practice. But few of them had possessed the spine of steel of his companion.

Underneath it, though, she remained all woman, caring and honest. A combination to make him glad to be a man.

She moved with effortless grace, placing her feet on the carpet and pushing herself upright. "Where are we?"

"The sky."

She frowned, and he relented, saying, "Somewhere over Kansas."

"I don't feel like Dorothy."

"And you don't look like Toto."

"Thanks," she said, swiping a hand across her eyes. "I think."

"Of course, with that hair—"

"If you say anything about the Wicked Witch...."

"Wouldn't dream of it," he said. "The Wicked Witch never had hair like yours."

She colored, and it chased away paleness and left behind a heightened stain of blush. If he'd ever seen a woman more beautiful, more desirable, Doug didn't remember the occasion.

The flight attendant appeared at their side. "Can I get you anything?"

Doug ordered coffee for himself and Arielle. "Make the lady's with a sugar." When the woman moved away, he caught Arielle's look. "I'm trained to be observant."

"About coffee?"

"Especially coffee. Habits, tastes, they're all clues."

In less than a minute, they had coffee and privacy. Arielle turned to stare out the small window. Her sigh wound a ribbon around his heart, a ribbon he'd have given nearly anything to untie.

"I take it back," she said. "I do feel like Dorothy, and everything seems unreal." Slowly she turned to face him once more.

Doug raised his brow, waiting for her to continue. Ghosts haunted her eyes again, as he'd known they would.

"How long will we be in Colorado?" Her voice dropped. "And how long until I can call my mom and dad to let them know I'm okay?"

Self-recrimination laced her tone, stirred in until it was part of the whole, much like the sugar in her coffee. He recognized the tone, had heard it before, emerging from his own throat.

And from the weight of experience, he knew only time healed the guilt. If it ever happened. "You tell me, Arielle," he said. "I'm not an ogre. Granting the fact we both want the same things, your safety and the safety of your parents, what's the best course of action?

"Earlier, you were psychoanalyzing me," he continued. "Give me your take on what we're dealing with."

"But—"

"Take a shot." God knew, Doug had been the recipient of enough of those today. She might as well get in a couple, too. And in the interim, she might find some inner peace. If she did, he hoped she'd share.

She sipped from her coffee cup, then swirled the porcelain between her hands, creating a miniwhirlpool. The same kind he'd been sucked into.

Arielle's assumptions about him this morning hadn't been far off the mark, much as he hated to admit it. She'd proved perceptive and intelligent. He actually found himself waiting for her answer.

"I paid a man for a hit," she began.

"Go on."

She looked at him. "You're serious about this."

"Serious as the metal that damned near deprived me of hair."

"He tried to kill me outside your office, then again in the alleyway."

As she spoke, her voice left behind the dullness of desperation.

"He should have been satisfied with that."

"Should," he said, prompting her.

"But he wasn't. He tracked down my parents—" She tripped over the last word, then lifted the cup to her lips with an unsteady hand.

Then, obviously having taken a drink of courage, she added, "He wants me dead, Doug."

He didn't respond. There was no need.

"It's like he has something personal to gain, he takes his job seriously."

"Assassins usually do."

She shivered.

"The thrill of the hunt, the glory of the kill."

When her coffee sloshed over the rim, he reached for a napkin, wishing he could take back the words. "Sorry."

"Don't apologize," she said, looking at him. "I didn't want it sugarcoated."

Good thing. When it came to reality, he was a diabetic.

"Does money talk louder than the thrill?"

Suddenly his sweet tooth had a craving. Without missing a beat, he lied to her. "Yeah," he said. Experience had taught him that often the only way to get rid of an assassin was to send him on a short trip with a one-way ticket, six feet beneath the ground.

Better the hired gun than Arielle.

"What are we going to do?"

We. A single syllable, a powerful word. They were a team; she'd cooperate. Mission accomplished.

So why did the victory echo with hollowness?

"I've had Brian call in some favors. We've got your parents' home under surveillance. They're being shadowed when they leave the premises. Only Brian's budget is tighter."

"Thank you," she whispered.

Her gratitude filled the space between them. He took it in, holding it in his soul, letting it illuminate the darkness residing there.

"I can't contact them," she said brokenly.

"It's your call," he said, laying the facts on the table. In the beginning, he'd underestimated her. Never again. "You know the risks. If they know where you are, they may be in danger. Your assassin is making up the rules as he goes along. He's capable of anything."

He reached into the seatback in front of him and withdrew his cellular phone, placing it on her tray table. "Your call," he repeated.

She stared at the phone for a long time, tears balancing at the corner of her eyes. "Put it away."

Tilting her chin, she turned away from him—from temptation, he imagined. For long minutes, she looked out the window. How easily he could picture the demons tormenting her.

And guilt would be the worst. He was aware how insidiously it crept up on you, sucking you into an unwinnable hand of what-ifs.

He left her alone with her struggle, knowing it was one of the more difficult tasks he'd ever performed. He'd been raised to be the protector. And when he failed at that…he failed as a man.

Night had long since swallowed the sun when Arielle turned to him, dry-eyed and resolved.

"We have to do whatever it takes."

He nodded. "I owe you an apology for leading you straight into a trap."

She shook her head. "I thought the guy was after me. We both thought I was the target. You owe me nothing, especially an apology."

"Brian will get him. As well as your assassin."

She fought for a brave smile.

And when she didn't say anything else for a few minutes, he didn't rush to fill the silence. She was forgiving of him. More so than he was. She was a trouper, and he admired that.

"You said we're going to Colorado…."

She trailed off when the pilot's disembodied voice interrupted, announcing possible turbulence as the plane flew over the Rockies. "What's in Colorado?"

"Rhone's safe house."

She sighed. "And how long will we be there?"

"Long enough to master the finer points of cribbage."

"Cribbage?"

"TV gets old."

"You've been there before."

"A couple of times." He only hoped this situation worked out as well as Rhone and Shannen's. And anyway, Doug was an ace at cards. He should be, after his years of practice.

"And when we're there, do we just sit and wait?"

He shook his head. "We formulate a plan of action, go

over every event, every detail of the man you contacted. We outplan him. We outsmart him.''

''Tell me what to do,'' she said.

He grinned. ''That's my girl.''

''Anyone ever tell you you're a chauvinist?''

''No.''

Her eyes had narrowed. ''I'm telling you now, Mr. Masterson. You're a sexist.''

''Do I talk too much?''

She nodded.

''So how are you going to shut me up?''

In that instant, the air rushed from Arielle's lungs.

Their bantering had replayed earlier words, but those had ended in a kiss. Self-protectively, she wrapped her hands together. She didn't dare kiss him again, didn't dare open herself to the emotions that being in his arms caused. She liked it, wanted to stay there.

But she knew better.

Doug Masterson wasn't a man who easily fell into relationships, according to Shannen. And neither did Arielle. She'd never tried to hide the fact that she wanted a home, children, and a loving husband.

Doug definitely didn't fit that profile.

He was a loner, intended to sail to the Bahamas alone and remain there indefinitely. She couldn't deny her attraction to him, but that was where it started and ended.

If—when—they emerged from this waking nightmare, she would probably never see him again.

''Arielle?''

When he looked at her like that, with something she didn't want to name smoldering in sea green depths, her objections eased down her insides, settling into a warm pool of wishes.

''Doug, I...we...'' She licked her dry lips.

He waited and waited.

''I've never... That is, I haven't...''

Showing mercy, he quietly asked, "Never taken the initiative?"

Her lips dried to parchment.

"It's easy," he encouraged. "First you lean closer, then you put your arm around my neck."

She shouldn't. She wouldn't. She leaned closer.

Doug did the same. And then she put her arm around his neck.

Pushing away insanity, she instead clung to him, this time with a different sort of desperation.

Arielle inhaled the stamp of his cologne, subtle strands blended with his own aura to create a mixture that seeped into her consciousness. It was a scent she knew she wouldn't ever forget.

"Then you brush your lips against mine."

Her heart tapped a timed tattoo.

Their gazes met, and she drank encouragement from his eyes. When she feathered her lips across his, he whispered her name. Feminine triumph surged through her, leaving a wake of wanting.

She pulled back a little, looking at him. His eyes had narrowed, a furrow winking between his brows. A pulse ticked in his temple. If she was drowning in sensual awareness, she hoped she would bring him down with her.

"After that, you deepen the kiss, asking for what you want."

Instead, daringly, she brushed across his lips a second time.

"Arielle, has anyone ever told you that you're a tease?"

She licked her lower lip, imagining the taste of him there. "I suppose you're going to."

"You're a tease."

"And you talk too much," she said, leaning into him.

"Then shut me up."

This time, when their lips met, it wasn't a glancing touch.

Instead, it was driven by the simmering awareness bubbling inside her.

She trailed her hands through his hair, finding the rich texture and letting the strands seep through her fingers. Her nerve endings ignited, fanning the flame.

He opened his mouth, inviting her inside. He hadn't taken over, but instead he offered quiet confidence. At his urging, she reached out with her tongue, tentatively tasting and touching.

He groaned.

The raw sound sent a spike of pleasure through her. She'd made him react, and that knowledge filled her with awe.

She felt him reach around her, placing his palms against her back. He pulled her closer and closer, until his arms enveloped her and her breasts pressed against his chest. Her nipples beaded in response, making her react in a way she'd never before experienced.

She blamed the danger that dogged their every step, the same danger Doug seemed to thrive on.

Until recently, she'd never been reckless.

And she only seemed to be compounding this streak that she hadn't known she possessed.

She sought comfort from him, and heaven help her, she also asked for a taste, just a taste, of excitement. He gave everything she wanted, responding to her kiss, parrying his tongue with hers.

Pulling him closer, she allowed the kiss to deepen, spinning her thoughts crazily out of control.

Whatever was wrong with her, she didn't want to resist it. Instead, she wanted to savor and enjoy, heady in the knowledge that she was capable of providing him with the pleasure he'd given her.

The plane bounced, jolting her to her senses.

Reality rushed back, and she ended the kiss.

She released her hold, unfurling her fingers and feeling a lingering tingle.

Doug drew away.

Warmth had surged into her lips, sensitizing them. She missed having him against her, missed the solidness of his body, missed the musky scent he wore.

What had she been thinking? Worse, what had she been doing?

Her boldness shocked her, making her aware of a part of her nature that she hadn't imagined existed. It was as if, with a few carefully chosen words, Doug had peeled back the protective coating within which her heart lay encased. The knowledge excited her, and simultaneously filled her with fear.

Was she learning how to live, only to have her life ended?

A cold chill crept over her, and she reached for the blanket, dragging it around her shoulders. Strange how the only time she felt warm was when Doug's arms wrapped her in security. Desperate for something to do, she grasped her cup and lifted the lukewarm remnants to her lips. Cool dashed against heat—exactly the way she felt inside.

Doug's hand curled around hers before she set the coffee down.

He looked at her with enigmatic eyes, a hint of teasing blending with the remnants of passion.

She started to speak, only the words wouldn't emerge. What could possibly be said to a man who unlocked secrets she didn't know she kept? "Thanks?" "Go away?" "Please don't leave?"

Confusion panicked her. Her life, the physical, as well as the emotional, twisted into tortured turmoil. And she didn't know how, or if, it would end.

"You can shut me up anytime," Doug said.

She looked at him, and her mouth dried up. His words were light, but their meaning rang with reality.

The thing that terrified her the most was that part of her actually wanted to take him up on the invitation.

Chapter 7

"Hi, honey, I'm home," Doug said, groping for the light switch. When several hundred watts flooded the living room, he held open the door for Arielle.

"Is there someone already here?" she asked.

"Just us. But everyone says that when they walk through the front door, don't they?"

Shaking her head, she moved past him, her elbow brushing his arm. Her touch was light and innocent, probably accidental, but that didn't make his purely male response any less potent. It wouldn't take much to reignite the spark that had been flickering ever since she entered his office.

Kissing her had been wonderful. Kissing her had been a mistake. Having her kiss him had nearly been a fatal error. One he shouldn't repeat.

She was an assignment, he was her protector.

Even if it took a hammer blow to his skull, he needed to remember that. And if he didn't, the inevitable nightmares would remind him.

"Rhone and Shannen have a lovely home," Arielle commented.

He checked to make sure the door latched securely, then turned the dead bolt and slid home the security chain. For good measure, he turned the regular lock, too. After that, he set the alarm.

She stood with her back to the cold hearth, arms wrapped across her middle, as if to ward off the Colorado chill. He'd have bet dollars to dinghies it didn't feel like this in the Bahamas.

"The house is ours for as long we need it," he said. "Has all the comforts, coffeepot, running water, forced air, fireplace."

"Big-screen TV?" she teased.

"Yep. With a VCR. Television reception isn't great, so there's a library of movies. All the necessities," he added. "Including a cribbage board."

She gave him the ghost of a smile, and it was then that he noticed the toll events had taken on her. Her complexion was stark, escaped hair drooped down her forehead, and his clothes hung from her, too big and bulky, making her seem smaller than she really was. Her eyes were wide and tired. Her purse hung from her shoulder, and all her worldly possessions were wrapped in leather, and not a single complaint.

That familiar clawing of failure crept up on him again. He meant to keep her safe as a babe in arms, but so far he'd done a miserable job of it.

Moving toward the fireplace—and her—he said, "Shannen's about your size. You can borrow some of her clothes until I take you shopping."

For the first time that day, interest sparked in her eyes, bringing her a trace of animation and making him wonder what she was truly like. Did she laugh often? Did she tease? And when she made love, did she close her eyes? Or did she leave them open, allowing her expression to be read?

"Shopping?" she asked.

Doug groaned—the age-old sound of masculine suffering. Unfortunately, there weren't any other males around to provide sympathy. The woman needed to shop, and he was the designated driver.

At least he could hope she approached shopping with the same single-minded determination she did everything else. They'd be in and out of the stores in a snap.

"I heard that," she said, placing her purse on the coffee table.

"What?"

"That heavy sigh. Actually, it sounded more like a groan."

"I enjoy shopping, even for groceries, which we're in desperate need of," he said defensively. "At least I enjoy it as much as the next man."

"But you'd rather have a root canal."

"Without anesthesia."

Her smile died—rather tiredly, he imagined—before it fully formed.

Their ride from the small airport had taken more than an hour, over lumpy roads and around hairpin curves. She'd grabbed hold of the dashboard for stability several times but, stoically, hadn't uttered a single cross word.

Unfortunately, the same couldn't be said about him. More than once, he'd cursed with a flair of jungle color. When he glanced at her apologetically, she'd reminded him that she was a teacher versed in playground duty.

There were many facets to the woman he'd agreed to guard. He had no business wanting to expose each and every aspect of her to the light of day.

Experience had taught him that mixing business and pleasure made combustible matter. When it exploded in his face, the shrapnel had zeroed in, like a radar-guided missile, to pierce his heart.

Doug didn't like bandages, so he'd decided to avoid being hurt. Simple as that.

"Why don't you sit down?" he said. "I'll light a fire and get you something to drink."

She didn't wait for a second invitation.

"I'll be back in a few minutes."

He hazarded a glance over his shoulder to see that she'd kicked off her shoes and pulled her legs beneath her. Slowly she closed her eyes.

Doug dragged his gaze away, but had less success in tearing his thoughts away from temptation. The woman, and her strength, were sexy as sin.

And he was a sinner.

There were cures for that, his grandmother had always told him. Doug, though, hadn't been much interested in being cured.

Moving from room to room, he made certain nothing looked out of place. He checked all the locks and window seals. The two-story log home was as tight as Fort Knox, but when it came to safety, that wasn't good enough.

No place was impenetrable.

He'd pulled off Rhone's rescue in Colombia because others made that very same, faulty assumption. A single slip, that's all it took. It could work for you. Just as easily, it could destroy you.

Doug went upstairs, opening every door, even the one to the linen closet. He inventoried the location of each piece of furniture, the placement of knickknacks, the angles of pictures. And he reached a conclusion he knew Arielle wouldn't like: They would be sharing the master bedroom.

None of the rooms connected with one another, and he refused to let her out of his sight. In the master bedroom, she wouldn't be more than a half-dozen steps away, even if she needed to use the rest room.

He'd tell her later, when the time was right. As he closed the door, he admitted the truth to himself. He'd tell her when she was too damn tired to object and couldn't form a coherent argument. He'd tuck her in, climb beneath the covers on the other side of the bed, then sleep like a baby. By tomorrow, their sleeping arrangements wouldn't be a concern.

Just to be sure, he repeated the assertion to himself.

Downstairs, he punched in the code to disarm the entrance to Rhone's office. Doug pushed open the door, allowing it to click behind him.

A personal computer sat on a desk, protected by a plastic dustcover. A shortwave radio dominated one corner, and two phones, each on a different line, one secure, one not, sat within arm's reach on the desk. The fax machine had already spit out a piece of paper, and he reached for it. From Rhone. No surprise there.

Shannen had been forced to tell Arielle's parents a part of the story. Rhone recommended that Doug have Arielle call her parents at Rhone's Washington, D.C., home. Much as Doug hated to take any chances, he realized his ex-partner had a good point. Fear obliterated reason. Faxing back a response, he disarmed the control panel, left the office and secured it behind him.

Arielle was still dozing on the couch, looking innocent and trustful in sleep. Had he ever been trustful? Even as a child? He doubted it. His home had been built on a lot of things. Love, respect and trust weren't among them.

Crouching in front of the fireplace, he reached for several newspapers, saving the comic strips for later. He wanted the last laugh for himself. He wadded the business section. Then he saw the travel insert, featuring a cruise to the equator. With great enthusiasm, he twisted the pages into a spiral. Then he torched the four-color photo of a South Seas sunrise.

After making sure the flames were licking at the pine logs, he crossed into the kitchen and brewed a pot of coffee. As the carafe filled, he looked around. It had been a while since he was here. Rhone made the house available to his friends. Doug had used it a couple of times, once for an impromptu vacation.

His first trip had been made to help Rhone and Shannen find their child. That had ended well. The second time, his enforced vacation had been taunted by visions and flashbacks, and he'd left Colorado only marginally better than he found it.

When he carried the cups, spoons and sugar into the living room, Arielle blinked.

"You don't have to wake up."

She yawned, stretching as he juggled with putting the cups on the table.

"I shouldn't let you do all the work," she said, pushing herself upright.

"You make an excellent point."

"But I guess I'll let you wait on me. If you're ever looking for a new job, we could use you in the teachers' lounge."

"They drink a lot of coffee, huh?"

"The entire staff combined doesn't drink as much as you."

"Caffeine's one of the basic food groups," he protested.

"Along with chocolate," she agreed, her voice rubbed raw by the lack of sleep and abundance of stress.

She stirred sugar into her coffee, the spoon still turning endless circles long after the crystals had dissolved. Doug took a seat in an armchair across from her, watching and waiting.

Silence slipped over the night, leaving behind a wake of uncertainty. The scent of pine filled the air. The wood bubbled and crackled, and he knew damn well he was postponing the inevitable.

"Rhone and I have arranged for you to call your parents tomorrow."

Her spoon abruptly stopped. She smiled as if he'd given

her the world, and for that moment, he felt as though he had.

"But how, when?"

"Rhone has a secure line here, and another at his home in D.C. Shannen will take your parents there."

Slowly, like the sinking of the sun into an endless sea, her expression changed, the smile fading. "That's a long way."

"Not when Rhone's the pilot."

"He'll fly them to D.C.?"

"I think he's anxious to play with his new toy. You know what they say about men and boys."

She didn't even attempt a smile. Instead, she held on to the cup as if it represented a lifeline to sanity. "They have to be scared witless."

"But you'll have the chance to change all that."

Peeling her fingers, one by one, from the porcelain, she slid the untouched coffee onto the table and drew her legs onto the couch. With effortless movements, she rested her chin on her knees.

It seemed she never experienced sorrow for herself. Instead, she saved it for others.

"I keep hoping I'll wake up and this will have all been a bad dream," she whispered.

Arielle wasn't looking at him. He suspected she wasn't talking to him, either.

"Do you ever wish that?" she asked him.

"Yeah, Arielle." He took a long sip from his coffee. "I do."

"You needed that trip to the Bahamas."

"Nah," he lied. "It'll be there next week." Unless a hurricane wiped it out. That'd be his luck.

"I should have understood."

She looked at him then, and the depth of emotion in her eyes walloped him in the gut.

"I should have waited for Brian, like you said."

Unable to sit there, seeing her pain, Doug shoved his cup onto the table, not caring that coffee sloshed over the rim. Standing, he crossed to her.

"I'm a big boy, Arielle," he said, capturing her shoulders in his hands. Instantly he gentled his touch. "I make my own choices." He feathered wayward bangs away from her forehead, and she tipped back her head to meet his gaze. "I'm here with you because I want to be. Don't mistake that."

"But—"

"Arielle, you're talking too much."

She closed her mouth.

Doug wasn't certain he could take tasting her again. She incited a primal need he'd thought conquered. And the force of his own weakness stunned him.

Before he could change his mind, Doug released her. Pivoting, he crossed to the fireplace, too restless to sit. Inside, hunger churned, a hunger he didn't dare assuage.

She might not like the idea of sleeping with him tonight, but the idea of having her so near terrified him. He'd never felt such a consuming need before. And, without a doubt, Arielle Hale was the worst person for him to be attracted to.

Tension, in time with the staccato of his fingers drumming on the mantel, settled over the room.

"We'll get through this, won't we?"

"I promise," he said. And this time he meant it. Now it was personal. He had something to prove.

"There's something I've been meaning to ask you."

"Shoot." He winced at the image. He'd been the target of one too many shots already today.

She looked at him through her long lashes. "Who's the man that wants you dead?"

Her directness socked him in the solar plexus. He'd known her questions were coming, and he knew he owed her answers. But to be faced with them so bluntly threw him off balance...the way he'd been since lunchtime yesterday.

He ceased the drumming and returned her directness. "Samuel Pickins," he said, the name burning on its way out, just like the ulcer he was sure he was developing. "He was in my unit in the Marines."

"Were you friends?"

"Yeah. Found out I didn't know the meaning of the word."

"You do now."

Thanks to Rhone and Brian, he did.

"What happened?" she asked.

He wanted to leave the past buried beneath the memories that suffocated it. But she'd been in the line of fire today...because of him. Made them about even, an eye for an eye, a bullet for a bullet.

But he'd asked her to bare her soul last night, demanded honesty of her. He could give no less himself. "As you've already learned, he's an expert in munitions. Had a lot of talent, could blow up damn near anything. One night he was playing with explosives, experimenting..." The deafening roar slammed through the space of two decades and pierced his eardrums. The sights, the tortured screams.

He became aware of Arielle softly saying his name, her voice sliding hypnotically through his senses with the support he needed to drag himself back through layers of the years.

Doug blinked. Sometimes he managed to forget the details of the horror that still lingered. Since then, he'd survived untold hell. And he'd survived because nothing, nothing, had ever been worse than watching the deaths of men he was responsible for.

"Two men, two *good* men, died," he said hollowly.

Unerringly she found the heart of the matter. "And you didn't cover for him?"

"I testified against him." Doug swallowed. "Said it

wasn't an accident.'' He'd had no choice. His code of justice had demanded he do the right thing, no matter the pressure he received not to sell out a buddy.

And one thing was certain—he'd do it all over again. The quest for justice still drove him. In a matter of moments, he'd lost some of his men. He still paid the bill some nights, with sleeplessness and nightmares.

Arielle had moved without him being aware of it. Reality returned with the feel of her hand closing around his wrist.

The unselfish touch of human warmth surged through him, bringing a flame flickering to life where he'd believed not even ashes still smoldered. Her own ache came from deep inside, and she carried the scars in her eyes. And yet she reached out to offer comfort and support.

She amazed him.

And if he hadn't kissed her before, he knew, he would have succumbed to the urge in that instant.

''He wants revenge?'' she asked.

''For the years he lost, the career I ended, and for what he probably sees as a betrayal of loyalty. *Semper fi.* Always faithful.''

''You were loyal to the right cause.''

''Not everyone sees it that way.''

''But you do. And that's all that's important, Doug.''

Their honesty bred an intimacy unlike anything he had experienced before.

''It's not always easy to do the right thing.''

''No,'' he agreed. ''It's not.''

''But it's always the right thing to do.''

Retreating from the intimacy, like the coward he tried not to be, he did what any sane male would do. He changed the subject. ''Earlier you were in the wrong place at the wrong time.''

''I usually am,'' Arielle admitted. ''In the middle of spitball wars, struggles between parents and administrators, budgets and taxes. I don't look for trouble. It finds me.''

He believed that.

As if aware of the tenderness with which she still held him, she removed her hand, dropping it to her side. With its absence, Doug noticed a chill in the air. Only a moment ago, he'd thought it was warm.

"I should have been able to foresee something like this."

"Just like I should have been able to prevent my brother's accident."

"It's not the same thing. You weren't there when your brother was injured."

"Is that why you're hiding from the world?"

A second slingshot to his solar plexus. The woman showed no mercy. She did it so well, hitting his weakest spot when he was the most vulnerable. What was it about her? His eyes narrowed. "Is this that shrink thing again?"

"No." She shook her head. "It's not that at all."

"I'm not running, Arielle, and I'm sure as hell not hiding." His words emerged with the sharpened edges of a Chinese throwing star.

"I'm not trying to make you into a case study."

"Good thing. I don't make an interesting study."

"I wouldn't necessarily agree with that."

It was back. That unwelcome flare of something that made him open up, tell things he had no business repeating. Too bad for her that she wasn't a mind doc. She'd make a good one. He'd even hand out business cards for her. God knew there were enough people who could benefit from her services. Trouble was, they were all his friends. Absently he wondered what that said about him.

"If you ever want to talk…"

"I don't." He could think of a dozen ways to pass the time with her. Talking didn't make the list.

Seeming to accept his curt dismissal, Arielle crossed back to the couch. He stoked the gasping fire, and when he returned to his chair, he caught Arielle in a yawn. Which brought him to another problem: their sleeping arrangements.

"The master bedroom's at the top of the stairs," he said.

"Is that where I'll be sleeping?"

He nodded. "It connects to a bathroom, and has a fireplace."

"Thanks." She stood and gathered their cups.

He figured he could tell her now or wait till she got back. Rationalizing that it'd be best if she didn't drop the dishes, he waited.

Then wished he hadn't.

When she returned to the living room, the rubber band drooped from her index finger, leaving her hair to float around her face in silky disarray. Shadows of exhaustion darkened her eyes, and she'd removed her shoes.

"Good night," she said. "I appreciate everything you've done for me."

But he'd done those things with great reluctance, he realized.

She turned and started up the stairs, her hand cupped around the banister.

"Arielle."

Stopping, she glanced over her shoulder.

"There's something you need to know."

He saw the breath she sucked in. Her eyes opened wide, as if fear once again replaced tiredness.

"Your bedroom...."

"Yes?"

"That's where I'll be sleeping, too."

Her mouth opened a fraction of an inch. "You can't be serious."

"You're paying me to be your protector."

"I'm not paying you to sleep with me."

His fist clenched at his side. "You've got to trust me on this."

"How many bedrooms does this house have?"

He knew he was being led into a trap. "Four."

"Then I'll take one of those."

He waited until she reached the top of the stairs. "If Pickins or your assassin comes gunning, do you want me near you?"

"That's unfair," she said.

"So's life." Even from a distance, he saw the slight tremor in her body. She'd reacted to him earlier, opening her mouth and responding to his kiss. She'd led the dance of initiation, and he suspected she didn't know what to do with the taste of her own sensual nature.

But none of that changed the facts. And the fact was, she was living with a death sentence poised like a guillotine. He just hoped she believed him to be less of a threat than her assassin. "Let me do my job, Arielle."

She sighed. "Will you sleep on the floor?"

"Bad back."

"Shannen told me you'd slept in the jungle."

"That's where I got the bad back."

"Do you know the meaning of defeat?"

"Yeah." Across the expanse of night, their eyes met, and he read weariness in her gaze. "But only when I claim it from others."

"You'll argue until you win."

He nodded.

"Uncle," she whispered, her shoulders dropping a fraction of an inch.

"I'll be up in ten minutes."

Her steps dragging, she turned and went into the bedroom, closing the door behind her.

He'd wanted to win. So why did the victory lack satisfaction?

Doug switched off the coffeepot and loaded their cups into the dishwasher, aware of her motions above him. He'd guarded plenty of people before, so why did this seem different? He was no stranger to the intimacy of isolation. Arielle's undressing shouldn't bother him.

But it did.

He was losing the edge. There'd been a reason he planned a one-way voyage from shadows to sunshine. He'd been a fool to let emotion stand in the way.

And if he didn't put it aside now, he'd be an even bigger fool.

Grabbing a flashlight from the pantry, he headed outside. Crisp Colorado air assaulted him, cleared his senses. Tuning in to the sounds of night and looking for signs of human predators cleared his mind.

Ten minutes later, confident that they hadn't had any two-legged visitors, he returned to the house. Inside, he locked the door, set the alarm and started up the stairs.

He knocked on the door. When he heard no sounds, he entered the room. The dim glow from the hall light cast her in a dark silhouette. Her chest rose and fell, but the uneven pattern meant she was feigning sleep.

Suited him fine. One woman, one man, one bed... His earlier thoughts returned to haunt him; he could think of a dozen ways to pass the time with her, and talking didn't make the list. But he'd get through it, the same way he always did—one night at a time.

Doug pulled his shirt from his waistband and tossed the cotton on the end of the bed. When he sat down to take off his shoes, she sucked in a shallow breath.

He unsnapped his jeans, leaving the zipper high and tight. Then he pulled back the covers and slipped beneath the sheet. Heat from her body whooshed onto his side of the bed. While the width might have been perfect for Shannen and Rhone, the bed was a third smaller than what Doug was normally accustomed to. And he was used to having the whole mattress to himself.

Almost imperceptibly, she scooted away, momentarily curving her derriere toward him when she did.

He glanced at the darkened ceiling, silently saying that there was no need for him to be led into temptation.

He could find it all by himself.

Chapter 8

Arielle's heart pounded, and her eyes burned. She hadn't gotten much rest last night, and that made it about three weeks since she'd slept more than a couple of hours at a time. Exhaustion had exacted a toll from her, physically, as well as emotionally.

She had little left to give. And the small part that still remained needed to be funneled to her parents.

"Ready?" Doug asked.

She met his gaze, drawing strength from him.

Last night had been difficult, more difficult than she might have imagined. Doug had slipped beneath the sheets, the coolness of his outdoor-fresh body seeping over her. She'd scooted away from him and been rewarded with the sound of a triumphant male chuckle. He'd known she was awake. Mercifully, he'd said nothing.

Even though she lay awake until a grandfather clock chimed midnight, she hadn't heard him fall into a restful sleep, either. So how did he manage to look so refreshed and alert?

"Arielle?"

Her throat went suddenly dry. She wanted to talk to her parents, reassure them that she was okay, but was she, really? She'd been shot at by the man she'd hired to kill her, then again by Samuel Pickins.

She was secluded in a mountain hideaway with a man who offered more danger to her, mentally and emotionally, than either of the assassins. Arielle searched for something to say to her parents. How could she offer them reassurance, when she had none inside herself?

"You don't have to do this," Doug said, his tone devoid of its customary teasing.

"Yes, I do," she said.

He cocked his head in understanding, then dialed the number, offering her the receiver. "Keep it short."

She nodded woodenly, nearly dropping the phone because her fingers trembled so badly. The sound of the first ring shattered through her senses. Doug didn't leave the room. Instead, he sat in a wooden chair and tipped it back on two legs, crossing his booted feet on top of the desk.

The second ring made her heart jump, and then the sound of Rhone's voice made her composure start to crumble. She tried to say something, only to have the words lodge in her throat.

"Arielle?" Rhone demanded.

"I'm...here." She glanced over at Doug, and he gave her a thumbs-up. Taking courage from his action, she cleared her throat.

"I've got your mother here," Rhone said.

"Put her on," Arielle whispered. She wound the phone cord around her finger while rehearsing the few lines she'd composed this morning.

The few seconds between Rhone handing over the phone and her mother saying Arielle's name seemed like minutes.

"Ari, honey, are you okay?" Frantic appeal raced

through Mona's words, the sentence shifting into a solid mass.

"I'm fine, really," Arielle said, choking on the lie.

"Where are you?" Mona Hale asked. "They won't tell me where you are."

Arielle squeezed her eyes shut, trying to keep the tears from falling. Her mother had been crying, and her voice was rubbed raw by emotion. Arielle had heard that tone before, when Mona lost her son.

Doug had coached her before picking up the phone, and she'd agreed to his dictates. "The mountains," she said, the half-truth formed in words as dry and bitter as ash.

"I need to see you, honey. Daddy's worried about you. When...when are you coming home?"

"I don't know," Arielle admitted. Silence slid down the line after her pause, echoing back at her. The answer obviously wasn't enough for Mona. "When this is all over. Soon."

"Now, Ari, don't be telling me lies."

As always, Mona possessed a mother's infallible instincts. "Mom, I just needed you to know that I'm okay. There's no need to worry."

"And that's supposed to make your mother feel better?"

A headache built behind Arielle's eyes. Mona knew exactly what line of work Rhone and Doug were in. "I'm in safe hands, Mom."

"Ari, please. Please come home."

Arielle heard her mother struggle for a breath, and she knew her actions were hurting her, even though nearly two thousand miles separated them.

"Whatever it is, your father and I can help you with it."

There had been a time when she believed that, a time she believed everything could be healed with a piece of Mother's apple pie and a loving hug.

But that had been a long time ago, before Danny's death crumbled the foundation of their lives, before her own life spun dizzily beneath her, destroying all the values she held dear.

"Come home, darling. We need you."

The desperation in her mother's voice tore at Arielle, ripping her heart into a hundred shreds. What had she done? How could wanting to spare her parents have resulted in so much hurt? Never in her life had she wanted anything more than to reach out to her mother, offering comfort and promises. Yet, if she did that, her parents would become targets, as surely as she was.

That was the only risk she was unwilling to take.

Despite her most valiant efforts, a tear trickled from between her lashes and traced her cheek. She heard Doug's boots thump onto the floor and quickly opened her eyes. He offered her a box of tissue along with a wry grin.

Arielle reached inside herself for a measure of strength. Her reserves severely tapped, she knew it was Doug's nearness that supplied what she needed. She closed her hand around the faded soft material and clutched it against her. Taking a deep breath, she fought for control. But it was too late. The last of her composure crumpled. "I'll call you again, Mom, when I can."

Doug moved instantly, taking the phone from her nerveless fingers. He propped the phone between his shoulder and ear, and moved behind her, placing his hands on her shoulders. Gently, but with undeniable force, he guided her into the chair he'd just vacated.

She wasn't aware of what he was saying, she only knew that he was using his gift of words to soothe her mother. And at the same time, he worked his magic on Arielle, too. He moved his fingers in gentle massaging motions, working out the knots.

Her head fell forward as he glided over the tightness in her neck, settling near her nape. Grateful for him taking charge and caring for her, Arielle allowed the rest of the tears to fall.

Seconds later, he left her while he hung up the phone. Then she heard nothing but the anguished sounds of her own heart breaking. Fully expecting that he'd given her privacy, she pulled her legs onto the chair, wrapping her arms around her legs.

But he hadn't left. She heard his footfalls, inhaled the scent of determined masculinity.

Arielle froze.

She opened her eyes to see him crouched in front of her. Then, tenderly, he swept a finger beneath her eyes.

"We'll get you through this," he said.

Her breath coming in labored bursts, she blinked and wiped her eyes. Doug reached for one of her hands, but it was his gaze, full of compassion, a gaze that she was certain saw into the depths of her soul, that made her heart skip a beat.

"Your parents have the best surveillance around."

Gulping at the pain of having harmed the only people she truly loved, she confessed, "It hurts."

"Yeah." He nodded. "And it would have hurt them a hell of a lot worse if they lost you."

"But—"

"You'll be back in the safety of their arms soon enough. It'll be a nightmare, and nothing more."

"Thank you. Thank you for letting me call them." Doug's words did more than offer her hope, they promised peace. Holding on to both emotions like the lifeline they were, Arielle blinked away the last of the tears. "I'm sorry for being so weak."

"Sweetheart, you don't have a weak bone in your body."

She met his gaze through her watery one.

"Everyone's entitled to cry."

She saw the anguish that lurked in the depths of his own eyes. Through her own ache, she recognized his. "Even you?" As soon as she asked the question, she recognized her error. She'd already pushed at that invisible barrier he had erected. Just because she'd exposed her emotions, that didn't mean he would.

Without answering her question, he said, "You can use the upstairs shower."

"Doug, I didn't—"

"I'm going into town in twenty minutes. Does that give you long enough to get ready?"

His eyes had turned cold, like snow in January. He'd said she didn't have a weak bone in her body, and now he was expecting her to prove it. Tamping down everything but the fire of determination, she stood, forcing her legs to support her weight. "I'll be ready."

She started toward the door, only to be halted by the stunning surprise and sweetness of his approval.

"You did good."

"Thanks," she said, not looking back. He wanted her at a distance, and Arielle heeded the warning. She shivered, afraid of what she might see if she looked at him again, if she saw what resided inside him.

Doug carried his wounds out of casual reach, but she recognized that they lay close enough to the surface to hurt everyone in his path.

Arielle pitied the woman who dared to unlock them. As for her, she didn't have the strength.

She suspected he'd seen enough devastation for two or three ordinary men. But Doug was no ordinary man. What he lived with would consume most people.

Maybe that was why he never cried.

Doug released a deep sigh. She'd rushed in where angels feared to tread. And then she'd apologized for her weakness.

Weak? He rolled the word around in his thoughts. The woman didn't know the meaning of the word. Compared to her, a tiger could easily be tamed. But Doug didn't care much for being clawed.

He thought he'd made it quite clear his personal life was off-limits. She didn't respect his No Trespassing signs. Hell, she probably skied out of bounds, too.

A nagging inner voice told him that if any woman could tear down his defenses, it was her. That was more dangerous than a knife to the heart.

He shoved aside thoughts of Arielle and reached for the phone. He had work to do. Work always kept his mind off females.

At least it used to.

"She's getting to you," Rhone observed a couple of minutes later, when Doug's mind had wandered yet again.

"Who?" Doug asked.

"Tall, long hair, thin, with curves in all the right places, that's who."

"Try sleeping next to her," Doug said. "Without touching."

"The things a man has to do when he's on the job."

"It's like being in a candy store and being on a diet."

"Wouldn't let her hear you say that."

Problem was, with the sensual kiss she offered, Doug had already had a taste. It was temptation and forbiddenness, all rolled into an irresistible confection and topped off with a dusting of powdered sugar.

"You're gone again," Rhone said.

"Plotting revenge on my ex-partner. If you'll recall, you sent her my way."

"It's hard to exact revenge when you're in the Bahamas."

"Try me."

Rhone whistled. "You're in deep."

"Throw me a rope, friend." Doug became aware of the sudden absence of sound, which meant Arielle had turned off the shower faucets. Now maybe he could concentrate.

The thought of her naked beneath the pulsing spray had caused more than one lapse in concentration. "How many men do you have at the Hales' house?"

"Three. Twenty-four-by-seven."

Three men, on a twenty-four hour detail, seven days a week. Rational thinking told him it was enough. Instinct—and he didn't dare think it was anything more emotional than that—told him it wasn't enough. "Add another."

Rhone didn't say a word.

"Send me your bill," Doug said.

"Like hell. If you want another man, consider it done."

Doug dropped his feet to the floor. "If you see anything suspicious, move her parents underground."

"Got it."

After another thirty seconds, Doug signed off. He leaned forward, staring at the phone and drumming his fingers on the yellow legal pad where he'd made notations.

He didn't have any feelings for Arielle, he told himself. At least none beyond those between client and protector. She was just another job, a name in his files.

Picking up a pen, Doug wondered if he'd always been this good at lying to himself.

Absently he moved the pen across paper, sorting through the things Rhone had said. The ink formed lines and shadows. Slowly a picture emerged, Arielle's likeness, each stroke a creation he wasn't aware of forming.

A few minutes later, he glanced down. He'd shaped her in softness and strength, with grace and grit. An odd paradox, as intriguing as the woman herself.

In the picture, her hair flirted with her shoulders…the way it had last night, when he went to bed.

Doug turned over the pad, slamming it on the desk.

His sketches always revealed what resided in his heart, even when his mind refused to acknowledge facts. He saw her many facets. But that didn't mean he was attracted to them. Sure as hell didn't mean he needed them.

"Doug?"

He looked up. Her approach took him by surprise, meaning he wasn't as sharp as he should be. That could get a man killed. Or, worse, captured.

"I'm ready to go."

He clenched his jaw. Shannen's clothes were marginally too big for Arielle. She had cinched a belt around the jeans, and the blouse she wore was pulled up at the elbows and fastened close to the throat.

Doug barely resisted the urge to flick open the button.

Instead of wearing her hair wild and free, she'd pulled it into a braid. Except for a sheen of nude gloss, her mouth was bare and...kissable.

He stood. "Come here."

She hesitated, folding her hands in front of her. "Doug, I..."

"Arielle, I showed you how to use the equipment on *Destiny*. You need to know the code to this room and how to get hold of Rhone in an emergency."

"Oh." She dropped her hands to her sides.

He knew what she was thinking. And he had to admit, the same thing had crossed his mind when he saw her there. Her gloss had one purpose—for him to kiss away.

He wondered how she'd react if he shared that little piece of information.

Shoving the legal pad beneath the computer monitor, he indicated the chair to Arielle. She took the seat, and he moved behind her, reminding him of the way he'd rubbed her shoulders earlier. The shape of her nape, the gentle arch of her back, the feel of her, had seemed natural. He'd offered comfort and, strangely enough, he'd found some of his own.

"This phone, as you already know, is a direct line to

Rhone's place in D.C. It also rings at his office. If there's no answer, it forwards to his cell phone.''

"More toys?"

"Rhone's offices are a veritable playground of gadgetry."

She looked over her shoulder. "You're smiling again."

"I like to play."

She nodded, and he caught a whiff of flowers. It sure as sunshine didn't smell like his extrastrength brand, and it beat the hell out of the eau de trash can they'd both worn yesterday. She'd probably experimented with one of the half-dozen or so bottles of shower gel that Shannen kept on the bathroom windowsill.

Doug wondered if Arielle would have a chance to use every one of them. He decided he might not mind critiquing each scent. If this was danger, it had never smelled so sweet.

She glanced away, and he pointed out the phone next to the one he'd already indicated. "This line is unsecured. If you're using it, I'm assuming I won't be around to stop you."

"You mean…"

"No telling who might be listening in. If you use this phone, you won't care who's listening. And the only way that'll happen is over my dead body."

A shiver traced up her spine, shaking her shoulders. Good—a touch of fear went a long way.

"I've seen enough," she said, pushing back her chair and standing. "I'm ready to go."

She turned to face him, and Doug immediately regretted his harshness. She wasn't Kerry, he reminded himself. Arielle was intelligent and, more, was blessed with common sense.

"One more thing," he said. "The alarm to Rhone's office."

"Doug, do I really need to know this?"

He folded his arms across his chest.

From deep inside, she sighed. "Are you sure I won't wake up from all this?"

If she did, he hoped to be there beside her. He gave her the code, saw her mentally file the numbers in memory, just the way she had when they were chased in New York City. Even though he knew he didn't need to, he asked her to repeat the alphanumeric sequence. She got it right on the first try. Bingo. "And you reverse the code to set the alarm. Try it."

She closed the door and punched in the code, smiling when the digital readout announced that the system was engaged. "I think I could grow to like toys."

"The value of play is underrated."

"Like cribbage, I suppose."

"Like cribbage," he agreed. Along with a few other things that came immediately to mind. Nice thing about them, they didn't require a board, a deck of cards or rules. And with the way she recalled numbers, she'd have a distinct advantage in any card game. Doug disliked being at a disadvantage in anything, especially his own games.

Following his instructions, she set the house's main alarm. A disembodied voice announced that the system was set. She'd done good, every step of the way.

Their drive into town was accomplished in a shroud of silence, and he saw her anxiously looking in the sideview mirror every few seconds. Fear again. He was starting to loathe the feeling.

The parking lot was nearly full, the huge variety store not only drawing the locals, but also those from the surrounding communities. Inside, Arielle headed straight for the jeans section, walking past a circular rack filled with denim skirts. When she grabbed the fifth pair, he went in search of a buggy.

By the time he returned, she'd added several sweaters, sweatshirts and blouses to the pile.

Retail therapy.

He shrugged. At least the fear had been temporarily banished.

Doug dutifully trailed her to the lingerie department. When he saw the potent combination of a lacy red teddy slipping from a padded hanger, his long-neglected libido reminded him he was a man.

A picture of Arielle in that oh-so-tantalizing scrap of fabric punctuated his thoughts. Whistling, he turned away. He hazarded another glance when she tossed a couple of packages in the buggy. Panties. Serviceable cotton, in stark white.

Sensible Arielle. Even the pajamas she chose were conservative. Surely someone had uncovered the passion he knew existed. Yesterday she'd kissed him. And he hadn't had to work at coaxing a response from her, she'd given it naturally. She was a study in contrasts, temptation buried beneath practicality.

Doug wanted a shovel.

She tossed socks on top of the heap, then said, "I need toiletries."

He nodded, not mentioning the fact she hadn't purchased any bras. Wasn't any of his business.

He'd taken a couple of steps before he realized she'd stopped in front of a rack of bras. She snagged red, black and purple from the rack.

Doug swallowed. Toiletries. Right. They needed toiletries.

Still, while she shopped, his gaze was drawn again and again to the array of colors splashed across that serviceable white. Sleeping in the same bed with her tonight would be far more difficult than last night.

They headed for the shoe department, passing hardware. A shovel. Yeah. A shovel. He'd thought he'd need it to dig away her secrets. Turned out he'd need it to dig himself out of the hole he'd fallen in.

Ten minutes later, she'd selected shoes. He grabbed a few things for himself, and they headed toward the checkout. They both started to unload the cart at the same time, their fingers glancing off each other's over the lingerie. She stopped, meeting his gaze.

An embarrassed flush crept up her face, and she lowered her eyelashes. "Thanks," she said, her voice hardly audible.

Doug wasn't a liar. He couldn't say it was no problem. He placed the kaleidoscope of color on the conveyer belt, satin slipping through his fingers.

While he unloaded the rest of her purchases, she grabbed her purse and pulled out a credit card.

"Put it away," he said.

"But—"

"I'll pay cash."

She drew her shoulders back a couple of inches. Trouble. He saw the storm brewing in her eyes, and barely resisted the temptation to turn away from it. He'd rather duel at dawn than face a woman with a purpose. And in a duel, you had ten paces between you and your opponent. Barely a dozen inches separated him from Arielle.

"Cash or charge?" the cashier asked.

"Charge."

"Cash."

The woman looked helplessly toward Doug.

"Cash," he repeated. The cashier nodded and started scanning the price tags. "Credit cards can be traced," he told Arielle quietly. "The colder the trail we leave, the better." The only happy trails he knew of were ones he followed.

Her eyebrows drew together. "But—"

"You're paying me to keep you alive." He captured her shoulders and added, "Let me do my job."

"I can't allow you to pay my expenses."

"I'll invoice you." Out of the corner of his eye, he saw

the colorfully arrayed bras drop into the bottom of a brown paper bag.

The fire in Arielle's eyes died, and her resistance went with it.

The cashier announced the price, and he reached for his wallet. After giving him the change, she tore off the receipt.

"I'll take that," Arielle said.

The cashier shrugged apologetically at Doug.

Arielle grabbed a couple of the bags, leaving Doug with the most dangerous one. A lady's lingerie had never mattered before. It shouldn't now. So why in a Colorado winter did it?

He opened the car door for her, handing the bag to her. He wouldn't have wanted to get rid of a grenade any faster than he wanted to dispose of the images her clothing conjured.

At the grocery store, they crisscrossed each aisle, tossing items of personal taste or necessity into the basket, pausing twice to argue over brand-name preferences.

He'd always considered grocery shopping a have-to chore, performed only when his cabinets and fridge were empty. Shopping with Arielle gave him a different and unexpected perspective, one, he decided, that he wasn't entirely comfortable with. The humor he could handle. It was the none-too-subtle hint of...intimacy, he decided, for lack of a better word, that bothered him.

His thoughts took a detour, and for a few seconds he entertained the images. After Kerry, he'd roadblocked Domestic Avenue, from both his mind and his future plans, never expecting, never wanting, to travel that direction again.

Did he want to now, with Arielle?

The question hung suspended, and for once, he found he was content not knowing an answer.

The drive back to the house was silent, punctuated only by the sound of rubber on pavement.

Braking to a stop in the driveway, he glanced over at Arielle, seeing her staring sightlessly out the windshield. The tender area beneath her eyes was still bruised. Sleepless nights, turbulent days and talking to Mona had all exacted a toll on Arielle's emotions.

His dictatorial ways hadn't helped, either.

He'd pushed and pushed, and she'd responded, rising to his every challenge, picking up and carrying on. But for most there came a point when nothing remained, when the adrenaline rush crashed to a stop. He'd seen it happen. Seen it happen? Hell, he'd gotten a T-shirt, he'd made the trip so many times.

He knew how to handle the inevitable letdown. Arielle did not.

And now, for her sake, Doug had to draw on his shallow reserve of patience, hoping against hope that the reserve didn't dry up. She deserved more than she'd been getting from him.

Doug shut off the engine and pulled out the key.

"Since graduating from college, I've never had anyone tell me what to do," she admitted. "I'm not good at it."

"Don't need to be for much longer." He shrugged. "I live a structured life, a by-product of my training, not my upbringing. I know I'm demanding as hell. I won't apologize for being accustomed to giving orders and fully expecting them to be followed. The lives of others, yours and mine included, depend on it."

Expectancy pulsed in the vehicle's cab. The scent of flowers mingled with leather and the coolness of a mountain morning, seeped into the car. He turned in his seat, his knee brushing hers.

Wide-eyed recognition took him by surprise, and it was an unpleasant one. His attraction to Kerry had led to disaster and devastation. A single serving of that combo plate was more than enough for his palate.

"I'll try to be better at taking orders," she said, her voice low but powerful, affecting him like the slap of a wave against a moonlit bow.

"And I'll try to remember to discuss what I can with you ahead of time."

"Thank you." She closed one hand around a paper bag and reached for the door handle with the other.

He held a caveat among his cards, and had no choice but to lay it on the table. "But there may be times, Arielle, when you have to trust me."

She let go of the door handle. And when she looked at him, it was with that same steely determination that had led her to him in the first place. "Trust is a two-way street, Doug. I've learned that lesson the hard way, standing in front of three dozen students. Trust isn't given, it's earned."

Her voice dropped an octave, demanding—and, more, holding—his attention as she finished. "Don't ask anything from me that you're not willing to give yourself."

He clenched his jaw. Trust? He could name, on two fingers, the people he trusted. All the others had let him down, betrayed the commodity he'd so reluctantly given. Trust again? Not in this lifetime.

Without another word, she climbed from the vehicle, closing the door behind her, leaving him to carry the last bag. The one representing temptation.

She offered temptation and demanded trust. How much worse could this assignment get? Looking heavenward, he offered a quick prayer that he wouldn't find out.

"Doug?"

The quiet urgency in Arielle's voice slammed into him. Instantly he dropped the bag and unholstered his pistol. Face pale, she pointed toward the alarm box.

"When we left, wasn't this little light blinking?"

Chapter 9

Arielle's hands went moist. Doug motioned her to one side, and she moved willingly. His eyes met hers.

"And to think I was ready for a cold one."

She gulped.

"We talked about trust."

Her answer emerged without hesitation. "I do trust you."

He gave a quick smile that didn't animate his face. Motions cool and controlled, he braced his legs apart, his nine-millimeter in his hand.

When she indicated the light on the alarm, he'd dropped the bag and drawn his gun with smooth efficiency, a forceful reminder, again, of the differences between them. Her lingerie had spilled across the front walkway, an obscene spike of color against dull white concrete.

Arielle looked around, not sure what she was searching for and hoping, hoping, that she didn't see anything.

Doug checked the alarm. "Back door has been opened. We'll go in here."

"I could wait outside," she said, fighting not to betray her cowardice.

"My clients don't get to play sitting duck. Chin up, Arielle."

She nodded, hoping her small measure of courage could compete with her unrestrained fear.

"I'll tell you when to follow me."

She took strength from his quick smile, from his attitude. Glancing skyward, she offered another brief thanks that he'd accepted the assignment. Without him, she didn't know where she'd be. More, she didn't want to find out.

He closed his hand around the doorknob and slowly turned it. Her heart raced, the muscles in her legs weakened. Soundlessly he pushed open the door, then eased himself inside.

Arielle clenched her hands, her pulse pounding. The couple of seconds when she lost sight of him seemed the longest she'd ever endured. She wanted to burst in behind him, see if he was okay. Reminding herself of the promise she'd made, she waited.

He reappeared a couple of seconds later. "Clear so far. Let's go."

At the door to Rhone's office, Doug paused to check the alarm there, then silently advanced into the house.

Arielle followed, her senses strung taut. "Doug?" she whispered.

He hesitated without turning back to her.

"Your coffee cup is gone."

He nodded curtly then continued. At the bottom of the stairs, he stopped and swept his gaze across the landing, gun poised.

Her heart continued to jump, and she wiped her palms on her jeans.

Near the kitchen, Doug halted. After making sure she was behind him, he nudged the door open.

Then he sighed. "Is it Wednesday?"

She nodded. Then, realizing he couldn't see her, she forced out a soft "Yes."

Motions controlled, he sank the gun back into its leather nest. "The second Wednesday of the month." Slowly he turned toward her.

"Doug?"

"It's not nice to point weapons at the cleaning lady."

"Cleaning..."

The sudden absence of adrenaline had her leaning against the wall for support.

"Could have done with a reminder from Rhone."

Her breath rushed out with relief, leaving her lungs burning.

"You'll like Betsy," Doug assured her.

Arielle's head swam. He switched gears effortlessly, leaving her to feel like a stalled clunker next to a sleek sports car.

"Honey, I'm home!" Doug called out, then pushed the door open the rest of the way.

Arielle's first glimpse of the older woman would stay with her a long time, she knew. Betsy's eyes were open wide, and her hands were closed around a butcher knife. The breaths she drew came in labored bursts, reminding Arielle of herself.

"Put down your weapons and come out with your hands up," Doug said easily.

Betsy's features were transformed, and a broad smile chased across her face. "Douglas Masterson, you rascal, you. You scared me to pieces. Rhone didn't tell me you were coming to Colorado."

"Just as he neglected to remind me you're here every other Wednesday." Closing the distance, he reached for the knife's handle. He slid it onto the counter, to safety. "Glad to see me?" he asked.

"'Bout as glad as I am for my gout."

"She loves me," he said with a boyish shrug in Arielle's direction.

"They all do," Betsy said, nearly scooping him up off the ground and pulling him against her ample form in a bear hug. "When I heard whispering, I knew it wasn't Rhone and Shannen. Those little ones, bless their tiny hearts, can't keep quiet when they come home. No siree. Lordy, Lordy, Doug, you gave me a fright. Thought for sure someone was coming after me."

"Only me sneaking up on you," he assured her. "I've been trying to catch you for years, but you keep up this talk about your husband."

This side of Doug enchanted Arielle. She'd seen him serious and sarcastic, but never carefree. She realized that no matter how deep his scars ran, he wasn't a man to let them ruin his life. He'd faced his torment and beaten it. Now if only she could do the same.

When Betsy released Doug, her wide grin encompassed Arielle.

"Why, you really are a rascal," Betsy exclaimed. "You finally brought a girl to meet me. I'm Betsy, honey," she said, pushing Doug aside and advancing on Arielle. "Glad to see you caught this wily guy. He swore he'd never be getting with no woman ever again—'cept for me of course—but I just knew otherwise. Mark my words, I told him."

Before Arielle could explain about the relationship, she, too, had been caught up in the whirlwind that was Betsy.

"And what's your name?" she finally asked.

Arielle labored for a breath, after nearly having her ribs crushed.

"Arielle," Doug supplied. "And she's my client."

"Your—"

"Client," he said again.

"Not your wife?"

Doug shook his head, and Arielle did the same.

"Child, what is wrong with you?" Betsy demanded of Arielle.

"What's wrong with me?"

"Now that you've got him, you're not going to let him get away, are you?"

Arielle never stammered, not when facing angry parents, a frustrated principal, or a demanding school board. But there was something about the directness with which Betsy made her statement that seemed to cut through everything and go for the guts. "I hired Doug to..." She trailed off. What else could she add? Save her from an assassin's bullet?

"Keep her out of harm's way," Doug supplied.

Betsy frowned. "That don't mean you can't keep him after you're done being his client. Good-looking man like that."

"Show some mercy on the woman," Doug said easily, moving across the kitchen and helping himself to a cup of the coffee Betsy had made.

Betsy folded her arms across the stretch of her chest and said, "And you could do worse yourself, young man."

Doug choked on his coffee, and Arielle didn't try to hide her triumphant smile. He always seemed so strong and secure. Yet this large, grandmotherly woman made him fight for balance.

"You're enjoying this," Doug said to Arielle.

"Yes." She poured herself a cup of coffee.

"You're not getting any younger, you know," Betsy supplied.

Arielle wrapped her hands around the cup and rested her hip against the countertop. She wasn't getting any younger, either.

For a few seconds, a few stolen seconds, Arielle allowed herself to imagine Doug in the role of husband and father. Friend and lover.

Her lover.

Wants and needs, basic and vital, surfaced in a rush, at once clearly defined.

She shifted away from the counter, placing distance between herself and her tormentor, only to find no relief—there was no escaping her imagination.

"And this house is a great place for a honeymoon," Betsy added with a wink.

Doug slipped his cup onto the table and ran his fingers through his hair, dislodging strands. They fell forward, dancing with his eyebrows. Arielle struggled with the impulse to reach out and finger back the hair, wanting to feel the texture against her skin.

She sipped from her sweetened black coffee, needing the distraction more than the dark liquid.

Doug wasn't a man she should fantasize about, not even for a few seconds. She had old-fashioned values, believed in the sanctity of marriage and children.

Doug didn't.

Plain and simple, he was a man with a mission. He was her reluctant protector, saddled with her more as a favor to a friend than from anything else.

And after the pain she'd endured twice before with other men over the same issues, she had no desire to subject herself to it again, even if Doug was interested.

"There isn't going to be a honeymoon, Betsy."

"No?" She narrowed her eyes.

"Sorry," Doug said.

"If there ain't gonna be a marriage, how come you're both sleeping in the same bed?"

Doug closed his eyes for a second. The nighttime arrangements had been Doug's idea, so Arielle left the awkward explanations to him.

"We're not sleeping together."

Her eyebrows knit together. "Only one bed has the covers mussed. How you gonna explain that?"

Doug's smile lacked enthusiasm, his frown better expressing the internal argument he obviously waged—about whether to explain or to bluntly tell Betsy it was none of her business.

"We're not…involved. We're sharing a room for her protection," Doug said.

"You really believe that? A lovely single woman in bed with a gorgeous man? Only a matter of time." Betsy tutted.

This time, Arielle choked on a sip of her coffee. Heat crept up her neck as two sets of eyes focused on her. "I, um… It's only a business arrangement. Really," she managed.

"Uh-huh. Well, as I been telling you, a man don't take care of a woman by sleeping with her, 'less they're married, of course."

"Of course," Doug echoed in a dry tone.

"I just don't know what this world is coming to anymore." Betsy shook her head, gazing into the distance. "These days, people sleep with anyone. Me and Harry, we waited till we were married, you know. Not that we weren't tempted, mind you. But that's the way we did things back then."

Arielle met Doug's gaze. He seemed torn between laughter and frustration. Another new side of him. How many more were there?

"So," Doug interjected helplessly, "how about a game of cribbage?"

Tall, jagged, snowcapped peaks obscured the sun as it moved from its afternoon position to early evening.

Despite the fact that he'd been planning an extended vacation, inactivity was weighing on Doug.

"I'll be back," he called to Arielle, grabbing his jacket and disarming the alarm. Once he was outside, the cool Colorado air cut through his jacket. After resetting the code, he swept a cursory glance around the area, then started toward the back of the grassy area that had been painstakingly sliced from the forest.

A wooden swing set sat in the middle, next to an empty sandbox. Dump trucks, along with pails and plastic shovels, decorated the area, testimony to the Mitchell family's shared happy times.

It was a place to heal, or so Rhone said about the land.

It had been successful for Rhone and Shannen. Maybe the magic would work for Arielle, also. Doug hoped so. She deserved peace. Hell, didn't everyone?

He found the crude trail that led deep into the forest. Tall pines protected the path and the vegetation that would soon lie dormant under blankets of snow until spring. How long had it been since he traveled these woods with Rhone and Shannen, on a desperate search for their baby son? And, more, how long had it been since these trees were the only thing solid in a world gone crazy?

On his last trip here, he'd screamed his grief to the sky, learned to mourn in the answering silence.

Why, Doug wondered, at this point, did he no longer feel whole? He'd thought he'd healed. Was it an illusion? Like the Bahamas?

He carefully looked at the trees, searching for any sign that there'd been visitors since his last check, earlier this morning. Instinct told him there was nothing out of the ordinary, but that didn't encourage him to return to the house.

Nearby, water that he knew would soon ice over flowed with a lazy constancy. The river rushed in spring, ambled in summer, trickled in fall. Seasons changed. So had he.

He laughed a lot, joked often. But standing near the stream, he realized the truth. It was a cover. And Arielle had seen that which he tried hardest to hide. He didn't have half the energy he used to. Brevity cloaked, but didn't eliminate, the dark lurking inside him.

He'd thought he'd faced up to his guilt and responsibility

in Kerry's death. He'd railed at God and the universe, his enemies and fate. Colorado had been a last-ditch effort. A place to heal.

Until now, he'd thought he had. Until now, he'd believed he was whole. Until now. Until Arielle.

She hadn't hidden from her pain. She'd cried, confessed her fear, trembled in his arms. Through it all, she'd remained steadfast in her belief. She'd walked into his office, confident of his ability not only to save her, but to stop the hit she'd hired.

They'd talked of trust, and she'd said it was a two-way street. Funny, till now he hadn't thought of that. He'd demanded her blind faith, and even though she'd said trust had to be earned, she'd placed it in him.

Her honesty and openness humbled him.

Their lives were a study in contrasts, light and belief against shadows and secrets. Which, he wondered, would prevail? Which, when pitted against the other, was stronger?

He released a heavy sigh. He'd wanted to turn down the assignment, give it to Brian. A part of Doug wished he had.

But then he thought of the feel of her against him, soft and feminine. She'd kissed him, drawing a reaction he hadn't known he was capable of. It went beyond physical, bordered on something more—

Doug silenced the thought, picking up a rock and hurtling it into the water. The stone splashed, then sank, sending skitters to the shoreline. Much like the ones Arielle had sent through him last night.

Somehow, she was starting to get to him. Even when they played cribbage earlier, he'd been unable to concentrate. What was it about him? *What was it about her?*

After concluding his perimeter check, he returned to the house to find Arielle staring out the back window. She'd been watching him, he knew. But just how much did she see? And why did the thought of her looking past the facade he presented to the world terrify him?

"I made hot chocolate," she said. "And we have some marshmallows."

Hot chocolate. How often had he had that fantasy as a child? That he'd walk in the door after school to a warm house, a hot drink and a caring mother.

But it had never happened. By the fourth grade, Doug had realized that it probably never would. His mother had never been there. He'd rarely had a hot meal, let alone a cup of cocoa. Still, that hadn't stopped him from hoping and wanting, the same way he had for birthday presents and parties.

"Would you like some?" she asked.

He shrugged out of his jacket and draped it across the back of the chair. Steam wafted from a pan on the stove, and Doug remembered his first trip to the grocery store as an adult. He'd bought a box of instant cocoa mix, boiled some water and burned his tongue. The taste hadn't lived up to his expectations, but then, life rarely did.

"Doug?"

"Sure," he said. He'd had enough coffee, and the wind's chill had seeped beneath his skin. "I'll take a cup."

She poured him a large, frothy mug, then dumped two puffy marshmallows on top. He accepted the mug and looked at the drink. It didn't look watered-down and tepid. Couldn't be hot chocolate.

He took a long sip, amazed at the richness and creaminess of the texture. Slipping past his guard, it warmed him in a way only his fantasies would understand. "No artificial flavor and preservatives?"

"Don't tell me you've never had real hot chocolate before?"

"Where's the little packets you rip open with your teeth? You already put them in the trash?"

She smiled, shaking her head. "I remember calling Mom

from college after our first snowstorm. I wanted some of her love, even if it was long-distance. More than anything, I wanted some of her hot chocolate.''

Arielle's eyes took on the same mist they always did when she spoke of her parents. *What* was it like? What would it have been like to sip from the cup of parental love and kindness, even once?

It made him that much more aware of the magnitude of what she'd done, of how devastated Arielle's parents would be if anything happened to their remaining child.

''The next day I received a care package, sent overnight and costing Mom a small fortune. And she shared her recipe.''

''So did my mom.''

''Boiling water and artificial ingredients?'' she asked incredulously.

''Nothing but the best for her son.'' The bitterness of the words slammed against the sweetness of his cocoa as the past collided with the present.

She reached for him, cradling a warm hand around his wrist. A bolt of something suspiciously like lightning charged through him, settling in an unnameable place. Lord, the power she possessed over him. A potency stronger than gunpowder, and just as explosive.

''Doug, I'm sorry.''

''Don't be. She never was much of a mother. I interfered with her plans in life.''

Even as the confession rolled from his tongue, Doug wondered what was wrong with him. He had never shared such thoughts before, not even with Rhone. And Rhone knew Doug better than anyone.

His words hung between them, an uneasy shroud to cover an already uneasy day. Betsy's words had loomed between him and Arielle, making him question the solo course he'd charted for the rest of his life.

Being alone and lonely no longer held any appeal. Until

he met Arielle, he'd had no idea he was a lonely man. But her hand touched him, offering reassurance. He realized that, having experienced its wonder, he didn't want to give it up.

Their gazes met, then ricocheted off each other. She slowly released his hand, then turned over her own to study it. Looking for…what? Did she feel it, too? The warmth… the sunshine?

Telling himself that his reaction was normal—a natural male response to a desirable female—didn't seem to help. Having once had a taste, he wanted more. A touch wasn't enough. A kiss wasn't enough. A glance that measured 8.5 on the Richter scale wasn't enough. He wanted her light, her energy.

Just as surely, though, he couldn't have it. He'd consume her, stomping out the very things he sought. He could look, but not touch. Unfortunately, he was a very tactile person. Furthermore, he'd never been good at following rules, not the ones made by others and not the ones made by himself, either.

"She has a secret ingredient."

He heard the whisper, and felt its sensation across his chest, settling in his heart. He shouldn't ask. He knew better. Meeting the honesty her gaze offered, he couldn't stop himself. "And what's the secret ingredient?"

"Love."

He turned away. He fixed his gaze out the window and into the distance. A place to heal? Sure. If that was the case, why did he feel broken?

Long seconds of silence dominated the room, sucking out the heat and sapping his thoughts.

"I think that was something she said to make me feel better," Arielle said, the tone of her voice not as strong as it had been earlier. He felt, rather than heard, her steps as she retreated to the far side of the kitchen. "But my hot chocolate has never tasted quite as good as hers."

Doug turned and moved to stand in front of Arielle. "Don't tell your mother, but I'm certain yours is better."

He reached out, his thumb following his gaze to the corner of her mouth. Her breath, warm and whisper-soft, caressed his skin as he wiped away a spot of froth.

Memories roughened his tone when he spoke, and his voice dropped lower still with the impact of a simple act that meant more to him than she could know. "I *know* it's better, because you are the one who made it for me."

Something had happened between them when she communicated her compassion, something strong and sizzling. He'd felt it, and obviously, so had she. He planned to keep his reaction to her under lock and key. That was the only safety device he could think of. And maybe he could dump the entire box of emotions overboard as soon as *Destiny* set sail…watch them sink to fathomless depths.

As long as they didn't take him with them…

Hot chocolate. How had that gotten to be a euphemism for so much more? He'd seen it coming, just like that locomotive. He'd been smart enough to dodge the first, but not the second. Maybe he could send his reflexes out for a tune-up.

"You may want to check in with Brian," she said, her tone slightly shaken. A reaction to his touch? He'd like to think so. "He called while you were outside."

Doug cocked a brow.

"Suggested you give him a call when it was convenient."

Convenient—their code word for *Privacy needed*.

He gave a curt nod. "You answered the call?"

"You showed me how."

Doug smiled, pleased in spite of himself. She was a woman who wanted to master her own destiny. He admired that, found her tenacity appealing.

Arielle crossed the kitchen. Apparently looking for

something to do, she reached for the wire whip and thrashed it through the simmering cocoa.

He ached to move behind her, reach out to her and still her frantic motions. But the blinding illumination of danger brought him up short, held him in place.

The fight-or-flight mechanism triggered, somewhere deep inside. And, like any rational male, he heeded it. "I'll be back in a few minutes." Escape. Another word for sanity.

She nodded without looking up. Before he left, he noticed she'd released the whisk to cradle the hand she'd touched him with.

The image of her haunted him as he closed the office door behind him and propped his feet up on the desk, leaning back in what he realized was false relaxation. How could he relax, when his gut churned with want and need? Betsy had spoken of marriage, home and hearth...values honored by other men. Not by him. Not anymore.

Once upon a lifetime, he'd wanted stability, even yearned for it. But he'd since learned that his career and stability could never be one and the same. This time, though, the story he was living would have a different ending, a happy one. Arielle would walk away alive. Doug would simply walk away.

Brian Yarrow picked up on the first ring. "Took you long enough, boss."

Good-natured ribbing wasn't on his agenda. Usually it didn't have to be scheduled. Today it did. "Got something for me?"

"Yeah, department store out here is having a sale on a thing called a sense of humor."

"Did you pick up one?"

"Sure," Brian said easily.

"Send it back, it's defective."

"Maybe we can get a quantity discount." Brian whistled. "Rhone said you had it bad for her."

Refusing to take the bait, Doug said nothing.

Brian laughed. "Guess he was right."

"Is that department store running a blue-light special on quitting while you're ahead?"

"Gotcha."

"Did you call for any reason other than harassment?"

Instantly the atmosphere of the call changed.

"Ran a make on that license number Arielle got on the van."

Doug sat up straighter in his chair and said, "Go on."

"Seems it's registered to one Samuel Pickins."

"Hell."

Brian didn't say anything else. There was no need.

The repercussion sank into Doug, like a lead weight thrown into the ocean. Pickins. The man was out of jail and had a vendetta. Doug was the bullet's target. Not Arielle.

"Watch your step."

Doug hung up the phone without responding. The hum of machinery thundered into his thoughts and echoed through his mind.

"Doug? Is everything okay?"

He looked at her through blurry eyes.

She stood in the doorway, silhouetted by the overhead lighting. She was so real and vibrant. So alive.

She took another step into the room, and he inhaled the freshness of summer-drenched flowers. Another scent... lilacs?

"What is it?" she whispered, clenching her hands in front of her in a way that betrayed her inner turmoil. "Remember, we said trust was a two-way street."

They hadn't said it. She had. And he was no longer certain he wanted to drive down that block.

"Whatever it is, I can handle it."

Doug dragged his fingers into his hair, tossing a lock across his forehead. How could he possibly tell her? And what, exactly, would he tell her? The truth? Or something slightly less than that?

Trust hung between them. He'd demanded it from her, he owed her no less. Still, he needed a deep breath before he admitted, "Brian tracked down the owner of the van."

"And?" she asked breathlessly.

"Arielle, I'm sorry." His hands fisted at his sides in mute testimony to his anger, frustration and, more, his clawing, cloying guilt. "You came to me for protection. Pickins owns that vehicle."

From the space separating them, he saw her deep swallow. Confusion painted across her blue eyes, darkening them. He'd have done anything to take it away, to keep her safe and secure in her little world. Instead, she'd boldly entered a realm she had no recognition of.

And if Doug had ever made a more difficult confession than the one he was about to make, he couldn't remember the occasion.

"You weren't the target yesterday in New York. There hasn't yet been an attempt on your life." He paused, then finished, "Arielle, in seeking me out, you may have signed your own death warrant."

Chapter 10

Doug's words stole Arielle's breath. In seeking him out, she'd signed her own death warrant?

Her shoulders shook as thoughts collided. That day in New York, the man hadn't been shooting at her? He'd been aiming for Doug? And she'd been in the way? More, the man she was terrified of hadn't found her yet?

She struggled through the implications. It was impossible, inconceivable. Someone was after Doug, the man she'd hired to save her? The man she'd blindly given her trust to?

Her knees weakened.

"I'm sorry," he said, the words ragged and real.

Arielle looked at him, into his eyes. Pain laced their depths, and, more, guilt loomed there, stealing from the vibrancy of their green.

As she warred with her own internal demons, she saw that his lay there, in his eyes, undiluted and exposed. He felt responsible. But it wasn't his fault. Compassion rising to the surface, she extended her hand, palm up. "You couldn't have known," she whispered, her tone as unsteady as his.

"That doesn't excuse it." Doug stood and exhaled. In a couple of steps, he'd crossed to her, capturing her trembling shoulders between his hands. "I meant to protect you."

"You did," she said. With the addition of his strength, her body steadied. It amazed her how much more power she felt when he stood near. "You did protect me. You got me out of harm's way."

"You should never have been there."

"We didn't know that at the time. Quit blaming yourself."

He flinched.

"You can't take care of everything and everyone, Doug. It's not possible."

They hadn't stood this close for a long time. She hadn't been in his arms since she kissed him. Arielle tried not to think about how right it had felt to have him hold her, how wonderful, how safe. The scent of cool evening clung to him, mixing with the spice of aftershave and the potency of masculinity.

Instinct urged her to run, yet something else, something she was hesitant to explore, held her in place. She reached up, tracing a finger down his cheek, feeling the sensual drag of his afternoon shadow.

Yet it was his eyes that held her completely captivated. They were haunted and guilt-ridden. But it seemed deeper than that, as if this burden had brought something buried and unhealed to the surface. "You're only human."

"Yeah," he admitted, the admission sounding like a failing.

To Doug, she realized, humanness was a failing.

"I came to you," she said softly. "And you tried to send me away. It's not your fault. If it's anyone's, it's mine. I should have listened, should have—"

"No." He shook his head.

Her hand stilled on his skin, but then she followed her heart and curved her palm around his squared chin. "If I can't play what-ifs, neither can you," she said. "You did your job. There was danger, you got us out of there."

"You're not safe."

Her pulse began to pound. Surely, after all this, he couldn't be thinking of sending her away. "Would I be safer without you?"

"You would."

"There's still someone out there looking for me."

"I haven't forgotten. Not for a second."

"If you send me with Brian, then he can't work on finding Pickins for you." She hadn't moved her hand, and for a moment, it was as if time had ground to a shuddering halt.

"Are you always so logical?"

The idea of being left alone, even with Brian, to fight the demon chasing her terrified her more than anything. "I try to be," she admitted.

"I'm not leaving you, Arielle."

He leveled his gaze on hers, and she felt the stirrings of response somewhere deep inside. She didn't want to want him this way, didn't want to need him.

She'd always prided herself on strength and independence. But Doug brought out a different side to her, brought out her weakness and vulnerability...made her feel incredibly feminine. No other man had had this dizzying effect on her. She found she liked it. She also hated it.

She needed Doug. It was that simple, and that complicated.

"You're stuck with me," he said.

She released her breath in slow, relieved measures. "I'm glad."

"I can be harder to get rid of than a hangover."

"I've never been one much for drinking." She offered a smile that he didn't return.

With reluctance, she dropped her hand, but her skin tingled as if they were still touching. "I'm not sorry we're here together," she confessed, wondering just where that statement had come from and how it had snuck past her carefully constructed defenses. She'd sworn never to let another man in, but with Doug, she feared it might already be too late.

"Aren't you, Arielle?"

She sucked in a shallow breath of air. "I trust you, Doug."

He swallowed, and she saw the way his Adam's apple moved. "Don't—"

"Shh..." she said, moving to place her finger across his lips. "I have no regrets."

Slowly, as if aware of the tightness of the grip with which he held her, Doug uncurled his fingers, one by one. "I'll take care of you," he swore.

"I know."

Tension sizzled in the atmosphere, as if so much more needed to be said. But her tummy had tightened, a female response firing through her and igniting a fire that she knew Doug's presence would surely fan.

Self-preservation kicked in. She needed to retreat to safety and hide there. She licked her lips, hoping her voice wouldn't betray her. Whenever things got hectic at school, when testing and grading became too much, she concentrated on mundane matters. Maybe it would help with Doug. Heaven knew, something needed to. "Betsy left a stew on the stove," she said.

"I'll be there in a few minutes." Doug dragged a lock of hair back into place.

She watched his movements, and wanted nothing more than to dislodge that lock of hair again, to regain the intimacy that alternately attracted and frightened her. "You have more work?"

"I need to update Rhone."

She nodded. With great reluctance, she blinked, severing the connection that flared and flamed between them. Her heart hadn't found a rhythmic tempo, and her throat still felt dry.

At the doorway, though, the sound of his voice halted her.

"This morning, while I was in the shower, you went outside for a walk."

She turned to face him. "How did you know?"

"I was watching."

A shiver slithered down her spine.

"Next time you need to step outside, let me know first."

"I stayed in the backyard."

"Where you go, I go. This is not open for negotiation."

Her back teeth met each other. "Does this mean I have no freedom?"

"Arielle," he said, a stroke of warning in the word. "You're my responsibility."

"But—"

"I'm not asking."

His brows were drawn together, a study in seriousness. He meant what he said, and she knew it. She'd seen guilt paint a picture on his face. He blamed himself for the attempt on her life, and now he'd be doubly vigilant. She wondered whether she could take it.

Arielle reminded herself that she'd practically begged him to take her case. She had no right to dictate how he did that. Still, that didn't mean his attitude didn't chafe. "I understand," she said.

He gave her a curt nod of dismissal. She recognized the authoritative gesture. The school's principal used it after performance appraisals.

Outside the room, she rested her shoulders against a log wall and expelled a shaky sigh. Within a few seconds, she heard the drone of his voice, resonating with strength and power—the two things she needed, the two characteristics that irritated her the most.

His words had bothered her more than she cared to acknowledge. She wanted everything to be over, didn't want to consider the consequences of another threat. She'd been so certain that going to Doug was the answer to her problems. But her determination might be the one thing that made them worse.

It didn't truly matter, though. They were in this together now. There was no one she'd have trusted more with her life. And that was exactly what this had come down to— her life. Maybe his, too.

How did he do it? How did a man live with constant threat and danger? The terror sometimes held her paralyzed. Doug lived with it every day of the week.

He worried that he'd placed her in jeopardy, yet hadn't given a second thought to the risk to his own life. She knew so little about him. Her heart wanted to know more, no matter what her mind said.

Hearing the sudden absence of sound, she took another breath and pushed away from the wall. She wouldn't fall apart, couldn't.

In the kitchen, she carried the pan to the table and served the stew, adding extra to Doug's bowl. She sliced the bread they'd bought in town and waited for him.

He walked into the kitchen without her hearing his approach. It was the movement of his chair in her side vision that drew her attention to his presence. Unlike the rambunctious adolescents she was accustomed to, the man moved with stealth, nearly able to sneak up on her. A useful trait, she mused, in his line of work, although nevertheless disconcerting.

For a fraction of a second, before he hid it, she saw past Doug's tough outer shell and into the realm of vulnerability. She saw frustration and guilt, and maybe a mixture of annoyance, along with a definite gleam of defiance. It was there in his eyes, but obviously, when he realized someone might see it, he schooled it away.

"How do you do that?" she asked.

He took a seat and picked up a spoon. "Smells good," he said.

"How do you manage to hide your feelings so well?" she persisted.

"Do I?"

"You do." She sat across from him. "Like right now. The chandelier could crash and you wouldn't blink."

He leaned toward her, as if letting her in on a great secret. "Cribbage," he said. "You've got to know when to force your opponent to take a risk, got to know when to take one yourself."

"Cribbage?"

"A poker face," he supplied. "I won earlier, didn't I?"

"Only because I'm a beginner." He was a master of deception. She realized she was learning about Doug in tiny fractions, uncovering aspects of his personality only when he wasn't conscious of giving them away.

"But you won't be a beginner soon. And I'll still be winning."

"Is everything a game to you?"

He put down his spoon. "Sweetheart, nothing is a game. Everything in life is a gamble."

He'd shared more about himself in that one statement than he had in the past couple of days. Earlier, she'd decided she wanted to get close, wanted to uncover the things locked away in his soul. Now she was no longer sure she wanted to.

She shivered at the coldness in his eyes, a layer of ice covering green...a contradiction to the lightness of his words. She reached for her cup, only to discover that the coffee was cold, as well.

They'd been drinking hot chocolate earlier, hot chocolate that he'd never had before. In her school, she often saw students, boys and girls, struggling to see how and where they fit in, kids wondering whether anyone cared, whether anyone would be at home when the dismissal bell rang. Kids like...

She looked at him, wanting to see into his past again.

Kids like Doug might have been?

"What do you see, Doc?"

His voice had dropped to a dangerous level, as if he knew exactly where her mind had wandered. She trod delicately. "I told you I'm not a psychologist."

"But that hasn't stopped you from psychoanalyzing me. Repeatedly."

She shifted in her seat. Doug saw more than she wanted him to, digging deep and trying to expose her innermost thoughts. "I deal with numerous pupils every day."

He picked up his spoon, but didn't stick it in the steaming stew.

"I see a lot in their eyes."

"You teach gifted students."

"Doesn't matter. People are people, no matter the age. And all of them—us—face problems. It's in their eyes.

"Mirror to the soul," she added softly.

"And your point is?"

"Sometimes it's there, Doug, in your eyes. The pain, the past, the guilt."

Metal clattered against stoneware. "Are you sure you don't have a license?"

"The bell rings at three, some kids jump up and head out the door, laughing, so excited to go home they're barely able to remember their backpacks and jackets."

She saw that she had his complete attention, so she continued, "A couple reach for their pencils and slip them into the spiral of their notebooks, then they zipper the notebook into the backpack. They put on their jackets a sleeve at a time. By this time, half the class is already gone. They give me a last, longing look, then slowly open the door.'' She paused. ''Which were you, Doug?''

A long minute of tension uncurled. She began to think he'd change the subject, laugh it off, treat it as a game, when it was anything but.

Finally, he said, ''If you were a betting woman...''

Her heart thundered. He'd left her an opening, as well as an invitation to walk through it. She only hoped there was solid ground on the other side, not a crumbling precipice. ''If I were a betting woman...''

''Go on.''

She drew a breath. ''You cleaned chalkboards for your teacher.''

Doug swore. He stood abruptly, toppling his chair. His eyes darkened as he glared in her direction. Then he turned and stalked to the far side of the room, leaving behind a wake of anger and frustration.

She'd shoved too hard in trying to topple that barrier. Why hadn't she realized that if she pushed at bricks, some might fall on her?

He stood with his back to her, staring soundlessly out the window.

She speared a piece of potato with a fork and realized she had no appetite. ''I did it again,'' she said with a sigh, lowering the fork. ''Spoke without thinking. I'm sorry.''

Slowly he turned. ''I asked.''

''But I have no right to pry.''

''Are you telling me I can't bluff when I play against you?''

She carefully entered into her answer, determined to undo what she'd already done. ''You can bluff anytime you want, Doug. You're able to hide what you don't want anyone to see.''

''But you see.''

''Only when you're not aware of it.''

''Some things are better locked up.''

She nodded. "And some things are better unbottled."

"And what if the stopper won't go back in?"

"Is that what you're afraid of?"

"I'm not afraid of anything, Arielle. Especially something that isn't real."

The words fell with finality. Only she knew better, knew that he'd voiced a lingering fear, even if he wouldn't admit to it. "Things that aren't real," she asked, "like your feelings, your emotions?" Things like cleaning the chalkboard because it was better than facing reality at the front door to your home?

Her heart ached for him. No matter how she told herself it wasn't any of her business, she couldn't make herself not care. That thought crashed on the heels of another. Caring for him might be more dangerous than facing an assassin's bullet, because living with emotional loss was often the toughest endeavor of all.

"When we get back," he said, "I'll have a shingle made for your office."

Effectively, he'd changed the subject, keeping his answers under lock and key, the way he said was safest. "I keep telling you, I'm not a psychologist."

"Yet."

The storm had passed, but she would now be able to recognize the warning sounds. Maybe in future she'd stay out of its way. If she was smart, she would. "Bet I can win at cards tonight."

"Bet you won't," he said, crossing back to the table.

"I teach math."

"Are you confessing to counting cards?"

"You might have won once, but it won't happen again," she answered, hedging.

"I bluff."

"I have an excellent memory."

He sat across from her, and she gently exhaled. Walking over cut glass would be easier than getting Doug to reveal facts he wanted hidden. She managed to eat a few bites while Doug finished off his bowl.

It didn't matter how many times she told herself not to pry, she couldn't help it. Betrayal had made her swear off men...all men. So why did nothing tempt more than the forbidden?

After dinner, they washed dishes together, their conversation light, if they spoke at all. The silence in between was a comfortable bonus. Then, in the living room, Doug struck a match to the dried timber in the fireplace and found a deck of cards.

Two hours later, she won her first game of cribbage. Gleefully she stabbed the peg into the final hole. "Skill beats treachery."

"Sometimes," he conceded, reaching into the popcorn bowl. "And sometimes I let someone win, just to throw them off balance."

"You didn't let me win. I beat you fair and square."

"Did you?"

She frowned.

"You'll never know, Doc."

She intended to prove it. "Shuffle the cards, Doug."

"So you do like to play."

"I like to win," she countered.

"That makes two of us. Winning isn't everything—"

"Yeah, I know. It's the only thing. So let's make it interesting."

"A wager?" he asked. "Like strip poker? I'll show you mine if you'll show me yours?"

Her mouth dropped open.

"Cards, Arielle, I'll show you my cards if you show me yours—at the end of each hand, of course. You didn't think I meant anything else, did you?"

Doug offered her a piece of popcorn. She held out her hand to accept it, but he shook his head. "Open your mouth," he said. "Like you did when you made a faulty assumption about what I meant."

"Faulty assumption?"

"Open your mouth, Arielle. For me."

She sucked in her breath. With patience, he waited. Time dragged on in miserly moments. He didn't blink, remaining focused on her as if she were the only woman in the world. Finally, sanity battling invitation, she did as he asked.

He leaned toward her, cards sliding across the coffee table. She closed her mouth around the popcorn, as well as his finger. The taste of salt and butter mingled as the popcorn melted in her mouth. Suddenly she realized that he hadn't moved away.

Intimacy crackled along with the burning pine in the fireplace. Embarrassed, she parted her lips and pulled away from him. Her face felt as warm as the sparks shooting across the logs, and her insides became molten.

It had been so long since she felt desire for a man, longer since she contemplated doing anything about it. What was it about Doug that made her want to wrap caution in kindling and hold it to the flickering flames?

Idiocy, it had to be. And maybe a need to really live. Being on the edge mentally and emotionally threw her off kilter. The knowledge that someone was out there, watching her, wanting her dead.

The illusion of safety shattered. But Doug hadn't sensed it.

"Good?" he asked, easing back his finger.

Popcorn had never tasted like that. And neither had temptation.

"Everything okay? You look like you're suddenly miles away."

She'd never been with a perceptive man before. She knew he saw through things, noticed things no other man would. And he called her a psychologist? "Fine," she said, curling her palms around her shoulders.

She trusted Doug, she really did. But that didn't stop fear from creeping in when she least expected it, leaving behind a trail of vulnerability.

Fear changed her, she realized, changed who she was as a person. When she looked in the mirror each morning, someone different stared back. Things she had once taken for granted no longer seemed so easy. She'd assumed she'd be going to school every morning, assumed she'd have dinner with friends once a week, assumed she'd make it to exercise class on Saturday. Now nothing was sacred, not even the next moment.

But it had another side, too. One that made her appreciate each and every thing she had. She marveled in the morning's sunrise, in the way the branches of an aspen swayed in the afternoon wind. And she thrilled to Doug's touch. Her senses seemed heightened, every event a sensory onslaught. She'd never surrendered in a man's arms the way she had in Doug's. She'd never responded to a man's kiss the way she did to Doug's. She'd never offered herself to a man the way she did to Doug.

When you wondered if each second was your last, each was special.

"Where did you go?" he asked.

"Go?"

"Your eyes went on a journey. One second you were here, the next you were gone. You need to take me with you. That's my job."

"I'm okay."

"Scared?"

"No." The lie nearly choked her.

"You're shivering."

How did she explain that her cold came from the inside, from a place that couldn't be warmed with blankets?

Without saying another word, he added another log to the fire, sending sparks shooting up the chimney. He crossed the room, but didn't sit across from her. Instead, he settled on the couch next to her. As close as they might be if they were—

She ruthlessly cut off the thought. She wasn't intimate with Doug, and certainly didn't plan on becoming intimate with him. Normally, she wasn't given to flights of fancy. But since she contacted that nameless man, nothing had been normal.

"Come here," Doug said, placing his arm across her shoulders.

She wiggled closer to him, tamping down the warning from deep inside.

Against her better judgment, when he urged her closer, she went, resting her head on his chest. His body radiated heat, as well as power. It blended into a heady combination that appealed to her on a basic, womanly level.

"I've seen cold like this before," he said softly.

She waited for him to continue, wondering if he'd reveal another facet of his complex personality.

"In the jungle."

"The jungle?"

"Fear doesn't care about the outside temperature."

A breath froze in her throat. Instead of revealing himself, he'd cut through the part of her that she'd been trying hardest to protect. "You're ruthless, you know that?"

"Truthful," he countered.

"About everyone except yourself."

Beneath her ear, his heart missed a beat, then continued on.

"You want to hear about the jungle?" he asked, his tone raw and hurt.

She didn't answer, didn't know what he expected her to say.

"Rhone was there," he said. "Being held prisoner in a hole in the ground."

She gasped.

"They'd had him so long, he didn't know what month

it was, barely remembered his own name. When I found him…'' Doug paused. ''When I found him it was eighty degrees and ninety-percent humidity. He was shivering so hard he couldn't stand up. And when I cut him free, I was shivering, too.

''There were gunshots and shouting, the stench of gunpowder and sweat and terror. We lost a couple of men, and Rhone and I barely made it out alive. The knowledge of what they'd done to him, what they'd do to me if we didn't get the hell out of there… My blood ran cold. Until then, I didn't know it could. But it does.''

She remained silent, her heart aching for him. When he continued, she feared her heart would surely break in two.

''I know what it's like to be cold inside, Arielle, because I've taken the trip myself.

''I know what it's like to fear life more than I fear death.''

Chapter 11

"No!"

"Arielle," Doug said softly, soothing a hand down her back. "Wake up."

She thrashed in her sleep, kicking, barely missing Doug's groin. He winced. Her aim had been a little too close for comfort.

She cried out again, twisting in the sheets, pulling them off him. Frigid air snapped at him, and her hand caught him across the face. Blood rushed to his cheek where she'd smacked him.

Not his lucky night.

Figured—he was in bed with a very desirable woman, and she'd finally reached out to him. Maybe he should have been more specific about how he wanted her touching him. "Wake up," he said again, surrounding her wrist on her second attempt to backhand him.

In the moonlight that spilled through the bedroom window, he saw her blink. "You're having a nightmare. Maybe about Rocky Balboa?"

Her teeth chattered and Doug knew he was going to get another wish. He was going to hold her. Unfortunately, he was no longer sure that was a good wish. Certainly, it wasn't a smart one. Keeping his hands to himself meant a chance for a better grip on reality. But that didn't stop him. He'd never been much for reality, anyway.

Doug closed his arms around her and pulled her against him.

"I'm okay," she whispered, keeping herself rigid and holding her head an inch or so above his arm.

"Sure you are. A regular one-man army." Confounded woman even lied in her sleep. She'd lied to him earlier, when she said she was okay, and she'd lied to him again just now.

Doug had a lot of useless skills, and a couple of useful ones. Recognizing lies was a specialty he particularly relished. It had saved his butt. And it had gotten his arm around a beautiful woman earlier, in front of the fire. Not that he'd minded. If circumstances were different, if he actually wanted a relationship, if she was anyone but a client....

"I was dreaming," she said softly into the anonymity of night.

He stroked a hand down her back, feeling the soft slide of satin beneath his fingertips. Slippery material snagged on the roughness of his skin. Another contradiction. As if there weren't enough.

"You're safe, Arielle."

"He was going to get me. He had a knife. I couldn't see his face, but I felt his hatred and resolve. A stench surrounded him and gagged me." Her voice choked on a sob. "I don't want to die that way."

Doug's jaw clenched. Who had she seen? The assassin she'd hired, or Pickins? The question stuck in Doug's craw. Pickins wouldn't have wanted a piece of her if she hadn't walked through the doors of the Masterson Agency.

Doug's motions stilled, and she rested her cheek against his bare chest. She wiggled once or twice, trying to get comfortable, ending up with her hair fanning beneath his chin and down his arm. Her left leg crossed his knee—an intimacy he hadn't shared with anyone, not since Kerry.

The thought of Kerry made his back teeth gnash together. She'd been young and unsuspecting. Worse, she'd been trusting, offering so guilessly what he demanded from Arielle. The thought of failure slunk insidiously into his mind, gathering force as it lingered.

Determinedly he banished the possibility. He wouldn't fail. He would keep Arielle safe. Rhone was in on the case, Brian had been on it since the beginning. The safe house was remote and didn't have easy access. Doug had alerted the local sheriff to be on the lookout for unusual visitors to the area, and had given the man a full description of Pickins.

And if Pickins got past all the safety measures, Doug had a score to settle. If he had wanted to be used for target practice, he'd have painted a bull's-eye on his chest.

"Don't leave me."

"Wouldn't think of it."

Within a minute, he felt, rather than heard, a change in Arielle's breathing. She'd found sleep. He knew he wouldn't even be able to hunt it down. She shifted slightly, her hair tickling his chin. He moved his hand in rhythmic motions across her shoulders, offering comfort, offering a promise.

He marveled at the feel of her womanly softness pressed against his harder contours. Man and woman. The way he'd once believed it should be.

He stayed like that for a long time, holding her, caressing her, inhaling the scent of freshness and vulnerability. *Vulnerable* wasn't a word that came to mind in the daytime hours when he thought of Arielle. She was strong, masking any weakness with determination.

The thought of her life ending, before it really had a chance to begin, before she had children of her own—Doug chopped the forming image in half. She'd live to a ripe old age, if he had anything to say about it.

The moon dropped lower in the sky, yielding to day. He realized she hadn't moved in the past hour or so, and his muscles had started to tense. Rest, evidently, was for the innocent. Which meant he might as well brew some coffee.

Knowing she'd never know if he succumbed just once, he didn't resist temptation. Instead, he dropped a light kiss on her forehead. A smile ghosted across her lips, and then she snuggled closer into him.

If he gave in a second time, kept her cradled against him, he'd be a goner, drowning in the very emotions he wanted to avoid. He refused to allow that to happen.

She murmured in protest when he moved away. Truth to tell, he wanted to. A long-denied part of him wanted to lie there with her snuggled against him. Her hand had curved around his shoulder, and it wasn't until he headed for the shower that he realized he craved the touch.

Beyond caffeine, Doug hadn't craved anything in years. So why now? More, why her?

He closed the door to the bathroom and stood under the stinging spray of mountain water. Comforting her hadn't been without its consequences. Ten minutes later, reasonably sure he wouldn't embarrass himself if she was awake, he zipped his jeans, tucked the pistol between his waistband and spine, then walked back into the bedroom.

She still slept, her chest rising and falling by peaceful measures. He stood at the foot of the bed for long moments, staring at her. Her hair spilled across the pillow, and she'd tucked the sheet beneath her chin. Long lashes barely distracted his notice from the bruiselike darkness beneath her eyes that sleep hadn't been able to vanquish.

His respect for her nudged up a notch. She didn't complain, did what she had to do and dug deep for guts that she probably never knew existed.

Having spoken to Rhone and Shannen, Doug knew Arielle was precious to her parents, as well as her students. He resisted the emotional tug that told him she was precious to him, as well. Doug didn't do precious. That knowledge didn't give him the power to turn away from her, though.

Only the demands of duty did that.

With reluctance, he finished dressing. He did a cursory check of the upstairs, glanced at window locks and the positions of curtains and blinds, then jogged down the stairs two at a time, doing a visual sweep on his way to the coffeepot.

He carried a mug into the office, hoping a fax or update had arrived. No such luck. He typed an e-mail to Brian, sent another to Rhone, knowing not all Internet firewalls were sophisticated enough to keep out hackers, then went outside.

Cold Colorado autumn nipped at him, the predawn hour making the chill worse. No prints marred the gravel driveway, except those of a deer who bolted when the beam of Doug's flashlight startled her.

Twenty minutes later, satisfied, he returned inside to find Arielle on the couch, with her legs tucked beneath her and her nightgown pulled over her knees. Her hands circled a cup of coffee, steam bathed her face, and the smile she offered barely curved her lips.

He bolted the door, the click echoing through the living room.

"I didn't dream it, did I?"

He raised a brow, taking a seat across from her.

"That you held me last night?"

"You had a nightmare."

"And you saved me from it."

He shrugged. "Had to protect myself. You've got quite an aim."

She flushed, the color standing out against the paleness of her features. Even though she didn't complain, she couldn't have denied that events had taken a toll on her. The sooner this was resolved, the better. She should be at the head of a class, not locked behind a safety door and looking over her shoulder.

He'd get her through this, no matter what it took. "How do you like your eggs?" he asked.

"I don't like to eat this early."

"Scrambled, boiled, poached, sunny-side up? You've got a fifty-fifty chance of it turning out okay if I need to flip them."

"Doug—"

"You need to keep up your strength."

She wrinkled her nose. "You asked for pancakes that first day on your boat."

"Yacht. She's a yacht."

She nodded. "If I make pancakes, will that work?"

"Do you know how to make French toast?"

"Can you be bought?"

"The way to a man's heart…"

"Is through his stomach. Is that true?"

"Try me."

She made breakfast every bit as well as she played cards. And he had to admit, her coffee was better than his, too. Maybe that was why some men got married. Cold cereal and eggs held limited appeal.

For the rest of the day, he didn't let her out of his sight. She frowned when she went into the bathroom later that afternoon for her shower, scowled when she found him sitting on a chair when she walked into the bedroom wearing only two towels, one on her head, the other wrapped around her body. Pale blue had never had so many possibilities before.

"Do you mind?"

He raised a brow.

"I'd like some privacy."

"This is as much as you're going to get."

"You're driving me crazy."

He studied the blunted tips of his nails.

"Since Brian called yesterday, you haven't left my side."

"And your point is?"

She sighed. "You're infuriating."

"You're still alive," he countered.

Arielle pressed her hands to her face, then slowly lowered them. "Doug, I know you mean well."

He waited. Goose bumps raised on her arms. Still, she stood there, facing him.

"I can't do it this way," she insisted. "You need to back off and leave me some breathing room."

Her words fired him. Doug stood and devoured the distance in three biting strides. Anger sparked. He stood close to her, his gaze searing into hers.

Doug tried to tell himself she was just an assignment. Tried to tell himself that their touches meant nothing, that holding her in his arms meant nothing.

But he could no longer make himself swallow that lie.

By the minute, his ability to resist her drew on shallower and shallower reserves. He wanted her safe, wanted her smiling, wanted her in his arms. He wanted *her*. "Make no mistake in this, Arielle." He ground out the words. "I will keep you alive. I'll do whatever it damn well takes to let you see your parents again and teach school."

Blood thundered in his temples, trampling tenderness. Her eyes were open wide, and she'd dragged her bottom lip between her teeth. Wisps of drying hair framed her delicate face. Yeah, he wanted her, all right, but he wanted a whole lot more than just her body.

That thought scared him spitless, reminding him of the

time he'd stood at the helm and stared into the hungry grip of a hurricane. Lowering his voice, knowing it matched the dangerous churning inside, he said, "I warned you you'd be sorry to be stuck with me. You took the gamble.

"And sweetheart, I hold all the cards."

Doug pivoted. He strode from the room, taking power and frustration with him, sucking energy from her.

When he slammed the door, a picture jumped on the wall. Her shoulders fell forward in the sudden silence. She felt as if the earth had been shaken, leaving her on a piece she'd never stood on before.

She dragged the towel around her more, keeping a tight grip on the terry cloth...something to hold on to, anything. Last night, she'd asked if everything was a joke to him. He'd proved it wasn't.

Arielle lowered herself to the edge of the bed, seeing his clothes from yesterday discarded in an untidy heap. The covers were mussed on his side of the bed, smooth on hers. She hadn't made her side of the bed. Rather, Doug had invited her to share the security of his.

She remembered waking up in a tangle of sheets and sweat, recalled a gentle voice that vanquished the demons chasing her. Doug. She took a deep breath and allowed it to ease back out. Stress management, they'd called it at the teacher in-service. Survival, she now called it.

He was a strong man, rigid and unmalleable as the steel of the gun he carried. He didn't want to be seen that way, so he made wisecracks and smiled easily. But that core of strength inside was undisguisable. He'd offered a glimpse of his humanness last night, allowed her inside to see his pain and uncertainty.

She was starting to care for him, she knew, woman to man. As impossible, irrational and illogical as it was, the fact hit her in the heart. She desired him, ached to be in his arms again.

Heaven help her, what was wrong with her? She'd never yet fallen for a man who could come close to giving her what she wanted. Doug Masterson, loner, could never offer what she needed.

She squeezed her eyes shut. Would she never learn? She couldn't want him, couldn't.

She'd lived with heartbreak before, and she knew she wouldn't survive it again. Which meant she had to stop the feelings now, before he swept her away.

Standing, Arielle reached into a drawer for underwear. The towel pooled around her, leaving her clothed in doubts and nothing more.

The routine of drying her hair and clipping a barrette around it provided some distraction. She jumped when he knocked on the door.

"You okay?"

"I'm fine, Doug."

"I'll be downstairs."

She'd been in the bedroom barely twenty minutes, and he'd knocked twice. His words of yesterday, when he'd indicated he would be her constant shadow, were proving prophetic. A part of her already regretted the power he held over her. Still, no other option existed.

After stalling for five more minutes, Arielle finished dressing, then made her way downstairs. He sat on the couch, remote control in hand, but with the TV volume muted. He'd been flipping aimlessly through channels until he looked up at her. With the touch of his finger, he zapped the picture. "I apologize if you think I was harsh."

She slipped her hands in her back pockets. "Are you apologizing for what you said?"

"No."

"I didn't expect you would. No regrets are necessary, Doug. You said what needed to be said."

"No grudges?"

She shook her head.

A fire blazed in the hearth. She looked into it, watching the flames flicker. The wood crackled and popped in the silence. A fire. Such a mundane thing.

At home, she might have held a match to kindling, then sat in front of the burning logs to grade papers. All across the country, people tossed wood on top of kindling, cooked dinner, prepared for the evening. Only here, even though she did all those things, nothing was normal. "How much longer?" she asked him.

When he didn't respond, she dragged her gaze away from the mesmerizing flames. "Doug?"

"I don't know. Since getting a trace on Pickins's license tags, there's been no more news."

She moved to the couch and sat. "How do you do this? All this waiting?"

"Get good at cribbage."

"I'm going crazy, Doug," she confessed, looking directly at him. "Even on summer break, I teach courses or take them. I've never had this kind of enforced isolation before. I've never had someone follow me around, watching my every move. I don't know if I can take it much longer."

"We're doing the best we can."

She wrapped her arms across her chest. "I'm not blaming you. I appreciate everything you've done and continue to do." She feathered her hair back from her eyes. "It's me, I suppose. Sorry about complaining. Mom always told me patience was a virtue."

"And you're not virtuous?"

"I guess not. I try, though. Mom still insists Mr. Right will come along, and that I'll give her grandchildren to bounce on her knee."

"Do you believe it?"

She didn't need to answer, could tell him to mind his own business. But for some reason, this seemed too important. "No. I believed it once upon a time, but not any-more."

"What happened?"

Maybe it was the night, or the flames, or the loneliness, or maybe it was Doug's presence. There was something about him that inspired confidence, the right amount of sympathy blended with an attitude for irreverence. Whatever it was, she admitted, "Prince Charming doesn't exist, at least not for me."

He waited quietly. Although she'd decided not to say another word, she continued anyway. "When I even hint at commitment, my phone never rings again."

"Any man would be a fool not to want a relationship with you."

She smiled, but it froze when she realized he wasn't joking. Slowly the smile faded. "You can't mean that."

"I do."

A log shifted on the grate, and the fire flared, sparking the room with intimacy. "Well, I've met a number of them. Went as far as getting engaged. I thought I loved him, thought he loved me the way I wanted to be loved. But when I mentioned that I wanted kids, several of them, he said he wasn't ready for fatherhood and supporting a brood."

Even now, after a few years, the wound on her heart still ached. She threw herself into her job with enthusiasm, treating the kids at school as if they were her own, because she'd probably have none of her own. "He asked for his ring back."

"Bastard."

"There has to be something about me..."

"Don't believe it. You just haven't met the right man yet. It can happen."

"Sure."

"I've seen it firsthand, with Rhone."

"Has it ever happened to you?"

Silence shrouded the room. Honesty had been replaced by a different kind of electrical charge. A pop exploded from the fireplace, making her jump. Doug wasn't going to answer, and she'd pushed too hard again, blindly jumping over that invisible line he constantly drew.

"Yeah, it happened to me, once."

Arielle sucked in her breath.

"Her name was Kerry." Rawness scraped through his words, as if he'd dragged them over a painful memory.

He turned from Arielle, staring into the depths of the flames.

"Did you get married?"

"Didn't work out."

She sighed in frustration. Doug was determined to shoulder his burdens alone, never sharing or opening up. On the other hand, he was never satisfied unless he'd dug out another person's innermost secrets. She'd have bet on his ability to wring confessions from hardened criminals... without ever giving away a thing about himself. "Did she dump you?"

"No, she didn't dump me."

"Then you dumped her."

"No, Arielle, I didn't dump her."

"Then?"

"Leave it be."

"You don't. You push and prod until you know every detail. You demand my trust, my belief, my complete honesty, and you're not willing to give anything in return."

Doug surged to his feet and swallowed the distance between them. She saw his anger. It brewed like an ocean storm in his eyes, whipping into deep swells.

"Leave it alone, Arielle."

On a surge of bravery, or stupidity—she didn't stop to analyze which—she pushed on. "What are you afraid of this time?"

He leaned in close, then closer. "I said, *leave it alone.*"

She should respect the boundaries he drew, should respect that line he warned her not to cross.

"You can run, Doug, but you can't hide. You can never hide."

His brows drew together, and his lips compressed. A pulse throbbed in his temple. Too late, she found rational thought. She wanted to retract her words, but she couldn't force them past her thundering pulse.

"Neither can you, Doc," he said, words containing nothing but granite.

She tipped her head back, her breath squeezing out in ragged little bursts.

At that, he caught her shoulders and said, "Anyone tell you you talk too much?"

There was no teasing in his tone, nothing but seriousness and frustration. "Doug, don't."

His lips caught hers.

She drew back, but he tightened his hold on her and deepened the kiss, demanding surrender.

He'd kissed her in New York to shock her, and other times with passion. But this was about punishment, for delving too deeply. She wanted to resist, wanted to stand there till he stopped, but she couldn't.

She'd started to care about him. With that had come the ability to see through his facade of anger to the anguish. Nothing was more painful than slicing open your heart and exposing it, and she'd asked him to do that.

She met his tongue, his thrust, with a gentle parry. Then she reached her hands around and clasped them behind his neck. He smelled of masculinity, of power, of determination. And beneath her hands, she felt the corded strength of him, but not the tenderness she knew him to be capable of.

Whatever had happened to Doug had very nearly destroyed him. Despite his actions, she remained doubly determined to find out what it was that had hurt him so badly.

He ended the kiss. Then he took a step away from her. "That shouldn't have happened." He dragged his fingers through his hair, raking it backward.

"Doug, I..." She pressed her fingers to her swollen lips. Her heart reeled with the intensity, the undiluted passion of his kiss. She'd never felt anything like it before.

"I've never kissed a woman out of anger. You shouldn't have been the first. I have no excuses."

He dragged in a breath. "You have every right to demand someone else protect you."

Chapter 12

Disgusted, Doug turned and strode to the window. Sightlessly, wordlessly, he stared out into the encroaching blackness of night. Tree branches snapped back and forth in the wind, tossed around like his insides.

What in the hell was wrong with him? Women didn't get to him. Beyond an occasional evening together, women had barely impacted his life in the past few years. He preferred the sweet song of the sea to the seduction of a sensual woman. The ocean in a storm was calmer than any woman he'd known.

Except Arielle.

Even now, when she had all the reason in the world, she hadn't uttered a cross word, hadn't fallen to pieces.

Just when had things gotten so screwed up? He'd always exercised taut control over his emotions, masking everything he didn't want people to see. Yet, with a few carefully aimed words, Arielle had found his heart and hit it with the intensity of an armor-piercing bullet.

In his years in the field, he'd seen the damage a piece

of shrapnel could cause. And now… He sighed. And now he'd experienced the soul-shredding impact.

The damnedest thing was, she'd found the truth he was trying to deny. He couldn't run, and he couldn't hide. It was always there, Kerry was always there, the guilt was always there. And he'd punished Arielle…for being honest.

When he turned, she was still sitting on the couch, a finger against her lips. Guilt clawed at him. Some protector. Instead of getting his protection, she needed protecting from him. Seeking, but finding no other option, he reluctantly said, "I'll call Brian and ask him to fly out."

She dropped her hand and surged to her feet. Her eyes were open wide and a flush crept up her cheeks. "You don't get it, do you? I don't want Brian. I want you."

"But—"

"Stuff it, Doug. You told me I'm stuck with you, and you're stuck with me. And when you're done hiding, let me know." Arielle rushed out of the room and ran up the stairs.

He braced for the sound of the door slamming, only to hear silence filter down the stairway. He released a deep sigh before shoving a hand into his hair. Where she was concerned, everything he said and did only made matters worse.

He wanted to escape her, but couldn't, not with the way the just-showered scent of her lingered in the air. More, not when the taste of her hesitation, her submission, then, finally, her gentleness, remained on his tongue. Even when he'd been stripped to his most male, most elemental reaction, she'd tamed him. She'd remained strong yet feminine, the paradox that defined Arielle's personality.

And so different from anything Kerry had ever been.

He'd been younger, and paid handsomely to protect Kerry. Emotions had gotten in the way. Foolishly he'd wanted to believe he was in love.

Unfortunately, the past seemed to be repeating itself. But

he knew better than to allow himself to fall in love a second time. He cared for Arielle, he was willing to admit that much. To a certain degree, it was inevitable.

Emotions were controllable...love was something that developed if fed by the right combination of passion, caring and wanting. No doubt, he desired her. He was human, a man. But he didn't want. Nor did he need.

He crossed to the window again. An image of Arielle seemed superimposed on the darkness, but when he looked again, he only saw a reflection of himself. She'd reached down inside him, finding a place that hadn't been touched in a very long time.

Doug definitely didn't like the fact that she possessed the ability to see inside him. It made him vulnerable. He'd vowed never again to be vulnerable.

Which meant he needed to solve this case. Soon. Soon he'd send her and her complex psychological probings back to her safe and secure world of class plays and parent-teacher conferences. He'd untie *Destiny* from her slip and sail out to the sea, preferably into a sunset.

Determinedly he strode into the office and punched in the phone number for his New York office. Yarrow answered on the second ring. "Give me something," Doug said. "Anything."

"A headache?"

"Got one."

"I'm gonna make it worse. Maybe you'll want to grab a bottle of aspirin."

His insides churned, but to combat that, Doug propped his feet on the desk. "Besides a headache, what've you got for me?"

"We've had a visitor. Left a couple of presents for you."

He'd always been a sucker for gifts. Nothing he liked more than returning them...twofold. After all, it was always better to give than to receive.

"Our guest ransacked the place. Left a message on the filing cabinet."

"Semper fi?"

"Yeah, clever little bugger painted a fire next to the word *fi*. Isn't he cute?"

"As a bug in a rug." Doug enjoyed smashing bugs. "Did he blow up anything?"

"Wanted to make sure you knew he still likes to play."

"How bad is it?"

"Insurance agent's here now."

As if Doug didn't have enough trouble, now his premiums would increase twice—once for the house, another for the office.

"He's saying something about cancellation. Does that mean anything to you?"

"Tell him up his—"

"Yes?"

"To up his rates. I'll pay 'em."

Doug drummed his fingers. "I want him found."

"I hired a couple of your friends."

"Pay 'em whatever it takes."

"You aren't going to like the tab."

As long as they didn't want a tip, too, it'd be fine. "It's worth it." He leaned back in his chair. Seemed Pickins didn't like losing. Well, neither did Doug. "Anything on Arielle's assassin?"

The sigh that slid down the line spoke of frustration and anger. Two things Doug related to. "Do you need extra help?" The load of two high-stress cases was enough for anyone.

"Got it covered. Do me a favor, though, check with Arielle, see if there's anything else she remembers. Distinguishing marks she didn't think of when you interviewed her before. I'll take anything, Doug."

"Yeah. So will I."

"Watch your back. Pickins didn't find any files or anything that gives a clue to your whereabouts, but..."

He leaned forward, a headache gaining force behind his eyes. "Don't worry about Pickins, find the damn assassin."

"I've been on the streets, in every fleabag hotel, every roach-infested bar."

Inactivity gnawed at Doug. "Find him." Doug slammed the receiver into the cradle, and the plastic phone vibrated with an offended jingle. He had three problems, an assassin on the loose, an explosives expert who enjoyed watching things go boom, and a woman—a client—who refused to talk to him. Couldn't get much worse. Unfortunately, out of the three, only one thing was remotely within his control.

Arielle.

He who never hesitated didn't have a clue what to do about Arielle. Go after her? Let her cool off? The second sounded better, more appealing to his masculine sense of conflict resolution. It also screamed of cowardice. He'd learned long ago that only courage combated cowardice.

He'd squared his shoulders and coldly stared at death, at torture, at despair. So why now did he prefer to cut open his chest and expose his heart, rather than face Arielle and her painfully accurate accusations?

Stalling, and knowing that was exactly what he was doing, he did another security check...finding not even a twig out of place.

A shroud of gray clouds hung across dark velvet skies, obliterating the moon. Tree branches shivered in the wind, and pine needles whispered of winter. Nature swirled and stormed, with Doug standing in the middle.

A matching restlessness churned inside him. He wished there was an alternative to sitting here, waiting, wondering.

He slammed a fist into his open palm. The need for action struggled with a sense of hopelessness. They were safer in Colorado than anywhere else. Obviously, Pickins was still in New York, and so, most likely, was the man hired to kill Arielle. Brian and Rhone were on the job, along with a host of Doug's colleagues. He was equipped with a cache of weapons and a state-of-the-art security system, as well as a remote, private location.

A snowflake sank onto his nose. And he'd thought things couldn't get much worse. Maybe it would be a dusting. With his luck, though, they'd be snowbound in hours. At least tracks stood out sharply in freshly fallen snow, he told himself. A silver lining.

He pulled in a deep draw of crisp air, then reentered the house. Warmth from the furnace blasted over him, making him realize that his rounds had taken longer than he thought. The scent of spices lured him to the kitchen, as if he were a condemned man walking inevitably to his doom.

Arielle looked up at him from where she sat at the kitchen table. She didn't say a word. Not that she needed to. Her eyes held a wary distance, and her arms were folded protectively across her chest. The unspoken warning to tread lightly came through loud and clear. "Smells good," he said.

"You can thank Betsy."

A pan simmered on the stove, the rising steam bathing the nearby window, and still the temperature seemed to drop a dozen degrees when he walked past her and reached for the coffeepot. Cold. No surprise there. Reluctantly he replaced the carafe.

"Did you make enough for two?" he asked, stirring the pot, then turning to face her.

Her eyes, her most readable feature, remained blank. "It would have been rude not to."

"And that's the one thing you never are," he said. "Rude."

"Rarely."

"But occasionally."

"Only when politeness fails."

"Ah," he said. "I see." But he wondered if he really did.

She released a soft sigh. "What do you want from me, Doug?"

"Nothing," he admitted. He had no idea what he wanted or if he had, how to go about getting it.

"You know, I haven't asked you for anything that I haven't already given myself."

Like a good commander. His respect for her nudged upward, along with his discomfort.

The buzzer sounded on the timer and she moved toward the stove, pulling on an oven mitt. "If you'll excuse me?"

When he didn't move, she smiled—a practiced little gesture that could have turned falling rain into an icicle.

"You're in my way," she said, the words packaged as a pretty, polite present.

Wisely he moved. Doug served the chicken and rice while she removed rolls from the cookie sheet. Unfortunately, those same biscuits remained untouched when she cleared the table after dinner, without having said another word.

While he brewed decaf and loaded the dishwasher, she went into the living room.

A few minutes later, hot cup of coffee in hand, he stood at the entrance to the living room, watching her. She sat on the floor in front of the fire's remains, chin resting on her knees, with her hands wrapped around her legs.

He took it as a good sign that she hadn't rushed up to her room. Then again, that might mean she wanted to finish their conversation. That thought sent chills down his spine.

Still, they couldn't continue this way. The tension grew with each minute. If it got much thicker, he'd need a hoist to lift the atmosphere.

Embers sighed in the fireplace, and wood chips simmered. He drank his coffee in the near silence, waiting for her to say something, anything. When, five full minutes later, she hadn't, he acted, moving across the room and sliding his empty mug onto the mantel above her.

"I need to ask you a few questions about your case." He didn't want to drag her into the past, but at least it was conversation, and at best she would provide the answers he needed.

She nodded warily.

"Brian's picked clean all the bones he found. He needs something new to go on. I know we've been over this, but I need to know, were there any distinguishing marks on the man you hired? Scars? Anything you didn't remember before?"

"I didn't see much."

Doug nodded.

"He had on dark green fatigues, I think. The sleeve was rolled up, like to his elbow. I was scared. I'd never done anything like that before."

"You're doing fine."

She swallowed. "Wait. He was missing a fingernail, I remember that."

Basically the same things he'd gotten from her before. The fingernail was new.

"Wait. There's something else...." She gnawed on her lower lip.

He waited.

"He might have had a tattoo, but I'm not sure. I just can't remember." She sighed deeply, the sound one of total frustration. "I've been trying, but I can't."

"It's okay," he assured her. "Let it come naturally." He wished he had access to a hypnotist—not that he was convinced it would do much good, but he was a desperate man. "Tell me if it comes to you."

She nodded, seemingly lost again. The same uncomfortable silence fell over them again, unsettling him. He had danced around what happened earlier, hadn't confronted it. Didn't much feel like it now, either.

"Time for another stroll outside before turning in—"

"I was thinking, when you came in earlier," she said, interrupting him, her voice barely audible above the gentle sizzle of charred logs. "About something you said."

He remained rooted to the spot. She hadn't looked up at him, and suddenly he wanted to go to her, wrap his arms around her and hold her tight. He wanted to see her eyes, read the emotion her voice concealed.

"I'm sorry," she whispered.

Sorry? She was sorry?

"I had no right to push you. Your past is your business. You told me to leave it alone." She twisted her hands together, but finally looked up, meeting his gaze clearly. "I should have listened to you."

He exhaled, slowly and completely. He had been the one who was wrong, not her.

"I won't pry into your life again."

That was what he wanted, right? Doug folded his arms across his chest, as if that might offer some measly protection for his heart. "I apologize for kissing you like I did."

"Don't. Your reaction was honest. That's more than most men have been with me."

He winced. So willing to accept his human failings, she humbled him. She made him want to live up to the unreal expectations she had of him, made him want to be a hero. "You didn't deserve that from me."

"Is it so very difficult for you?"

He frowned.

"Being human?"

"Yeah," he admitted.

She started to stand, and he offered his hand. For the pulse of a few seconds, he didn't think she'd accept. The last time he touched her, it had been with anger. He wouldn't blame her for politely refusing. Instead, she slipped her palm into his, her touch sending waves of awareness through him. It transcended the physical and cut into his heart.

Arielle trailed the fingers of her free hand down his face, lighting on his cheekbone, then outlining his chin. She paused, looking at him. "We're all human. Every one of us has faults and failings. It makes us real."

"Is that the teacher or the psychologist speaking?"

"Neither. It's the woman."

It was Arielle he wanted in his arms, in his bed—the teacher, the psychologist, the woman.

And he owed her. If nothing else, he owed her the honesty she'd given to him. Confession wasn't a conscious decision, but rather an inevitable one. Reaching up, he cupped his hand around hers. "You asked about Kerry."

Arielle blinked. "Kerry?"

"Yeah. The woman I cared for."

"You loved her."

Doug nodded. "I was young, invincible, and head over heels."

Quietly, she waited. Her fingers warmed his skin, her touch projected light on the darkness of his past.

He'd been interrogated before, under the worst of conditions. He hadn't cracked. Not even when they brought out the syringe.

What she wanted from him, though, was worse than an enemy cajoling secrets with a cattle prod. Try as he might, he didn't see her as the enemy, and that made her that much more dangerous. During his life, he'd been hurt by only three people. The three people he'd loved.

He told himself he didn't care about Arielle, that she was a client, nothing more. Maybe if he told himself that another dozen times, he'd actually believe it. "It was a long time ago."

With her free hand, she feathered blond strands back from her face, tucking them behind her ear. "Doug, I appreciate your willingness to talk, but I respect your privacy. You don't have to do this."

"Yes," he said as he released her hand, "I do."

Without saying anything, Arielle gently pressed her palms together and regarded him, the pale blue of her eyes offering a silent, sincere serving of compassion.

That compassion undid him. Pivoting, he strode to the far end of the room. Distance didn't help. Her presence went with him, the scent of her clinging to him, her warmth lingering on his face.

Turning toward her, he took a deep breath. "I was paid an ungodly amount of money to protect her. Her father was a businessman, dealing in as many illegal shipments as legitimate ones. Seems he messed with the wrong people. They went after his daughter to assure Daddy dearest didn't make any more mistakes.

"I guess people can be a little testy when coke turns out to be talcum powder. They wanted to powder their noses, not their behinds."

She smiled slightly, and the simple gesture sapped some of the chill from the murkiness of memory. Odd how she possessed that ability, that of shedding sunshine and scattering shadows.

"I took the assignment." He rested his hand on the phone stand, drumming his fingers near the enviable picture of Rhone with his family.

After a couple of seconds in which silence pulsed with expectancy, punctuated by his motions, he continued, "She needed to be protected, I needed the money. I'd just opened my own agency. I was an expert at everything, a kid who knew it all. I could protect her from a few thugs. Hell, I had already sent Pickins to jail. I'd dealt with every weapon known to man. Like I said, an expert."

"This was after the Marines?"

"And before Central America."

She shuddered, sinking into the couch. ''Kerry's the reason you went to Central America.''

''A death wish,'' he admitted, not surprised that Arielle had surmised what had remained unspoken. ''I didn't care if I never came back. There was nothing to live for.''

''She obviously meant the world to you.''

''She was my fiancée.''

He watched Arielle suck in a shallow drink of oxygen, followed quickly by another.

''We'd been engaged barely a week when her brother was executed, less than two weeks when they came looking for her.'' His hand formed a fist, and his knuckles whitened. ''Less than a month later, I went to Mexico and worked my way south.''

Arielle blinked—getting more than she'd bargained for, he'd have bet. He wondered whether his sordid past repulsed her as much as it disgusted him.

''It started as revenge. And it ended as with Rhone—a Colombian prison, and the government bailing me out in exchange for certain services.''

She swallowed. ''You said it started as revenge.''

He admired guts. Arielle had them, more so than he. ''I wouldn't rest till the guy that got Kerry was six feet under with worms as company.''

''He...he got her?''

''Yeah.'' His next words burned the back of his throat, searing with a bitterness not dulled by the intervening decade. ''Kerry died while she was under my protection.''

''Oh, God, Doug...''

Arielle's hand covered her heart, as if she felt his pain, experienced it and took it in. It went beyond compassion, went deeper than anything any woman had ever felt for him.

''It was a long time ago.''

''But it's still there.''

The psychologist, the woman. Arielle. ''It's still there.

You were right. I can run, but I can't hide. I learned that I didn't know squat, that letting your guard down for even thirty seconds gets you killed. Or worse. It gets the woman you love killed.''

"Guilt's a heavy burden to bear."

"Lady, you don't know the half of it." She didn't know about the nightmares, how he'd replayed the scene night after night, desperately searching for a different outcome, one that left Kerry alive.

"You would have traded places with her," Arielle guessed.

"Gladly," he responded, without hesitation.

"I would have traded places with Danny, too."

He drew strength from her lack of judgment, from her support. The light of trust in her eyes never wavered. He'd demanded that of her, unconditionally. Now that he'd received the gift, he was no longer certain he deserved the honor. Still, it gave him the courage to continue.

"I screwed up. I believed I was enough, that we didn't need more backup than the two people I'd taken with us. I believed they couldn't find us. More, I believed Kerry's father when he said he'd returned the money he owed. I believed him, Arielle, because they'd already killed his son. I thought Kerry meant the world to him. I thought the heat was off."

"It wasn't?"

"No. He lied."

"Doug, don't you see? It's not your fault, Kerry's father—''

"Don't. It *is* my fault. I had a job, an assignment. Her life was my responsibility." The breath he took burned with the fire of failure. "John trusted me with his daughter's life. I failed."

"Who forced you to be responsible for another human being?" Her voice dropped as she asked, "Who made you God?"

"She took a bullet meant for me."

A tear spilled from one of Arielle's eyes.

"Kerry died in my arms, whispering my name."

In an instant, Arielle was in front of him, her hand, soft and small, warm and tender, resting on his tightened one. "You couldn't have known. It's not your fault."

Had he done many things more difficult than making that telephone call? "Tell that to John Denning."

She gasped. "He blamed you for Kerry's death?"

That was an understatement. The nine-millimeter Doug had been forced to stare down the barrel of hadn't been a water pistol. Fortunately, he had seethed with the need for his own revenge, and that had preserved his survival instinct.

Despite the ugliness of his confession, Arielle remained steadfast, never recoiling in horror. He wouldn't have blamed her if she had. It was a testament to her inner convictions that she still stood there.

Now more than ever, he understood what had driven Arielle to hire the hit on her life. She felt as deeply for others as she did for herself. Not surprisingly, she'd rather face an assassin than a slow death that would destroy her family financially, as well as emotionally.

She amazed him.

"I'm sorry I forced you to relive it."

As she had earlier, she touched him on the cheek, leaving the top of his hand chilled. Interesting how he hadn't noticed her warmth until it was gone.

"My heart aches for you. You can't curse yourself for Kerry's death. If she hadn't been in danger, she wouldn't have needed you. You can't save the world, Doug, no matter how much you try."

"I won't let anything happen to you."

"If it does, I don't want you holding yourself responsible."

Anger spiked.

"I begged you to protect me, Doug. I didn't give you much of an opportunity to refuse. There's no way you could have known we'd both be targets."

Rationally, he realized she was right. But his protective nature told another story. Failure wasn't an option, ever again. "You're my responsibility, Arielle."

"No one can be responsible for someone else."

He closed his hand around hers, and his eyes captured her. "You're my responsibility, Arielle, make no mistake in that."

"I can't allow—"

"When the threat against you has been neutralized and you're back in school, my job will be over. And not until then."

"Doug, has anyone told you how infuriating you are?"

"Has anyone ever told you that you talk too much?" he countered.

A smile ghosted her features, banishing, if only momentarily, the ache. "Funny, I was just going to say the same thing to you." She rose on her tiptoes and brushed her lips across his.

His heart thumped, and response stirred in his groin. "Arielle?"

Their gazes met. Slowly he unfolded his fist.

"Kiss me, Doug."

He needed no second invitation.

Doug pulled her to him, claiming her lips. But this time he didn't want to punish, he wanted to accept the healing she offered. He needed Arielle.

Her tongue met his, melding, mating. He tasted the sweetness of forgiveness, the headiness of honesty.

With a groan, he deepened the kiss, pulling her against him. Nothing could have felt more natural, more right. Moist warmth invited and welcomed, encouraged.

It wasn't enough. God help him, the taste wasn't nearly enough. He wanted more, wanted all she had to offer. He'd sworn never to take again, never to ask again, but here it was, wrapped with powerful heat.

Her breasts pressed against his chest, the femininity of her making him harden.

She reached behind his neck, lacing her fingers in his hair. As she shifted, her thigh slipped between his legs, pressing against him.

Blood surged through him, vanquishing everything else. All that existed was now and here. Him and Arielle.

"I need you to hold me, make love to me," she said against his lips.

"Arielle, we can't."

"Can't or won't?" A shadow of hurt shaded her eyes.

"Can't," he said firmly. "I can't let my guard down, can't take a risk with you."

"I already told you that you can't save the world, Doug."

"But I can save you."

She looked at him with that unqualified trust he'd been demanding. It was a blessing as much as it was a burden. Instead of lessening the pulsation of desire, though, it only increased the urgency.

"I will save you, Arielle. No matter what it takes."

"Who will save me from myself?"

"Arielle." Resolve and patience tied into a knot and, together, slowly slipped away.

"I want you to make love to me."

Nobility demanded that he try again. Trying to think when her arms were around him, her body against his, became an act of total concentration. And his was about shot.

"Don't you want to make love to me?"

Her voice haunted him. She thought he didn't want her. "There's nothing I want more, but for your sake, we shouldn't do this." Quicksand seemed stable, compared with his insides. He'd wanted her in his arms, in his bed, for a long time. "This is your last chance."

She licked her lower lip in a nervous, sensuous gesture that made his gut constrict. "Then I'll pass."

He looked into her eyes and was lost. Nobility, after all, was for kings. And Doug definitely wasn't royalty.

Chapter 13

Doug's eyes darkened, from the calmness of an ocean bay to that of a stormswept sea. Indecision disappeared into the blazes of passion, and a tremor traced her spine.

She wanted this, but nothing had ever scared her more.

His grip on her tightened. He pulled her against him again, his lips descending on hers. She felt his hardness against her, his masculinity and power.

His tongue probed the deepness of her mouth, demanding her response. Willingly, she gave it. Her hands tangled in his hair as she tried to drag him closer and closer.

She savored his taste, the tanginess of desire. She reveled in the feel of him, sinew and strength. His scent, that of power, surrounded her, sweeping over her senses and consuming her thought.

She wanted to be in his arms forever, wanted the future kept away, wanted to truly live, wanted the horror of the past blocked by his presence. For a moment, for that moment, it was.

She'd come so close already to losing her life, and nothing at all was certain. A few weeks ago, she'd spent her nights writing lesson plans, grading papers, returning calls from concerned parents. She'd gone from that to the terror of a misdiagnosis, to the possibility that an assassin's bullet would find its mark.

Tomorrow wasn't a promise. She had no guarantees. Arielle longed to live for the moment, longed to have Doug hold her tight.

The kiss lasted just short of forever and not long enough, at the same time. When cool evening air bathed her moist lips, she shivered.

"Cold?"

She didn't answer, didn't know whether she could find her voice.

Doug eased away, stepping back a couple of inches. He plucked the barrette from her hair, then framed her face with his hands, pushing back wayward strands and looking deeply into her eyes.

"Are you scared, Arielle?"

"No... Yes."

His grin offered reassurance. "I'll take care of you."

"I know."

Slowly he moved his hands, untangling hers and then reaching beneath her to sweep her from the floor.

"Doug!"

"I've always wanted to do this," he said, holding her against him. "Humor me."

Her legs dangled in midair, her thighs supported by Doug's strength. "And I've always wanted someone to do this," she admitted.

He grinned, deducting worry and years from his face. She snuggled close and wrapped her arms around his neck.

The fire gave a small crackle, as if in encouragement, when he strode from the room.

He took the stairs effortlessly, each step jostling her and

igniting nerve endings. She was still fully dressed, but oh-so-aware of him as a man.

He kicked open the door, carrying her into the bedroom. Doug flicked the light switch, and a dim glow filtered across the darkness. "Do we really need the light?"

"I want to see you. Every inch of you."

Her eyes closed as she realized what he wanted from her…everything, with nothing held back. Just as he always did.

He paused at the foot of the bed, held her for a few seconds, and quietly said, "Open your eyes, Arielle."

Obeying the command was more difficult than she could ever have imagined. When she did as he asked, she saw an expression on his face that she'd never seen before. In his smile rested unadulterated approval. He wanted her for herself. Right then, she knew she cared for him…realized her heart was in danger of becoming forever lost.

Slowly he slid her down the length of his body. Her hands dropped to her sides. Now that they were here, she wasn't sure what to do, what to say.

"You're still with me?"

She nodded.

"Say it, Arielle."

"Yes," she whispered.

Her mouth went dry when he reached for the top button of her blouse. When he slipped the second free from the fabric, her heart added a second beat.

He opened the third, the one covering her bra, all without ever breaking the contact of their gazes. She saw his intensity, knew she was the recipient of the same energy and devotion he showed in all aspects of his life. She'd never received this kind of intensity before, and it overwhelmed her.

The fourth surrendered. And her knees threatened to buckle when he pulled the cotton free from her jeans, his fingers lighting on her midriff. She sucked in a breath at the feel of his hand on her bare skin.

The material of her shirt spilled downward, lying in disarray across her hips. Still, he hadn't looked away from her face. "Doug…"

"Shh. Anyone ever tell you not to disturb a man at work?"

"No."

"I'm telling you now."

Finally the last button was freed. The cotton gaped, and evening air nipped through the opening.

Instead of removing her shirt as she expected, Doug touched her chin. Silently he trailed his index finger down her throat, pausing there, at the hollow. Her pulse pounded beneath the brush of his fingertips, and she wondered whether he felt it, if he heard it.

Still touching her, he said, "I've wondered all day."

"What?"

"Which one."

"Which one?"

"Which bra you're wearing today. Red? Purple? Black?"

She shivered, in spite of the room's warmth. In maddeningly slow motions, he continued to trail lower, pausing when he reached the valley between her breasts where the lace covered her. Her breaths came in hollow bursts.

"In fact, I've been wondering the same thing every day since we went shopping."

At that instant, his gaze dipped, and her breath froze in her throat. She wanted to look away, but he captured her chin with his free hand.

"Red," he whispered, tracing the tops of the satiny, lacy material. Letting go of her, he eased the blouse from her shoulders, allowing it to puddle behind her, sinking on the carpet.

Even though she was still covered, she felt her nipples

harden beneath his perusal. She'd never experienced this kind of physical reaction before, this consuming desire to join with another person.

Leaving her still partially clothed, he continued his lazy downward exploration, causing her to suck in her belly. No, she had definitely never felt this way before, but then again, no other man was Doug Masterson.

With his thumb, he parted the button at the waistband of her jeans, then snagged the zipper tab between his thumb and forefinger. In the silence, each rasp of the parting metal screamed with the same anticipation that was singing in her.

Impatience swelled as her insides raged, tossing and turning. She kicked off her shoes as he maneuvered denim past her hips, snagging but not removing her panties.

In seconds, she stood before him, wearing only her lingerie. She experienced a twinge of shyness that disappeared when he inhaled sharply. Beneath his jeans, she saw his arousal, and her nerves stretched taut.

Her fingers trembling, she reached behind her for the clasp of the bra, brushing her hair out of the way, only to have him stay her movement with his hand. She wanted to hurry, wanted to join with him, but he refused to rush.

"Let me."

His fingers on her sensitized flesh made her murmur. "Doug, I..."

He kissed her, gently, with a promise of fulfillment.

The hooks parted, leaving her breasts unbound. Doug drew one of the straps from her shoulder, then removed the bra entirely, allowing it to sashay to the floor. Her breasts filled, seeming heavier than ever before. They throbbed and ached. But still he didn't touch her, and, oddly, that seemed to thrill her more than if he had.

He removed her panties, then took a step back. She'd never stood in front of a man like this, open and needful. Instinctively she crossed her arms over her breasts, then wasn't surprised when Doug reached for her, uncrossing her arms.

"You're beautiful, Arielle," he whispered.

Her eyes squeezed shut. She knew that wasn't the truth.

"You're beautiful," he repeated, in that husky voice that oozed down her spine.

"My breasts—"

"Are perfect," he said. And he meant it, she realized. To him, maybe she was beautiful.

He touched her then, cupping her breasts. Unable to help herself, she let her shoulders drop forward, spilling the weight of her breasts into his palms. His thumbs arched over her nipples, bringing them to a heightened sense of awareness.

And when he lowered his head, a tiny moan escaped. He circled one nipple with his tongue, while he gently squeezed the other. She cried out, her knees finally buckling.

As always, he was there, wrapping a supporting arm around her, protecting her, even when she could no longer think. Her hair hung down her back when she tipped her head, unconsciously granting him the access he wanted.

She was lost in a world that spun crazily with emotion, a world where nothing would ever be the same again. Her eyes closed when he moved to dampen the nipple of the other breast.

He grazed the darkened tip with his teeth, then shocked her by lowering his hand and slipping it between her legs. She cried out his name, and then, when he found her private spot, she gasped. "Doug, please."

Arielle knew she was going to come undone in his arms. "Make love to me, Doug." She raked her hands into his hair and, thankfully, he relented.

"I am making love to you...every inch of you. I want to know you, discover your secrets." Scooping her from the floor, he carried her the few feet to the bed, momentarily setting her down to haphazardly throw off the covers. He lowered her to the sheet, placing her head on a pillow.

In less than thirty seconds, he'd removed his own clothes and placed his gun within easy reach. He stood before her, a magnificent man who had shuttered away everything except the moment. She noticed his chest, the whipcord power, tanned and honed. His chest was shaded by hair, a band of it trailing lower, thinning as it went.

Unable to help herself, she followed the path, past his waist, his navel, and lower. She pulled her upper lip between her teeth.

He wanted her. He'd thickened, straining toward her from the thatch of hair. She hadn't imagined he'd be so...masculine. Arielle reminded her heart to keep beating as thunderous thoughts chased through her mind.

Doug opened the nightstand drawer and drew out a package before joining her on the bed. She knew she should make her final confession to him now, but couldn't find the words. In fact, she couldn't think, let alone talk.

He rolled onto his side, facing her, not letting her look away, and said, "Touch me."

Hesitantly she did, closing her hand around him. Doug sucked a breath between his teeth, and she tightened her grip. He removed her hand with a soft curse. "That wasn't such a good idea," he said, voice gravelly.

She smiled. He turned the tables quickly, though, stroking the inside of her thigh, encouraging her to open her legs. Then he found her warmth. She arched, lifting her hips from the bed and tossing her head to the side. He continued his motions, driving her insane. She wanted more, wanted him.

"No second thoughts?"

"No second thoughts."

He grinned cockily. For an instant, he left her, and she heard the sound of the small package being ripped open.

He returned in only a few seconds, continuing to caress her, arousing her to heights she'd never reached before.

He moved between her legs, poised at her entrance. He supported his weight on his elbows, then lowered his head and took her mouth. She surrendered. She'd longed for this moment her entire life, wanted to be made love to as if she were important, cared for.

Instinctively she lifted her hips to meet him. His tongue filled her with heat, obliterating all thought. Slowly he entered her, penetrating deeper, and she whimpered at the sharp pain.

Doug froze. "What the—?"

Her eyes opened, and she met the accusation in his stare, the tone of betrayal in his voice, that vanquished all traces of tenderness.

"Damn it, you're a virgin."

She swallowed deeply and tightened her hands on his shoulders. "It...it's okay," she said, fighting the fog of confusion. She'd been so ready, so willing.

He eased away from her and turned onto his side. She stifled a moan, her insides throbbing, and anguish tore at her heart.

"It's not like it's a disease," she said, trying desperately to make light of the situation, the way he usually did. But instead of his eyes lightening, they darkened another notch. Arielle trembled from the absence of his heat and the force of his anger.

"For crying out loud, why didn't you say something?"

"I didn't want to."

"You didn't want to?" he echoed.

"It's my body, my choice."

"I can't do this to you, Arielle. We can't do this."

"I asked you to make love to me, Doug. I'm a big girl." She reached for a sheet and drew it over her, huddling in it as if it could offer protection, as if it might shield her heart. "What difference does it make?"

Even in the room's dimness, she saw the spark of frustration that spiked in his eyes. He dragged his hand into his hair. "What difference does it make?" he repeated incredulously.

"I trust you," she whispered, knowing he wouldn't settle for anything less than complete honesty. "I want my first time to be with you."

He sighed. "No, you don't."

"Don't tell me what I think or how I feel," she said, sitting up and dragging the sheet with her.

"Arielle, do you always act first, then think later?"

"No. Usually I'm very rational and reserved." Tears clogged her throat as all the horror of the past weeks closed in on her. "But I'm tired of living for tomorrow. I need to live for today." She struggled for a breath. "I've learned that tomorrow isn't a guarantee. Tomorrow may never come."

She held out her hand. "Don't you understand that? I want you to make love to me. I didn't tell you because I knew your sense of justice would force you to try and talk me out of it. I don't want to be talked out of it. I want to live. And *feel*." She paused. "And if we don't survive this, I don't want to die never having been held, never having experienced this."

His low response, a single word, wept with earthiness.

"Why me, Arielle? Why me?"

She stopped shy of telling the complete truth when she added, "I've never felt this way about anyone before."

"Don't. I'm no hero. I can't live up to the image you have of me."

"I'm not asking you to live up to anything. I have no false illusions. We're both human beings, nothing more."

"I don't deserve you."

Her heart aching, she finally finished, "I'm not asking for anything in return. I just want to be in your arms."

She worried her lip, wondering whether she'd said too

much. Outside, the wind howled, slapping branches against the windowpane and driving snow against the house's exterior.

In reaction, she shivered. Silence grew, and modesty became secondary to his rejection of her.

Catching a sob in her throat, Arielle flung back the sheet, scooting to the edge of the bed. She paused when she heard his softly spoken command.

"Come here."

In his tone, there was a mix of acceptance and…regret? Dear Lord, what was she doing?

"Arielle, look at me."

Wants and needs battled with logic and common sense. Reluctantly she lifted her gaze from the floor to glance over her shoulder, denial forming her lips.

The words froze in her throat as he reached out to her, his eyes warm and unwavering. She hesitated the span of one heartbeat, then another. Her nipples hardened once more. A single glance from him uncurled tendrils of desire that heated her lower body, made her ache, made her want.

She reached out to take his hand, locking her fingers with his.

Lying beside him, he whispered in her ear.

"Relax," he murmured, placing a kiss at her temple.

He'd surely asked the impossible.

Leaning over her, he kissed her forehead, then the tip of her nose, then her chin. He trailed lower and lower, and her back arched with each inch he covered. He stopped barely above the juncture of her thighs, lifting his head and making her cry out.

For a few seconds, he left her. Then she squealed when she felt him touch his tongue to the inside of her ankle. He kissed her calf, her knee, and then, when she tried to draw her thighs together, he lifted one of her legs and draped it over his shoulder.

"Doug, I…"

"You wanted to live, Arielle."

Her head tossed on the pillow, and her hands reached through air, seeking to find him.

"You wanted to feel."

She couldn't possibly have meant it. There was no way she could stand the exquisite torture, the heat flowing through her.

"Let me do this for you."

Gently he nipped at the tender skin, and her indignant reaction gave him the access he sought. His breath warmed her, even as the thrill of the forbidden seemed to snake through her.

He found her most sensitive spot, and she dug her nails into the mattress beneath her. He flicked his tongue over her, leaving moisture and neediness behind.

A moan tore from her throat when he reached up and, with his hands, cradled her breasts. Her head swam, and the earth slipped on its axis. She heard the thunder of her pulse, inhaled the heady aroma of their readiness and struggled for survival.

She hadn't known what she'd asked for, hadn't realized she'd asked to be swept away, to yearn with such hunger and thirst with such intensity.

His tongue tantalized again, leaving her trembling as though she were hanging by a thread. "Stop, please, Doug, I feel…"

"How?" he asked against her. "How do you feel?"

"Like I…I'm.…" One heel sank into the mattress, while her other leg sought balance against the slickened surface of his back.

She struggled to open her eyes, only to fail, flailing through a blackness broken only by vivid shots of bright light.

"Let go," he whispered, his breath feathering across her and driving her mad with the sensual onslaught.

"Take it, Arielle, reach for it."

Her nipples throbbed, then, as if heeding unspoken knowledge, his fingers closed around the tightened peaks. Perspiration trickled down her back as he encouraged her with relentless determination. She wanted it...him....

His thumbnails arced across her sensitive nipples, and she shuddered, calling out his name.

Emotion and sensation built, and Doug pushed her closer and closer to oblivion. Nothing mattered, right here and now, except Doug. The threat and the horrible sense of reality that rested beyond the front door faded.

Arielle had never felt more alive than she did at this very moment. She'd been right to wait, she knew...right to give herself to someone she cared so deeply for...right to love the man she made love with.

With a searing intensity, the darkness shattered with flaming energy as sensation after incredible sensation rocked through her.

Reality slowly returned. She heard the faint ticking of Doug's watch and became aware of the coolness of the temperature, the slickness of their bodies, the fact that Doug gently cradled her in his arms, offering himself as protection against the bite of coldness. More, she became aware of the look of concern and question on his face.

"You all right?"

She turned slightly toward him, reeling from their lovemaking, reeling from the knowledge that she'd finally had the courage to admit something to herself.

She loved Doug.

She loved him.

Yet the knowledge was tempered by pain. She had to keep it quiet, couldn't blurt out a confession. She'd promised she wanted nothing from him.

"Arielle."

"I..." She fought to find her voice. Dizziness slowly receded, and the room no longer spun around her. All her body sang with fulfillment, with the realization of her love. "I'm wonderful."

At her words, he grinned triumphantly—an expression of pure male satisfaction.

Still, she knew he had cared for her without taking in return. "But..."

"But?" he said into the silence.

Shyness no longer had a place between them, yet that was exactly what she was experiencing. "What about you? I mean, you didn't, we didn't actually, you know..." Words failed her under a cloud of embarrassment.

"We're not finished yet."

She trembled when she saw intent in his eyes. Even the dimness of the overhead bulb couldn't diminish the spark in his eyes.

"I'm going to let you lead, Arielle. We'll do as much as you feel comfortable with.... We can stop at any time."

She nodded. Maneuvering, he feathered his fingers into her hair. "I don't want to hurt you," he said.

"You won't."

"You're right, not if you're in control."

Holding her, he moved so that he lay beneath her, with her legs straddling his body. "Doug?"

"We'll do this at your pace."

Her knees rested on the sheet, her feet curved into the mattress. She placed her palms on his chest, marveling at the coarse texture of his chest hair beneath her hands. For a few seconds, she admired his body, the strength of his biceps, the lean power of his shoulders.

"Whenever you're ready," he said, the words hoarse and strained.

She drew a shallow breath, holding it for a few seconds. Then he slid against her, and she felt the tip of him.

Biting down on her bottom lip, she lowered herself slightly, hesitation battling desire. But her moisture made his entrance easier. By small measures, he filled her, stretching her, and she sucked in a breath. Gingerly, then, she wiggled down a bit farther.

Doug's groan made her look down at him. "Am I hurting you?" she asked.

"Hell, no."

She moved again until a pain cramped through her. She dug her knees into the mattress at his sides, lifting herself a bit.

He wrapped his hands around her waist, holding her steady.

"You said it was okay to do this at my pace."

"And we will," he said, gritting his teeth.

He'd closed his eyes, and Arielle knew enough to realize that holding on took all his self-control. Clamping her back teeth together, she thrust herself down. Pain ripped through her, and tears stung her eyes. He filled her uncomfortably, and she ached to pull herself away. When she started to move, Doug tightened his grip, holding her in place.

"Give it a second."

She nodded, against her better judgment.

"Try and relax," he said.

"I am relaxed."

"Then take your nails out of my skin."

She tried, then tried again. As the seconds passed, the pain inside her receded. Other sensations bombarded her instead, the way their bodies joined, her hips around his, her hands on his skin, the budding of her nipples, the way her buttocks rested against his pelvis.

This was about so much more than sex, she knew. It was about trust and belief. For her, it was about passion, honesty, and... The word stalled in her mind. For her, it was about love. She knew it completely.

"I'm okay," she told him, the lie covering up the realization she didn't have the courage to contemplate.

"That makes one of us."

Their gazes met.

"Ready?" he asked.

Arielle nodded, then lifted herself slightly, Doug's hands helping her. She eased back down, meeting his instinctive surge upward. Settling just for a second, she stroked upward, and was rewarded by the sight of him closing his eyes, much as she had earlier. She continued the motions, gently, getting used to the feel of him.

Each movement brought her closer to awareness, and the feelings she'd experienced previously returned. Ribbons of recognition fluttered through her. Doug reached up, cupping her breasts, making her nipples lengthen and goose bumps tease her skin.

By unspoken accord, their rhythm changed. The soft, sensual motions were replaced by longer, frantic ones. Her body dampened again, and she clung to him, the rocking of her thighs encouraging him the way he'd earlier encouraged her.

She saw his pulse ticking near his temple, felt a change in him where she rode him. Then she no longer noticed anything, as the need reached for her. Her eyes fluttered closed and her head tipped backward, her hair spilling down her bare back.

He reached for her shoulders, pushing her down as he surged up. She felt him throb, and at that exact moment, release ripped from her core, the force of the joining more powerful than what he'd given her earlier.

Time ticked by, with her barely noticing its passing.

Slowly she opened her eyes, to find Doug looking at her. He still cradled the weight of her breasts in his hands, still filled her.

Unaccountably, in the light of the aftermath, she felt a tinge of awkwardness. She hadn't known just how much she cared for Doug, hadn't realized that not only had she been saving herself, she'd been saving her love. "We survived," she said quietly, hoping her voice didn't betray the feelings that were welling up inside her.

"Maybe we could get T-shirts made."

She appreciated the light response. With a half smile, one that couldn't hide the ache that accompanied her dawning understanding, she said, "I don't even want to know what they'd say."

He smiled then, releasing his hold on her to take her by the shoulders and draw her down against him. "Sure you're okay? You're not hurt?"

"I've never been better." Physically, at least. Emotionally was another story.

All her life she'd dreamed of falling in love, of having a family of her own. She'd spent slumber parties giggling about the boys in high school, spent hours gossiping over coffee in college. She'd even believed herself in love, until talk of a home and family splintered her picket-fence dreams.

A sigh escaped before she could stop it.

Doug adjusted their positions, gently rolling from beneath her and pulling her against him. He stroked his finger across her damp lashes.

"Regrets?"

"No." She shook her head. Then she took a leap of trust by confiding, "I'm just scared that I'll never get to experience this again."

"You will. I promise."

He kissed her then, offering so much hope, hope that her heart clung to.

Doug pulled her into the security of his arms, protectively wrapping himself around her. She rested her head against his chest, determined to live each second to its fullest. She'd gained nothing by always holding back, but she was learning that loving was the greatest risk of all.

Doug had been called a lot of things in his life. *Coward* hadn't been among them. Until tonight. Until Arielle.

He poured a mug of coffee from the half-empty carafe

and stared into its depths. The moon stood silent sentry in the sky, stars still twinkled overhead. Along with the frigid temperatures, the occasional chirp of a bird promised dawn. And he hadn't slept for five minutes.

She'd moved but not awakened when he untangled himself from her and climbed out of bed. He'd leaned over and placed a light kiss on the top of her head, inhaling the freshness of the shampoo she'd used, some sort of fruit blossom this time. The scent of her, the feel of her, her trust and sweet abandon, all conspired to make him forget reason, to want to slip back in beside her...inside her.

Doug gulped a drag of coffee, unlightened and unsugared. At the moment, he preferred it that way.

He needed something bitter in his gut to replace the sweetness of Arielle. Who'd have figured her image would saunter across his mind as soon as he closed his eyes? Who'd have figured a woman might mean more than a quick release, and just who in the hell would have figured it would be her?

Dragging a hand across the nighttime shadow on his face, he exhaled. He'd had sex plenty of times, made love with Kerry, but even that hadn't reached the power he'd found with Arielle.

She reached deep inside him, tapped into a place he'd kept under tighter security than the Secret Service kept over the president. Bullets occasionally found a president, but until now, no one had found Doug's heart.

He'd sworn never to get involved again. Then she'd looked at him with huge eyes, asking him to make love to her. He'd believed he could separate the act from the emotion, just as he had countless other times. When he discovered the precious gift she offered to him, he should have known the cost to himself...it was more than a trip to the Bahamas, more than the loss of a vacation.

And, damn it all, he wouldn't trade half a night with her for half a year in the Bahamas.

He drained the mug, slamming the stoneware onto the countertop. The relationship could go no farther, no deeper. They were both in too deep already. Emotional waters were murky, dangerous, and he had no desire to be another fatal statistic.

"Doug?"

His breath froze. Slowly he turned to face her. One of his T-shirts skimmed her thighs and rode up when she stretched to brush tangled hair from her face. As if realizing what she'd done, she lowered her arm to her side.

She smiled at him, a hesitant smile that filled him with the sunshine his soul craved. He told himself he didn't need a lighter side to his personality, that he didn't need Arielle.

His body told him otherwise.

"I woke up, cold," she said, her statement sounding more like a question than an accusation.

Another point in her favor. She didn't cling or make demands. While he had loved Kerry, those were two things she'd done. In the end, those had been the things from which he couldn't save her. "You should be in bed," he told Arielle.

"Yes."

He was as drawn to her as a wave to the shore. And knowing he risked everything by venturing too close, he strode across the few feet separating them and placed his hands on either side of her head, spreading his fingers across her scalp, through her hair.

In seconds, her thighs straddled his, the softness of her breasts pressing against his chest.

"Are we going for another T-shirt?"

He smiled, needing her. "A matched set?"

"Hmm," she said, her neck arching gracefully when his tongue touched the pounding pulse in her throat.

Her arms went around him, and she leaned into him, asking with her body. Her reaction to him, honest and raw, flared a response inside. He hadn't had this much stamina since high school. Then again, he'd never met a woman like Arielle, a woman who'd put her own life at risk to save others from suffering.

That thought nearly paralyzed him.

The idea of Arielle putting herself at risk ever again... He gritted his teeth. Not while he was on duty.

Her hands trailed down his back, and she cupped her hands beneath his buttocks. He hardened. Denim chafed, and he wanted more of her...wanted what his T-shirt barely hid.

"You like romantic fires?"

"Doesn't every girl?"

"Even if there's no fire in the grate?"

"That means you'll have to keep me warm."

"Your wish is my command." He grabbed a handful of black cotton and tugged it over her head, noticing the way her nipples puckered in the coolness.

He couldn't resist laving them with his tongue, then easing a hand between her legs.

"Doug?"

"Yeah?"

"You've got too many clothes on." She reached for the zipper, the drag against him chafing.

"Hold on," he said, adjusting the front of his jeans.

"Now?"

"No time like the present."

Between them, they pushed denim past his hips, and then she closed her hands around him. He swelled against her palm.

"You said later," she reminded him.

"Yeah." He'd meant it at the time.

"It's later, Doug."

She began to move her hand, leaning toward him to place a kiss on his neck. Her trust thrilled him....

Trust.

Hell.

He'd been caught unprepared. He was downstairs, and the protection was upstairs. "Arielle, hold it."

"I am."

He squeezed his eyes shut, asking for strength. Fine time for her to discover a sense of humor. "Not that," he said. "The condoms are upstairs."

"But can't you...? I mean, if I, can you...?"

He was close to proving her right.

"Let me," she said, echoing his earlier words.

Their limbs tangled, they somehow made it to the living room couch before collapsing. Her hand still around him, she trailed kisses over his chest, then lower.

He'd never met anyone like her, so giving, with no thought of receiving.

Her hair brushed his stomach, and strands trailed over his thighs as she worked her way lower.

Nothing would happen to her, he vowed. Her sunshine, her trust, her belief, all were like a lifeline to a drowning man.

Until recently, he hadn't realized he didn't know how to swim.

How much more, he wondered, didn't he know? And how much more would she teach him?

"Is this right?" she asked.

He sucked in a deep breath. "Doug?"

"Yeah," he responded, through clenched back teeth. "You're doing fine."

"Can we get a T-shirt?"

Her breath feathered against his groin. "Anyone ever tell you talk too much?" he asked.

"Fine. I'll shut up."

And she did, leaving Doug to whisper a promise...a whispered promise that she'd have her tomorrow.

Chapter 14

"Room in there for one more?"

"Doug?" she called back to him, through the shower curtain surrounding the claw-footed bathtub. She looked through the fabric, seeing his silhouette. Her heart thumped. He couldn't be serious. The bath was barely big enough for one.

"Yeah, it's me. Who'd you expect, room service?"

"I was hoping." She pretended a sigh. "After all, I haven't even had my first cup of coffee yet."

Arielle hadn't expected him to walk into the bathroom. It spoke of a new level to their relationship, of assumed intimacy. The knowledge that it couldn't last filled her with pain, a pain she knew she had to hide.

"You mean you'd take coffee over me?"

Never. "Maybe when I've only had a few hours' sleep," she teased.

Bubbles frothed around her as she sank into hot water up to her chin. Her knees peeked through the foam, as did her toes, but nothing else showed.

He slid open the curtain, and steam seeped into the small room. He'd closed the door to the bedroom, making the atmosphere immediately intimate.

"Guess I'll never make you the offer of coffee, tea or me."

He stood there, bare-chested, with sleep-tousled hair in disarray that she longed to tame. She remembered his hair falling into unruly waves last night, when her fingers furled through the strands.

This morning, a forest green flannel shirt hugged his shoulders, making his eyes more vibrant than she'd seen them before. The scent of morning and the crispness of snow clung to him. He'd been awake for hours, she knew.

When the sunshine slipped through the bedroom window, she'd reached for him, only to discover that he'd risen. Feeling hollow and wishing he still held her, all the while telling herself she didn't have that right, she'd hurriedly pulled on her panties and Doug's shirt before heading for the soothing promise of a bathtub.

As she lay in bed, the remembrance of their lovemaking had sauntered through her thoughts. He'd been gentle, coaxing, wonderful. She knew she'd lock away the emotions, the memories, and store them for another time, when she could savor them.

She'd slept little, and he'd gotten up way before her. In spite of that, he appeared rested and ready for the day. Blue jeans snuggled around his waist, hips and thighs...just as she had been last night, and again this morning.

Her heart missed its next beat. She couldn't believe how wanton she'd been, how much she'd responded to him, couldn't believe how much the sight of him brought an instant awakening.

"You're in luck, I come bearing gifts." He held up his hand, fingers curled around the handle of a cup.

"That's for me?"

He crouched near the tub, the smoky green of his eyes

revealing the true lack of teasing there. His thighs were spread wide, giving her a view. More unsettling was the recollection of everything they'd shared. Passion and tenderness she'd only dreamed about were now a reality that made her yearn for more.

She poked her arm out to reach for the coffee, bringing them into closer contact.

"Blessings on you," she said.

"So, how 'bout it? I'm sharing the last cup of coffee. You gonna share your bath?"

She sipped from the coffee. It was hot and strong. She gulped as the accompanying thought scalded the roof of her mouth. Hot and strong...like Doug.

"Burn your mouth?"

If he only knew.

"Yesterday you used up all the hot water."

She tried to concentrate on what he said. "Are you trying to make me feel guilty?" she asked.

"Appealing to your sense of justice."

"Justice in...the bathtub?"

"My job is to deliver justice, ma'am, not quarrel with where the delivery takes place. Unless you're too sore?"

"Tender," she admitted, running her tongue across her teeth. "But not sore." The conversation should have flustered her, but it didn't. She offered the mug back to him. "Don't want it splashing all over us."

"Is that an invitation?"

She nodded.

He grinned, then took the mug, sliding it onto the vanity. From his waistband, he withdrew his pistol and placed it beside the coffee...a constant reminder of the threat. He'd been outside already, and as she headed upstairs, she'd heard the drone of his voice in the office.

If only she could pretend...

His jeans joined hers on the bath mat. His shirt settled on top of the pile, and she saw the evidence of his arousal.

"This is a small tub," she warned him, sitting up and scooting back.

"Yeah. I know."

"That's why you suggested it," she said, wondering how on earth they were going to make this work.

"Maybe."

"Maybe?"

"It's also wet."

Her insides melted at his husky words. This was the man she loved, a man she wanted for all time, a man with whom she shared only a brief interlude. She needed memories, as many as she could gather, to cherish on the long and lonely nights ahead...if she even had that much.

For now, though, he wanted her and she wanted him. That was all that mattered.

She pulled her legs closer to her when he stepped in, facing her.

He hissed in a breath. "No wonder there's no hot water left when you're done."

"It's not that hot."

"Unless you're a lobster."

She scooped a handful of suds and tossed them at him, the white bubbles clinging to his legs, to his...

His eyes darkened with intent.

"I didn't mean to do that."

"Yes, you did."

"Maybe just a little."

"Maybe," he conceded. "Come here."

"Where?"

He extended a hand. "Here. I'll collect my revenge in a few minutes."

Trustingly she slipped her hand into his, dampness against dryness. Warm water swirled around their feet and calves, and her body heated, even though cool air circulated around her.

For a seemingly endless amount of time, he looked at

her, and for that moment, she knew what it felt like to be loved. Surely he couldn't have looked at her any differently if he did love her.

"Did you wash?"

She shook her head.

He reached toward the window ledge for a bottle of shower gel. "Peach?"

Arielle nodded. It was the only scent she hadn't yet used.

"Hold out your hand."

She cupped her hand, and he poured a liberal amount of the gel into her palm. After putting the bottle back, he dipped two fingers into the gel and soothed the silky smoothness across her shoulders. A second dip, then he trailed some onto her belly, then more on her thighs.

"Turn around."

Each place he touched seemed to spark to life. Slowly she turned her back to him. He slicked some down her arms, then made a trail, tracing her spine from the base of her skull, making her glad she'd pinned up her hair, to the small of her back. He reached from behind her to take the remaining gel from her. He rubbed it between his hands, then cupped her buttocks and slid down the back of her thighs.

"Hmm...I think I like this."

"I know I do," he said, slipping the words into her ear.

He massaged her shoulders with gentle circular motions, bringing the slickness to a sudsy foam. He continued the motions downward, rubbing her buttocks and, for a hint of a second, slipping his hand between her legs.

She reached for the wall for stability when he said, "Open your legs wider for me, Arielle."

Trembling, she did as he asked.

He washed the insides of her thighs and gently worked his way down. It wasn't enough, and at the same time, it was too much.

"You can turn around again."

''If I can.'' When she did, it was to see stormy desire in his eyes.

His hands, so large and powerful, gave with such gentleness. He repeated his motions on her arms and sides, then spent an unbearably wonderful amount of time spreading lather across her breasts and her nipples, which pebbled with pleasure at his touch. Her breasts seemed to fill, throbbing as with last night's lovemaking, wanting more, so much more.

He motioned her to sit and joined her in the tiny space. Facing her, he said, ''Give me your foot.''

She raised her foot to his knee, and he gave her calves and feet the same sort of attention. The bubbles had disintegrated, and try as she might, she couldn't draw her gaze away from the part of him that communicated his desire, leaving her to wonder at the control he possessed. As for her, she didn't know how much more she could take. ''I can't,'' she said.

''Remember my revenge.''

''You're a monster.''

She reached for him, closing her hand around his hardness.

''Uh-uh,'' he said removing her hand. ''This was my idea.''

It would only take seconds for her to reach fulfillment and, maddeningly, he denied her just that.

After her other foot was washed, he continued upward, not stopping till he'd cleaned all of her. His hand effortlessly dipped between her thighs, completing the task he'd started earlier. Her muscles weakened. She wanted him now. ''Doug!''

''Still need to rinse you off.''

''I'll do it,'' she said quickly. Never in her life had she realized that such a state of craving existed.

He chuckled as she attempted to move away from him, quickly rinsing the suds from her sensitized body. Doug stood and stepped from the tub, grabbing a towel to hold for her.

The nubby material brushed her nipples, bringing out a small cry. He palmed his gun, then snatched away the T-shirt she reached for and said, "Don't bother."

In the bedroom, she pushed back the covers and lay on the bed, while he reached for a packet from the nightstand. When he kissed her neck, then started toward her breasts, she said, "Please, no more."

He chuckled again, the sound seeming to resonate from his chest as he put the shield in place. Shifting, he positioned himself over her, nudging one rock-hard thigh between hers to separate her legs. Strength and power rippled beneath her fingertips, tempered with controlled gentleness. She didn't want tender and gentle. Urgency thundered through her, and she wanted to lose control completely, wanted him to, as well.

She lifted her hips, taking him in, and within seconds, her world exploded. He surged deeper, taking her higher and higher. Then, through the tingling descent, she became aware that he hadn't reached the edge yet. She smiled with new confidence and wrapped her legs around him, holding him closer, tighter.

"Arielle!"

In seconds, she felt the pulsation of his release, and heard the deep-throated sounds he didn't try to hold back. Arielle rained kisses on his cheek, neck, shoulder, wanting the moment to be frozen forever, wanting to stay with him indefinitely. Yet she knew her only wish was the one thing she could never have.

He held her for a long time, as if he sensed that need.

The minutes blended together, and her eyes grew heavy, last night catching up with her.

Later, when the ringing of the phone shattered the warmth that cocooned her, she opened her eyes to see that he was gone. The ringing abruptly stopped, and she realized that with his absence, her body had cooled, and goose bumps now dotted her arms. Sitting up, she reached for the towel she'd dropped on top of the covers and drew it around her.

She heard nothing, not even the drone of Doug's voice. The silence hung so thick, she heard the constancy of her own heartbeat.

Sinking back onto the edge of the bed, she felt a wave of loneliness crash over her. Doug had been tender with her, patient, and just now driven by passion. None of it, though, was reality.

She loved him, but wasn't foolish enough to believe he could ever return it. Even if they somehow found a way to survive this, it wouldn't matter. They moved in different worlds. The world he existed in wasn't even close to anything familiar to her.

More, the scars entrenched in his heart ran deep and ragged, cloaked by the burden of guilt.

All the rationalizing in the world didn't help, though. She loved him, completely, totally, with all her emotions engaged. It left her needy.

A sob caught in her chest as she told herself that even a broken heart was better than never having experienced the joy of loving.

But if that was so, why couldn't she convince her heart?

She grabbed some clothes, then went into the bathroom, reaching for a glass and filling it with water to chase away the lump lodged in her throat.

The front door slammed, the echo of it tracking up the stairs. He'd gone outside, as he did every couple of hours, always on guard. Protecting her.

After dressing, she dried her eyes and straightened her shoulders. She had strength and courage. She'd call on them, no matter how difficult it might be.

A dark shadow crossed the mirror.

Her pulse leaped, and she swung around. Seeing nothing,

she told herself that she was being jumpy, that the stress of the past weeks had crept up on her, leading her imagination to play tricks on her. She reminded herself that she was alone in the house. Still, she curled her hands into fists and cautiously entered the bedroom. She saw nothing unusual or out of place.

Rationalizing that it had been a trick of the light, nothing more, she willed her heartbeat to return to normal. Returning to the bathroom, she applied a coat of mascara to her lashes, all the while keeping a constant watch on the mirror.

Finally finished, and knowing she had to face the day, as well as her pain, she made the bed, the very act reminding her again of their shared passion, passion she had never known existed.

Downstairs, she poured the last cup of coffee from the carafe and stared out the window above the sink. A blanket of snow decorated the landscape, a layer clinging to tree branches and covering the swing set. Several sets of footprints led back to the small opening in the surrounding woodlands. The wind had shifted, though, leaving certain branches bare and filling in some of the footprints. A drift was buttressed against the shed.

As she watched, wind whipped again, tossing snow from the roof and throwing it across the patio. She shivered, the temperature in the house seeming to drop a couple of degrees. Absently she wondered how Doug managed to stay warm. Knowing him, she figured he probably didn't feel it. At times, he seemed superhuman.

She decided to brew fresh coffee and turn up the thermostat a couple of degrees. He might not feel the chill, but she did, more so since her emotions were involved.

Suddenly, a shriek slashed from overhead speakers. A woman's disembodied voice calmly stated, "Intruder alert, zone three."

A scream rose and died in Arielle's throat. Hysteria battled rational thought as she frantically tried to decide what to do. Doug! She needed Doug.

A glance out the window showed no signs of him. Oh, God, something couldn't have happened to Doug…. Please, God, no, she prayed. She needed him.

A shiver lanced up her spine, a shiver of bone-chilling fear. Her pulse slammed into a frantic staccato. Had the intruder left, or was he there, behind her, staring at her? Was he there to kill her? To kill them?

Breath burned her lungs as she fought for calm. Panic solved nothing. But terror wasn't easily harnessed.

Her pulse pounded as the words *intruder alert* ricocheted around her and through her mind. She had to think. But how could she? Mouth dry and palms sweaty, she carefully made her way to the back door. Ripping it open, she rushed out back, nearly collapsing in relief when she saw Doug striding toward the house.

"Doug!" she screamed, running through the snow.

"Miss me?"

"Thank God you're back."

He frowned, wrapping her in the comfort of his arms.

"What's the matter? Need company in the shower again?"

She barely noticed the cold or the dampness on his jacket. All she knew was that he'd protect her. She hadn't realized how much the terror had paralyzed her until she saw him. She hadn't been capable of thinking straight. All she'd known was she needed him…trusted him.

"Arielle?"

"He's here."

"Who is?"

She gulped at the frozen air, her teeth chattering.

"Tell me once we're inside," he said, leading her back toward the house.

"No!"

"You'll get sick out here without a coat."

"I don't... We can't go inside."

Doug looked down at her and saw the same fear on her face that had made his insides curdle the first day. Whatever scared the hell out of her then had been real. But this time, it meant more to him. He cared for her, had a personal mission to save her, to right the wrongs of the past. His nostrils pinched as he surveyed the landscape.

He noted nothing different or unusual. Not that that came as a surprise. He'd checked the perimeter three times since dawn. Hell, he'd had to do something to burn off the energy that heated his blood.

He'd spent half the night and all the morning trying to get her out of his soul. But he'd failed. How could he embrace shadows again, after experiencing the brightness his spirit craved? A hike through drifted snow in freezing temperatures hadn't helped. The colder he grew, the more he longed for her heat.

He told himself the Bahamas sounded good. But now he wanted company on the trip. He was in deep, deeper than he'd ever been, and, boldly, he swam away from the lifeline his mind tried to toss in his direction.

He didn't want to be rescued.

Instead of clinging to the lifeline, he boldly ran toward a rope shaped like a noose. The closer he got to her, the tighter the knot became. He'd always been partial to his neck, just the way it was. So why wasn't he running like hell away from her?

He wasn't rich enough to be able to afford involvement with her, with any woman, but he cradled her against him, regardless. He held her for a full minute, maybe because it was what she wanted. Maybe because it was what he wanted.

"I saw a shadow in the bathroom mirror."

"Go on."

"When I looked, I didn't see anything."

Snow blasted around their calves and thighs, and he

knew the wind was biting through her sweatshirt and blue jeans. In her tennis shoes, her toes had to be curled against the cold, but she didn't complain. He extricated himself long enough to shrug out of his coat and drape it around her shoulders.

"You think I'm being hysterical."

"Arielle, you don't have a hysterical bone in your body." But this time, he hoped she was mistaken, that the stress had driven her to see danger in harmless things.

"The alarm said intruder alert in zone three."

His curse carried on the wind and fueled anger. He released his hold on her and unholstered the nine-millimeter. He carefully surveyed the landscape for the dozenth time, frustrated to note nothing out of the ordinary. This was a game of hide-and-seek. He didn't like games, especially when he was on the hiding end.

She shuddered, and he held her with his left arm, absorbing her shivers against his chest.

"Doug, he might still be in there."

Leave it to her to lay it on the line, stating what he'd rather keep hidden. Her honesty humbled him.

"What if he stood there, watching me?" Her voice dropped as she said, "Maybe he watched me getting dressed."

Doug's jaw clenched tightly. Damn it all to perdition.

"It may not be the jerk who's after you, may not be Pickins. Could be someone wanting shelter from the cold." He wondered if she'd take reassurance from the lie, or whether she'd see through it.

"But it might be the guy I hired," she countered. "He might have found us."

She had seen a shadow, then heard the alarm. So when and how had the perp gotten in, snuck past their defenses and Doug's vigilance? How long had the intruder been out there, watching, waiting to make a move? "I'm on it."

"I want to stay with you."

He shook his head.

"You can't lock me up."

He could and would. "You'll be safe in Rhone's office."

"I don't want to be alone."

"I don't want to be worried about you if there's someone in the house. I can't afford the distraction."

Softly, against his chest, she said, "I'm not Kerry."

"And I'm no hero."

"I disagree. To me, you are."

"Don't." He looked down at her, seeing the fright, but, layered above it, drowning it out, a serving of strength. She was right that she wasn't Kerry. She was so much more, meant so much more to him. And that left him defenseless. "Five minutes, Arielle. Give me five minutes."

He saw indecision in her eyes. She wanted to trust, but was afraid of that very thing. He knew what he was asking of her, knew what it would cost her.

Finally, she released a soft sigh of defeat. "Five minutes?"

"Not a moment longer," he promised. "Stay behind me. You know the drill."

She worried her lip.

Inside, he noted an untouched cup of coffee, air filtering through the overhead vents, and a trace of peach on the air. But it was the bite of fear that annoyed him. He didn't want Arielle to be afraid ever again. When he found the son of a bitch who'd scared her, Doug intended to extract cold, slow revenge.

Doug punched in the code for Rhone's office, then held open the door for her. Following, he grabbed a handheld shortwave radio and flipped the switch on the receiver that occupied a corner filled with state-of-the-art communication equipment. Before he headed out, he briefly explained how to operate the mike. "Don't use it unless absolutely necessary. Understand?"

At her nod, he pointed toward the secured phone. "Call Brian. Tell him I need reinforcements."

Her answering nod was more automatic than genuine.

With her safe, he headed for the front room, cold blasting through the open window. Carefully detailing the placement of furniture and knickknacks in the room, he went to the window. Pistol propped in his hand, he checked the grounds. Tracks. Damn it. They led away from the house, but there were none heading toward the house.

The questions remained. How the hell had he gotten in? And when? Had the faceless enemy been inside the house all night? Watching Arielle? Watching him? Watching them?

The alarm had been set the entire time....

Except when Doug brought in firewood earlier this morning. He cursed. A momentary lapse had been all it took. While he was in the shed, someone had walked into the house. That meant that the someone had been close, anxious for an opportunity to move in.

And Doug, her protector, had gone on a perimeter check, locking Arielle in the house with a madman.

The thought of what might have happened made a pulse thunder in his temple. Some hero. Some protector.

Vowing to redouble his efforts at vigilance, he checked the rest of the house, even though it was obvious that the perp had toyed with Arielle, then left. In one of the bathrooms they hadn't used, a metal tube of lipstick lay on the vanity, the insides smeared in the sink. The mauve tone, a subtle and becoming hint of color on Arielle's lips, was a blatant and obscene contrast against the white porcelain. Doug swiped the sink, removing the remnants of the crude innuendo.

Descending the steps two at a time, he reassured himself that for now, Arielle was safe, before allowing the urge for action, fed by the single-minded need to retaliate, to obliterate his need to be with her.

He headed outdoors, careful to arm the system, before hunting down the tracks to the nearest oak tree.

The tracks abruptly stopped, and a dislodged pile of snow covered the tree's trunk.

Whoever had been there had climbed the tree and jumped the privacy fence. Following the trail, he'd walked to the road...the road that had already been plowed.

Doug exhaled in disgust. Defeat and determination both gnawing at him, he returned to the house, to Arielle.

She was still on the phone to Brian, and she mutely offered the receiver to him. In answer to her raised brows, he shook his head.

She perched on the edge of the desk, her struggle for bravery evident in the curve of her shoulders.

"Understand you've had a visitor, boss."

"Lost him."

"I know you like good news.... Pickins was seen on a commercial flight out of Logan International yesterday."

Other than the Bruins, nothing much good had come out of Boston.

"Destination?" He didn't need to hear the answer. Denver.

"Your jet's fueled. I'm out of here in two minutes," Brian said.

"Rhone?"

"He's with me."

Doug reached to hang up the phone, only to have Brian's voice halt the motion. "Got some more bad news."

"Wasn't that enough?"

"*Destiny*..."

Doug rolled back his head. Grinding his back teeth, he inhaled deeply.

"He got her?"

"Big-time. Be prepared for some grumpy neighbors, not to mention your insurance agent. Your premiums will be supplying a chunk of change to the local glass company. The explosion blew out all the windows in a quarter mile."

"Job security."

"Not according to your agent. Says his loss ratio this year is in the toilet, no thanks to you. There's more, boss."

"Go on."

"There was a flag tacked to a nearby dock...."

"Marine Corps."

"No need to play twenty questions with you."

Doug was sick enough of games to be tempted to burn the cribbage board.

"Weird thing is that he spray-painted a picture of a pick on the flag, sort of like a sickle."

The Marine Corps flag was enough of a giveaway. Why did Pickins need to paint a pick on it? Pick had been his nickname. It was as if he wanted to be sure his identity was not mistaken.

"On my way, boss."

Doug hung up, facing Arielle.

"Brian told me about your boat. I'm sorry," she said.

"Yacht. She's a yacht." Then he corrected himself with a wince. "*Was* a yacht." The loss of *Destiny* didn't even begin to register when compared to the thought of something happening to Arielle. A boat...a yacht...could be replaced. Arielle couldn't.

"You didn't find anyone?"

He shook his head.

"Are we safe?"

"For now," he hedged. The knowledge that someone, maybe Arielle's assassin, had found them, made the tension three times thicker. He was out there, watching. Waiting?

Doug considered the possibility of moving her to another location, but if someone was there, anticipating a move, they might walk into a trap. Much as his instincts screamed for immediate action, he needed to wait for backup. The house was safe...or would be, as long as he didn't drop his guard for a single second.

"Would you pour some coffee?" He didn't want the caffeine, but she needed something to do.

She nodded woodenly, the motion automatic, rather than sincere. It didn't matter, though, as long as he kept her focused on moving forward.

In the kitchen, she took out two clean mugs and filled

them. Handing Doug his, she half turned to stare out the window and, as far as he could tell, looked at nothing in particular.

"I heard you say Pickins sank your boat," she said, steam rising from a cup to bathe her face.

"Yeah." He pulled out a chair to sit at the table. "Left his calling card. A flag with a spray-painted pick on it."

Her face drained of its remaining color. She sloshed coffee over the rim as she slid the cup onto the counter.

He stood. "What is it?"

"A pick?" she whispered.

He nodded.

"He had a tattoo...on his forearm."

Doug frowned as things clicked into place. "Who did?"

"The man I...the man I hired."

Doug's single curse singed his own ears.

"I'm sorry, Doug.... I was trying to remember, but I couldn't see well, and it was dark."

"It's okay," he said, striding to her. He gathered her close and held her tight. Bile burned his gut. "You couldn't have known."

He saw tears swimming at the corners of her eyes. "I hired the man who wants...to kill you."

The irony of it struck Doug. Pickins, just released from prison, had had no money and no means to exact his revenge...until Arielle innocently blundered into something she had no understanding of. And Pickins, probably laughing the whole time, wanted Doug to know that the woman he was protecting was the one who'd sealed his death warrant.

Pickins had played them all for fools, and Arielle was in more danger than Doug had ever imagined. The small amount that she had seen would prove a positive ID of Pickins.

He stroked the tears from her eyes.

"I led him straight to you," she said.

He shook his head. "Not likely, when the agency's listed

in the phone book. You simply provided him the monetary means to accomplish his goal. The fact that you unknowingly led him to me was a bonus for him.''

"But—"

"It's me who's at fault. I should have sent you with Brian. Pickins wants me, not you, not Brian."

"You tried to send me away. I wouldn't go."

The reminder didn't lessen the guilt.

"I wanted to be with you." She reached up her hand and traced his cheek with tenderness, with recollection. "You asked for my trust, I've given it to you."

His heart squeezed at the enormity of what she offered, both burden and blessing.

"And no matter what happens," she continued, "I'm glad we met. I have no regrets where you...we...are concerned."

His eyes closed.

"Doug, I don't expect you to feel the same."

He opened his eyes, seeing sincerity and more, love in her eyes.

"But I want you to know that I—"

He sealed off her confession with his lips. She didn't love him, couldn't love him. He didn't believe in the emotion. More, he didn't trust it.

Kerry had offered him her love, and he'd been unable to save her.

That wouldn't happen with Arielle. He deepened the kiss, and she made the confession with her body, if not her words. He didn't deserve her, he knew.

Didn't deserve her love.

Chapter 15

Arielle sighed in frustration and tossed down her cards. Neither she nor Doug had glanced at the cards since she dealt the hand, several minutes ago. The tick and tock of the clock echoed off the house's shadowed log walls, the overcast sky adding hours to the time, making it seem later than early afternoon.

Looking up at her, he asked, "Had enough?"

"Yes," she admitted, standing and wrapping her arms across her chest. "I feel like a fish in a pond, just waiting for someone to toss in a hook."

Doug had closed all the blinds, but they'd stayed in the kitchen, near enough to the office, where she could take refuge, and near enough to the action for him to respond instantly.

So far, since he returned to the house, she'd avoided asking the question uppermost in her mind, half-afraid of the answer. But the not knowing was driving her crazier than the truth. "You know who was in the house, don't you?"

"Someone who likes hide-and-seek."

"Doug..."

He threw down his cards. "I don't have proof."

"You've got a guess."

"That's all it is, a guess."

She gulped. "Do you think it was Pickins?"

"He likes games."

The breath that had coagulated in her lungs leaked out. "He's here? Somewhere nearby?"

Darkness hooded his eyes, made reading his expression impossible. "*Someone* is."

"What are we going to do?"

"Wait for Brian and Rhone. Then play our own version of hide-and-seek."

Fear for him held her momentarily in its frozen grip. "Is everything a game to you?"

"Nothing's a game where your life is concerned, Arielle."

"But what about yours?"

"I'll protect you," he swore.

He hadn't answered her question. His unspoken words contained more power than the ones he'd said. He'd save her, she knew, even at the cost of his own life.

She shuddered. Earlier, she'd tried to tell him she loved him, only to have him cut through her words with his lips. The kiss had tasted of passion and urgency, of trust, of belief, of promise and of determination. He'd released her, leaving her reeling, hardly able to stand.

And even though he'd cut off her declaration, sealing off her confession, she loved him, more than anything. She needed him, wanted him. She didn't want a hero...she wanted Doug.

Instinctively she rested two fingers across her lips. They'd made love, explored a part of her she'd never known existed.

The doorbell rang. For a moment, their eyes met, and

Arielle's heart sank. Doug's eyes were as dark and dangerous as they'd been that first afternoon, as they ran through the streets of New York.

He straightened his shoulders, reaching for the nine-millimeter that rested at his fingertips, and, in a single, effortless motion, stood.

Her hand went to her throat. "Rhone and Brian?"

"No. I don't expect them to arrive for another couple of hours." He moved into the front room and pulled back the drape with his index finger. "What the—? Stand clear of the door."

He glanced back at her, apparently making sure she'd moved away. Then, squatting, he reached out with his left hand, turning the knob. A flurry of snow blasted through the opening.

Arielle heard his sharp intake of breath, saw the odd-shaped object he'd retrieved from the doorstep. Backhandedly he swiped the door shut.

"Oh, my God, Doug, it's a grenade!"

"The safety pin is still intact." His voice was unnervingly calm as he picked up the explosive, gingerly wiping snow from the surface.

Hands gripped at her sides, Arielle watched.

Doug laughed, the short, bitter sound slicing through the tense silence. "It's not real."

"A toy? But why—?"

"I told you, Pickins likes games." He stood, tossing her the plastic replica. "Arielle, I've got to go after him."

Arielle dropped the fake grenade on the couch and rushed toward Doug. "No, please, don't go until Rhone and Brian get here."

"No time. I don't know what other ideas of fun and frivolity our boy has planned, and I'm not willing to risk your well-being waiting to find out."

"You don't know for certain that it's Pickins. You said so yourself earlier. And you don't know if whoever is out there is alone," she pleaded, unaware that she was squeezing his arm until Doug gently loosened her grasp.

Holding her hand in both of his, he kissed her palm, then curled her fingers over the spot his lips had touched. "I...know it's Pickins. I also know he's alone."

She battled tears, the reason for them a toss-up between his tenderness and consuming fear for his life. As his words sank in, she blinked away the moisture, welcoming the anger that had begun to build, replacing the fear.

Apparently he saw the gathering storm in her eyes. He shrugged. "After the incident this morning, I found a little message in the snow. One set of footprints."

"*Semper fi?*" Arielle asked.

Doug's gaze flicked over her. "Yeah."

A sense of betrayal lanced through her. "Pretty good deductive reasoning, Sherlock, for someone who wasn't sure his hunch was correct."

"Arielle—"

"You lied to me, Doug." A knot of tension settled in her shoulders. When she asked him if he knew who the intruder was, he'd told her he could only guess.

His eyebrows arced together as he looked at her. Latent energy pulsated from him, but she refused to back down now.

Arielle released a breath. "You demanded complete honesty and forthrightness from me," she said, struggling to hold her calm. "You didn't rest until you'd uncovered all my secrets and exposed them. You wouldn't let me run or hide from myself or from you."

"Arielle, no good could have come from you knowing about Pickins."

"So lies are better, is that right, Doug? Is it?" Her fingernails dug into her palms. "It's my fault he's here, my fault he's after you."

Doug shook his head. "It's not your fault. Pickins has

wanted revenge on me since the day my testimony sealed him behind bars. He'd have found a way to get it.''

''That doesn't change the fact that you demanded my trust and won't return the favor.'' Quietly, emotion rampant, she asked, ''We're in this together, aren't we?''

''For better or worse,'' he agreed. ''You're right about that, and nothing else.''

''Where am I wrong?''

''My job is to protect you—''

''Wait a second,'' she said, interrupting him. ''You withheld information from me to protect me? You've got it backwards. You said we're in this together, and I hired you, Doug. I'm paying for the protection. Surely that counts for something.''

''Get this straight, lady, I'm not working for you.'' He took a threatening step toward her. ''I didn't take a penny of your money. I don't want your money. I'm doing this because I want to, not because of the promise of a nice thick paycheck.''

Arielle swallowed. He'd never admitted how much he cared, but this, this, came as close as she might ever get. Tears stung at the back of her eyes, and she bravely held them back.

''You came looking for me, but when I agreed to help you, it was under my terms, my rules.''

''Trust is a two-way street. I'm not Kerry, I haven't fallen to pieces yet. You owe me the courtesy of belief. You owe me that much, Doug.''

''I owe you your life,'' he said, vanquishing the rest of the distance separating them and capturing her shoulders. ''I owe you a shot at survival.''

''I don't hold you responsible for me. I'm a big girl, I'll live with the consequences.''

''You're right,'' he said. ''*Live* being the key word. But while we're at it, get one more thing straight. I hold myself responsible for your safety.''

"You have to trust me," she said, feeling his fingers digging into her shoulders. He gripped her with barely restrained anger, and she didn't want to crack through the reserve. All she wanted was his faith in her. "The same way I trust you."

He kissed her. Long and hard and rich, with the same passion he'd coaxed from her last night, then again this morning.

When he released her, she leaned against the wall. The man weakened her, chased away logic. If this was love, she wasn't sure she'd survive it. She'd never before been through such turbulent emotions.

"Arielle, I want nothing more than to take you back to bed and prove how much I trust you."

She sucked in a shallow breath.

"But until this is over..."

He captured her lips again, her mouth, seeking her tongue. Willingly she melded with him, relaxing against him, feeling the hardness against her stomach that proved just how much he wanted to take her back to bed.

Anger evaporated, and all that remained was the honesty of her feelings and the beauty of her belief.

"We'll talk later," he promised, ending the kiss and leaving her aching for so much more.

She stepped away from him slowly, realizing that this might be the last chance they'd have to hold each other. The thought terrorized her, even more than the idea of losing her own life. She wanted to remain in his arms forever, pretend the future didn't exist.

But it did.

"The sooner this is over, the better."

She nodded, fighting for nonexistent bravery. He was right, even if that very fact broke her heart.

As much as she loved him, she knew she'd never fit in his world. Her life was filled with lesson plans and homework assignments, not guns and ammo clips.

Arielle choked back a sob as she followed Doug back into the kitchen. Trust her to finally find what she'd been searching for, only to see the possibilities fade like snow in the bright sun.

"You okay?" Doug asked, opening a map of the surrounding area.

"Nervous," she admitted.

She sat in one of the chairs at the table, drawing her legs close to her chest. Doug stood at the island, his gun in its holster under his arm. Even though his words were calm, she read carefully leashed energy in each motion.

He continually glanced toward the windows and doors, always on guard and alert. She should take comfort from that, she knew, but yet she didn't. In fact, she wondered if she'd ever be calm again. The East Coast no longer seemed like a real world, more like a figment of her imagination. Was it just a couple of weeks ago that she'd made a decision to increase the benefits of her life insurance policy? It didn't seem possible.

"There's nothing I can say to sway you to wait until Rhone and Brian arrive, is there?"

"No." Both his tone and the directness of his glance forbade argument or discussion. He straightened, refolding the map.

Doug strode through the downstairs rooms, pulling back blinds and drapes to look out each window. And with each moment that passed, her insides twisted a notch tighter.

"It'll be over soon," Doug promised, returning to the kitchen. "Pickins isn't patient. He likes to play, but always likes to be dealing. He wanted me to know he's here. Most likely he knows I have backup on the way. He won't be expecting me to hunt him down alone."

Needing to distract herself while Doug assembled extra ammo and checked the clip in his gun, she asked Doug, "Are you nervous?"

"Always the psychologist?"

She attempted a half smile in response to his lightness.

"Not nervous," he said. "Filled with anticipation, like it's a long holiday weekend. What does that tell you, Doc?"

"That you get entirely too much pleasure out of this."

His eyes took on a smoky darkness. "Among other things."

"Doug, I..."

He raised his brow, waiting.

She'd tried to make her confession once, but he hadn't wanted to hear it. And even though the words echoed in her mind, she didn't dare distract him.

"I need coffee."

"Is there anything but caffeine in your veins?"

"Adrenaline," she admitted. "And I'm scared it'll wear off."

Doug had been there himself. In Central America, he'd spent three days running on adrenaline, scared spitless it'd wear off before he accomplished his mission. He hadn't had time to rest, to eat or to sleep.

Yeah, he knew how Arielle felt. He'd been there. Hell, he was there right now. He'd let down his guard once, and Pickins had gotten in.

And now, while the cover of rapidly approaching darkness was more friend than enemy, Doug hesitated to leave. He could not ignore the intense feeling that something wasn't right. He'd learned years before to listen to his gut, rely on his premonitions. His life and others' had depended on it.

This time was no exception.

More than anything, he wanted the whole mess ended, wanted a well-deserved rest in the Bahamas. Of course, that meant he needed a new yacht. Better yet, maybe he'd fly. He had more of a chance of actually making it that way.

Arielle crossed to the counter, but didn't reach for the carafe. Instead, she looked at him. And the expression in her eyes robbed him of his breath. Her eyes wore the expression of trust, but mixed with reality.

No other woman possessed that capability, to be so open, even when faced with the truth. She was a gem, and he had been right the night before. He didn't deserve her, didn't deserve her love.

But, God in heaven, that didn't stop him wanting....

"Will I see you again?" Her words trembled on the air.

"Yeah," he said, wondering if he'd lied. Seeing her again might lead him straight to hell, because he wasn't sure he was strong enough to resist her. She had dreams, she'd told him, of a house with a split-rail fence. She dreamed of a family, of kids.

But Doug didn't dream.

And as much as he was willing to admit that he cared, he didn't have the right to rob her of her dreams.

"Anyone ever told you you're a lousy liar?"

"Anyone ever tell you you talk too much?"

She gave a shaky smile, and he admired her courage.

An explosion rocked the house, shattering a front window. Instantly he grabbed Arielle, placing her behind him. His body a shield, he whipped his gun from its holster. The alarm shrieked. Adrenaline slammed into his gut, and he pivoted toward the sound. Then, looking over his shoulder, he snapped, "Stay close to me."

She nodded, her eyes wide and her mouth open with shock.

"Arielle?"

"I'm okay." She nodded again. "I'm right behind you."

He started toward the front room.

Just then, another explosion ripped the atmosphere, followed by a third and fourth. Glass shattered, and the house shook. Doug ground his teeth together. Hide-and-seek. Damn it to hell and back again. Where the hell was Pickins?

Before he'd gone another step, a cold chill lanced him.

"*Semper fi,* buddy."

Doug froze, the coarseness of Pickins's evil voice creeping down his spine.

Arielle.

Doug executed a swift turn, leveling his gun at Pickins...and at Arielle.

Son of a bitch.

Cold sweat beaded on Doug's brow, and more dripped down his spine.

Pickins had climbed through the shattered patio door and grabbed Arielle around the throat. He held her in a choke hold, a beefy elbow tipping back her neck. Deadly black metal pressed into her temple, and her toes barely brushed the floor.

Her eyes were wide with terror, her breath coming in short, desperate little bursts.

For the barest hint of a second, Doug's pistol wavered. Pickins noticed it, though, a cackle blending with the piercing shrieks of the alarm.

History unfolded before Doug, a horrible replay of a situation he could never hope to win.

Guilt assailed him, cutting at his heart. He should have known Pickins would blaze back in, full of righteous indignation and glory.

The tattooed pick on Pickins's forearm flashed ominously toward Doug. Fear made his blood coagulate, dredging through his veins.

"What do you say now, *buddy?*" Pickins demanded, the unholy light of insanity radiating from his eyes.

"Whatever you want," Doug said.

"How's it feel to have someone you once counted on...*semper fi,* you freaking jerk...staring at you, holding the power of life or death in his hands?"

"You know how it feels."

"I wanna hear you, man. I wanna hear you tell me."

Pickins tightened his grip on Arielle, making her gasp.

And it hit Doug with the force of a rocket blast. He loved her.

He loved her with his heart and soul. Somehow, over the past few days, he'd fallen in love with her. And it wasn't a young, immature love like the one he'd had for Kerry, but a soul-deep love that transcended everything.

He'd sealed off her own confession, hiding behind his own lack of courage. He'd known then that he returned the emotion, but he hadn't had the strength to admit it. Hadn't had the chance to admit it. And now each second marked a lost possibility.

"I lost my girl 'cause of you, you righteous, self-important bastard!" Pickins yelled. "You sent me to prison, and my Rita said she didn't have no time to wait for no loser. She shoved my ring through the metal bars, threw it at me, like I was a piece of trash." Then his eyes lit again. "You ever lost a girl?"

Once. And Doug vowed it wouldn't happen a second time.

"Huh, Dougie boy? Have you?"

Arielle belonged in his arms, and Doug wouldn't rest until that happened. She belonged in his arms, in his bed, in his life. And he intended to tell her just that.

Rhone and Brian couldn't be far away. If Doug could only stall long enough, maybe they'd arrive and the situation would be resolved peacefully...without a hair on her head being touched.

"Got out of prison 'bout a month ago. No job, no one waitin' for me. Now I got something you want." He cackled again.

The alarm continued to wail, and tension tightened around Doug's neck like a noose.

"There's one thing I want, Sammy...your sorry, worthless butt six feet under. Shouldn't have gone for imprisonment, should have recommended they seek the death penalty. New York doesn't need your kind of trash wandering the streets.''

Pickins's eyes narrowed.

Doug surged on. "Only feel like a man when you're threatening a woman, do you? How about you act like a real man, go a round of one-on-one, just you and me?'' Doug didn't mean basketball, except for the part when he'd slam-dunk Pickins's skull.

Pickins pressed the barrel deeper into Arielle's temple, and Doug shut his mouth.

"Ain't gonna happen, my boy."

"You don't want her...you want me. Revenge, right? Let her go, Sammy.''

Pickins tutted. "Ain't gonna happen, not when it's my lucky day and all. I got twofers, got the little lady and you.'' He licked his lips. "Couldn't have afforded no plane ticket without her money. Now where's my manners? My mama would be ashamed of me for forgetting myself like that.'' He lowered the gun momentarily. "Thank you for the money, little lady,'' he said.

"Go to hell,'' Arielle said.

Pickins backhanded her. "Now is that any way to accept gratitude?''

Doug's trigger finger itched. Her eyes were wide and terrified, and she bit her lip when Pickins shoved the barrel against her temple again.

Though he fought not to look into her eyes, Doug lost the battle. Her eyes showed trust, belief, the two things he'd demanded of her, the two things he now prayed he could use to save her.

But more, beyond that, he saw the trueness of love. Last night, he'd known what she was about to say, and he'd stopped her. Now he desperately wished he hadn't. He needed her love. And he wanted to hear her say the words.

For a moment, Doug let down his own guard, allowed

the love he felt to be expressed in his own eyes. Did she see it?

She closed her eyes momentarily, and when she opened them again, he knew. He knew that no matter what else happened, she realized he loved her.

She gave a brief nod, their communication transcending the verbal.

"You know, I think I ought to be killing the missy and not you." Pickins laughed—more a giggle than anything. "Think that'd drive you crazy, you and your morals…ain't that what you called them on the stand, your *morals?* So damn many morals you sent me to jail 'cause of a little accident?"

"It wasn't an accident, Sammy, you killed innocent people, men who trusted you."

"Just as I'll kill the missy." He cackled.

The alarm went silent. And the tension in the atmosphere became palpable. Pickins would kill her, Doug knew, and take more pleasure in that than from murdering Doug.

"Word on the street said there'd been a mix-up, that she didn't want to die after all. Don't that just make it better?"

His grip nearly choking Arielle, Pickins backed toward the front of the house.

"Let her go."

Pickins laughed.

"Trade you," Doug offered. "Give me the girl and I'll give you my gun."

"Don't like your games, Dougie boy." His eyes sparkled with an unnatural light.

"Point-blank range," Doug told him.

"She dies."

Doug's gaze collided with Arielle's. "Shoot him," she mouthed.

He couldn't, wouldn't, take that risk. He'd bet his life on the turn of a card, but he refused to gamble with hers.

"Do it," she urged softly.

He gave a quick shake of his head.

Pickins chuckled. "Ain't this grand?"

Silently she mouthed, "Trust me."

Before he could react, tell her not to, she pulled her elbow forward and slammed it into Pickins's stomach. He roared and smashed the pistol against her head.

Arielle crumpled, and Pickins shoved her at Doug, letting her fall into his arms in an unconscious heap.

Chapter 16

Pickins fired.

The chandelier shattered. Protecting Arielle with his body, Doug grimaced as shards of glass spiked toward the ground, swearing when a dagger of crystal impaled his shoulder. Pushing past them, Pickins ran into the living room, leaping through the broken window.

Doug lay Arielle down, squeezing his eyes shut in momentary relief when he saw the consistent rise and fall of her chest. He dropped a kiss on her forehead, promising to return.

Grabbing the phone, he dialed 911. After identifying himself and Arielle's condition, he left the phone off the hook.

"Pickins!" Doug yelled, wincing as he yanked out the glass. He wavered momentarily, but the heat of anger drove him on.

He took the same path as Pickins, the image of Arielle lying on the floor making him run faster. Pickins wouldn't get a second chance to hurt someone Doug cared for. Not if he could help it.

The blowing and drifting snow partially covered Pickins's tracks, obliterating others. The semilit conditions, created by the snow-covered ground and overcast sky, were both a blessing and a curse, Doug decided, seeing his prey dart into the trees that lined the driveway. If he could see Pickins, then Pickins would surely be able to see him.

As he closed the distance, Pickins pointed his gun over his shoulder and fired. Fortunately, his aim was off. Well, so much for it being Pickins's lucky day. Doug intended to ruin it completely.

Slowing his pace, Doug tried to keep in the shadows of the trees. The tracks he followed suddenly blended with a herd of others that scattered in all directions. Deer. Most likely taking cover from the wind, Pickins had startled them. Doug cursed.

Squatting near the base of a tree, he closed his eyes to listen. He heard the subtle movement of a branch. Reacting—but not fast enough—he turned as Pickins jumped from above.

Caught in an iron vise of insanity, Doug struggled for air as Pickins tightened his hold on Doug's neck. The two rolled down an incline, Doug fighting to gain the upper hand, to position his weapon, even as blackness threatened to overtake him.

"Shooting to kill was too easy!" Pickins yelled, straddling Doug at the bottom of the hill.

Doug fought to raise the gun, and grimaced when it fell from his weakened grasp and sank into the snow.

"One-on-one does have its appeal," Pickins continued, his voice seeming to come from a distance. "I'm gonna choke the life out of you, you lousy bastard. But before I do, I wanna hear you beg for mercy."

The moment Pickins loosened his grip, Doug coughed

and gulped for air, at the same time bringing his knee up into Pickins's groin.

Fighting to hold the enraged Pickins away with one hand, Doug searched blindly with the other for his gun.

Pickins grabbed at the pistol. Reaching deep, dredging up determination, Doug's grip tightened on the handle as both fought for their lives and for control of the trigger.

Fury and pure hatred blazed in Pickins's eyes.

"Give it up, Sammy."

"So I can go back to jail?" He sneered. "I'd rather go to hell!"

Suited Doug fine.

"I'll see you there with me," Pickins promised. Despite the frigid temperatures, beads of sweat dotted his brow.

Staring Pickins in the eye, Doug knew the desperation that glinted there. Nothing more dangerous than a desperate man. And Doug had no illusions about Pickins. He'd killed before and protested his innocence. He'd hurt Arielle. And he intended to kill Doug.

"*Semper fi*, buddy, till one of us dies!" Pickins's demented laughter echoed through the forest.

A single shot rang out.

And Pickins was no longer laughing.

Wind rushed through the treetops, scattering snow over the ground. Then the unmistakable rustle of underbrush and the snap of a twig underfoot.

"Doug?"

He glared up at Brian. "About damned time you got here. What took you so long?"

Doug grunted as he rolled free from the still form lying next to him. Stumbling to his feet, he accepted Brian's steadying hand.

"Whiteout conditions. Closed roads. You know, the usual. Out of the ordinary, though, was an arsenal of explosives I stumbled across near a rock piling looking for you."

"I'm not surprised." Where Pickins was concerned, Doug experienced no emotion. He never liked having to use his weapon, would prefer to handle conflict differently. In the majority of cases, he regretted the loss of human life.

"Call the coroner, the black and whites," he told Brian.

Holstering his nine-millimeter, Doug headed for the house at a run, ignoring the dull ache in his shoulder. "How is she?" he demanded of Rhone, sinking onto the floor next to Arielle. Her eyelashes stood in stark contrast to her pale face. Doug had never experienced this mind-numbing, bone-chilling fear before.

"She'll be okay," Rhone promised. He'd been bathing her forehead and bruised temple with a damp cloth, and he offered it to Doug.

"Has she woken up?"

Rhone shook his head.

Doug took Arielle's hand between his. Cradling her wrist, he was calmed but not reassured by the steady beat of her pulse.

"Need to see to your shoulder," Rhone stated, moving away.

"Just a scratch."

"Three dozen stitches," Rhone countered.

"Two."

"You're on."

In moments, he heard the distant wail of sirens. Whispering softly, he confessed, "I love you."

He would have sworn a smile flickered across her lips. Even when the emergency response team arrived and started to work on her, he refused to leave her side.

"Sir, we have a few questions for you," a police officer said, placing a restraining hand on Doug's arm when he started to follow the stretcher from the house.

Rhone flashed an ID card and said, "Yarrow and I can answer anything you need to know. Go with her, Doug."

Thanking his friend, he climbed into the back of the ambulance.

The siren screamed, and Doug held her hand, looking heavenward. He'd never been much of a praying man. Until lately. Until he nearly lost the one thing that mattered more to him than anything else.

He'd gladly have given his life in order to spare hers. "I love you, Arielle," he said again, the husky tone of his words drowned by the wailing of the siren.

Light pierced through Arielle's skull, bringing a blinding headache with it. She heard the whir of machinery she'd heard before. And she smelled the unmistakable odor of antiseptic and despair.

A hospital?

But it couldn't be... She hadn't been in a hospital since Danny...

She fought to remember where she was and how she'd gotten there, but the harder she reached, the farther away the fragments of memory seemed to slip.

In frustration, she turned her head on the pillow. Pain exploded through her head, and she gasped. Arielle started to lift her hand to her temple, only to feel a slight resistance.

Slowly she opened her eyes, struggling to focus on the spinning room. An IV tube was taped to her hand, and her blue-and-white cotton gown had slipped from her shoulder.

Finally, blinking to focus, she saw Doug, slumped in a chair next to the bed, hair falling across his forehead. A day's shadow shaded his chin and jaw, and dark circles bruised his eyes. His chest rose and fell shallowly, as if he were barely keeping sleep at bay.

A sling held his left arm close to his body. He'd been hurt, and she wanted nothing more than to reach out to him. But as she tried to sit, the world whirled around her.

Cradled beneath blankets, memories returned in disjointed fragments. She remembered.... Pickins. He'd caused explosions, and then… Arielle frowned, and winced at the corresponding pain. She'd been following Doug. Pickins had grabbed her.

Above the pungent scent of disinfectant in the room, she could still smell Pickins. He'd shoved his arm around her throat, tipping back her head. She'd seen the tattoo grossly etched into his skin. And his breath… She closed her eyes again.

The pieces floated back, then, without her having to try. She'd told Doug to shoot Pickins, silently trying to communicate her trust, her belief and, most of all, her love.

Their gazes had met. And for a second she'd seen… It floated away. Then, teasing, it returned. She'd seen his answering love.

Knowing he'd never shoot at Pickins while the man had her hostage, she'd done the only thing she knew to do…she'd elbowed Pickins in the stomach. And then the world had gone black. It had stayed that way until just a few seconds ago.

Hadn't it? Her breath caught. A part of her wanted to believe she'd heard Doug confess his love. Had he? Or had it been nothing more than a dream, a wish?

The next time she opened her eyes, it was to see Doug looking at her.

"Sleeping Beauty," he said softly. "Welcome back."

Her heart leaped.

"If this is a way to make sure you get sympathy so I don't beat you at cards tomorrow…"

"Yes?" she asked.

"It's working." He stood, moving closer to her. Crouching, he reached for her hand and held it gently.

"What…" She cleared her throat and Doug offered her a sip from a paper cup. The water slid down her parched throat, and it was then that she realized just how weak she felt. "What happened to your shoulder?"

"I'm more worried about how you're doing."

"And I'm worried about your shoulder."

"Figures," he said. "Danced with a piece of glass. Tried to make sure it didn't step on my toes."

"So you offered your shoulder instead?"

"Whatever works."

"Did you get stitches?"

"Three dozen." He winced. "I won't be carrying you anywhere for a week or so."

They lapsed into silence, a thousand things needing to be said.

"How are you?" he asked.

She looked into his eyes, touched that he'd positioned himself near her, so that she didn't have to lift her head. "I think this counts as an Excedrin headache." Then she asked the inevitable. "What happened to me?"

"He hit you on the head with the butt of the pistol."

She swallowed, her mouth suddenly dry again. "And Pickins?"

"Isn't around to tell his side of the story."

A sigh of relief escaped her. Even though she didn't wish anyone to die, she wasn't sure she could have lived with the terror of knowing he was still out there, watching, maybe waiting for another chance.

A soft knock on the door halted any more conversation. Doug looked at her and she nodded.

"Come in," he said.

The door eased open, and Rhone entered, handing a small box to Doug. The men exchanged knowing glances, and Doug slipped the package inside his jacket. She would have frowned if it didn't hurt so much.

Rhone grinned at her, and she offered a wan smile in return.

"How're you feeling?"

"Like buying stock in aspirin."

"I'll send you a carton."

"Sure," she said. "And what will I do for tomorrow?"

"She's a trouper, Doug," Rhone said.

"Yeah," Doug responded, and she wondered if that was a note of pride in his voice. "She is."

"I'll be back later," Rhone promised Arielle. "Shannen's at the airport now, picking up your parents."

"Thank you," she whispered. "How can I make it up to you?"

"By naming your firstborn after me."

"Adios, Mitchell," Doug said. "You've gotta go now."

Rhone saluted. "I can take a hint."

The door swished shut behind him, sealing her behind the closed door with Doug. For some reason, the atmosphere was branded with an intimacy she hadn't before noticed.

"I almost lost you," he said, the words broken with emotion.

She hadn't heard him sound so raw, so rough, before. The scratch of huskiness in his voice brought a tear to her eyes.

"I'm not good at this sort of thing," he admitted.

Their gazes locked.

"But when Pickins had you..." He exhaled. "I'm a fool. It took me nearly losing you to make me see what I had. don't want to take that risk again." He paused for a breath. "I love you, Arielle."

Her heart turned over in her chest.

"I don't want to live without you."

The words hung there, between them. But she didn't dare hope...

"I want kids, as many as you do. You told me about a house with a split-rail fence. I'll get you one."

"But, Doug—"

"Will you do me the honor of being my wife?"

Heated tears chased down her cheeks.

"Arielle?"

She squeezed his hand tight. "I love you, Doug."

"Then...?"

"I'll marry you."

His whoop of joy made her smile.

He released her hand, drawing the small box from his pocket. "This ring was my grandmother's. She was a special lady, always there for me, when no one else was. I had Shannen get the ring out of my safe at home and bring it with her. I can get you another—"

"No, oh, no. Doug, this is perfect."

He extracted the ring, the pear-shaped diamond winking in the fluorescent lighting. Holding her hand toward his heart, he softly asked, "May I?"

"Yes," she whispered, her heart singing with the fulfillment she'd dreamed of but never dared hope for.

"I stopped you before you told me you loved me. Tell me now."

"With my heart and soul, I love you."

He smiled, vanquishing years and exhaustion with the single act.

Then he slipped the ring onto her finger. The band of gold fit snugly, the diamond sealing her love for eternity. She'd never take it off, she promised herself.

"As soon as I break you out of this joint, I want to get married."

"I need time to plan," she protested.

"Arguing already?"

"Simply stating facts."

"Anyone tell you you talk too much?" he asked.

"Maybe. Once or twice." She smiled. "So what are you going to do about it?"

As he cradled her face, the warmth and gentle pressure of his touch communicated the depth of his love. Leaning over her and whispering the words she'd longed to hear, he kissed her.

Epilogue

"Let's leave."

Arielle smiled, an act he never got tired of seeing.

"So how 'bout it—you and me, a bottle of champagne, and a berth on *Our Destiny?*"

"Doug," she protested, "the reception just started. This is only the first dance."

"So?" he asked, pulling her closer, reveling in the feel of her against him. "Our ship came in...or, correct that...our *new* ship came in. The guests have food and drink and a band. They won't even notice we're gone."

She looked up at him, then faltered in her steps. "They'll notice."

He wanted her so desperately. The doctors had kept her under good care, and she'd been busy planning their wedding. Graciously Doug had given her a week. But he wasn't an infinitely patient man. "Five minutes," he said. "Say your goodbyes."

"Doug!"

"I promised you the wedding of your dreams. Did I deliver?"

"The limo was wonderful. But you didn't need all those roses."

"You said they were your favorite flower."

"But twenty dozen for the sanctuary?"

"Smelled good."

"Yes." She smiled. "They did."

"Five minutes."

"But..."

"I didn't promise you a long reception." He drew her against him. "Did I?" he whispered, nipping at the top of her ear.

She sagged against him.

"Five minutes?" she asked.

"I'll have the car brought around."

From a vantage point in the corner, he crossed his arms over his chest and watched her move toward Rhone and Shannen. Arielle's gown was held together with tiny buttons, from the nape of her neck to the curve of her back. He couldn't wait to unfasten each and every one, then slip satin from her shoulders.

At the edge of the dance floor, she stopped near Rhone and Shannen. Bending, she drew Nicky and Jessy toward her. Seeing her with his godchildren made Doug ache to hold her. She deserved children of her own, and he intended to be a good provider. A man had to do what a man had to do.

"How come you always get the girl?" Brian asked.

"Maybe you can now."

"You'll still be available for consultations?"

Doug nodded. The agency would be in good hands—Arrow's. As for himself, Doug was going into business with Rhone. Less risk, but plenty of excitement, in the security field.

After their honeymoon, they'd go house-hunting, and Arielle had already considered the schools she'd like to teach at. The future looked bright. Not bad for a man who never used to believe in the future.

"Good luck, boss."

He shook Yarrow's hand. "If you get the girl, I want to be the first to know."

Yarrow grinned. "Don't suppose Arielle's got any cousins?" Offering his congratulations again, Brian moved toward the back table, where an attractive woman sat, alone.

Doug shook his head, smiling. When Arielle returned to him, Doug said, "I've got a gift for your parents."

"For my parents?"

"Come on."

Together, they searched out Mona and Jack, finding them sitting together between dances, holding hands.

"I thought you said your new husband was impatient for the honeymoon," Mona said.

"Mother!"

"He is," Doug assured them. "But Arielle had something she wanted to give you."

He offered the envelope to Arielle. She frowned slightly but took it, extending it to her parents.

"Open it, Jack."

With hands starting to gnarl from age, Jack tore open the envelope.

"Tickets for the cruise we've always dreamed of!" Mona's eyes filled with tears. "Kids, you shouldn't have."

Arielle hugged her parents and kissed them.

"Be happy, honey."

Arielle looked at Doug before saying, "I will, Mom. I will."

Mona extracted a promise that Arielle would call soon. But when they were out of earshot, Doug lifted her hand to his lips and said, "Not too soon."

"I can't believe you did that," she said, rising on her tiptoes to kiss him on the cheek.

"What, kissed you?"

"Remembered they wanted to go on a cruise."

Outside, he pulled her beneath the seclusion of a tree. "I remember everything you ever told me."

"Everything?" she repeated breathlessly, looking into his eyes.

"Including the fact that you wanted me to slowly undress you, then make love to you for the rest of the night."

"Oh, yeah?"

"And then you said you didn't want to get out of bed for the next three days."

"I didn't say any of those things."

"So how come I remember so well?"

"Wishful thinking?" She reached for his bow tie.

"Yeah, maybe," he said.

"Doug…"

"Hmm?"

Using the ends of the bow tie, she drew him toward her. "You're talking too much."

"So you think you can shut me up?"

With a grin, Arielle rose onto her tiptoes. "I know I can."

Doug slid his arms around her as she did exactly what she'd promised she would.

* * * * *

Return to the Towers!

In March
New York Times bestselling author

NORA ROBERTS

brings us to the Calhouns' fabulous
Maine coast mansion and reveals the
tragic secrets hidden there for generations.

For all his degrees, Professor Max Quartermain has a
lot to learn about love—and luscious Lilah Calhoun is
just the woman to teach him. Ex-cop Holt Bradford is
as prickly as a thornbush—until Suzanna Calhoun's
special touch makes love blossom in his heart.
And all of them are caught in the race to solve
the generations-old mystery of a priceless
lost necklace...and a timeless love.

Lilah and Suzanna
THE
Calhoun Women

**A special 2-in-1 edition containing
FOR THE LOVE OF LILAH and
SUZANNA'S SURRENDER**

Available at your favorite retail outlet.

CWVOL2

Take 4 bestselling love stories FREE

Plus get a FREE surprise gift!

Special Limited-time Offer

Mail to Silhouette Reader Service™

3010 Walden Avenue
P.O. Box 1867
Buffalo, N.Y. 14240-1867

YES! Please send me 4 free Silhouette Intimate Moments® novels and my free surprise gift. Then send me 6 brand-new novels every month, which I will receive months before they appear in bookstores. Bill me at the low price of $3.57 each plus 25¢ delivery and applicable sales tax, if any.* That's the complete price and a savings of over 10% off the cover prices—quite a bargain! I understand that accepting the books and gift places me under no obligation ever to buy any books. I can always return a shipment and cancel at any time. Even if I never buy another book from Silhouette, the 4 free books and the surprise gift are mine to keep forever.

245 SEN CF2V

Name	(PLEASE PRINT)	
Address	Apt. No.	
City	State	Zip

This offer is limited to one order per household and not valid to present Silhouette Intimate Moments® subscribers. *Terms and prices are subject to change without notice. Sales tax applicable in N.Y.

UMOM-696   ©1990 Harlequin Enterprises Limited

**Make a Valentine's date
for the premiere of**

♦ HARLEQUIN® **Movies**

starting February 14, 1998 with

Debbie Macomber's

This Matter of
Marriage

on  **the movie channel.** tmc

Just tune in to **The Movie Channel** the **second Saturday night** of every month at 9:00 p.m. EST to join us, and be swept away by the sheer thrill of romance brought to life. Watch for details of upcoming movies—in books, in your television viewing guide and in stores.

If you are not currently a subscriber to The Movie Channel, simply call your local cable or satellite provider for more details. Call today, and don't miss out on the romance!

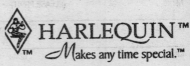

the movie channel. tmc
*100% pure movies.
100% pure fun.*

♦ HARLEQUIN™
Makes any time special.™

BESTSELLING AUTHORS
IN THE SPOTLIGHT

.WE'RE SHINING THE SPOTLIGHT ON SIX OF OUR STARS!

Harlequin and Silhouette have selected stories from several of their bestselling authors to give you six sensational reads. These star-powered romances are bound to please!

THERE'S A PRICE TO PAY FOR STARDOM... AND IT'S LOW

$1.99 U.S.
$2.50 CAN.
Special Offer

As a special offer, these six outstanding books are available from Harlequin and Silhouette for only $1.99 in the U.S. and $2.50 in Canada. Watch for these titles:

At the Midnight Hour—**Alicia Scott**
Joshua and the Cowgirl—**Sherryl Woods**
Another Whirlwind Courtship—**Barbara Boswell**
Madeleine's Cowboy—**Kristine Rolofson**
Her Sister's Baby—**Janice Kay Johnson**
One and One Makes Three—**Muriel Jensen**

Available in March 1998
at your favorite retail outlet.

PBAIS

DIANA PALMER
ANN MAJOR
SUSAN MALLERY

MONTANA MAVERICKS Weddings

RETURN TO WHITEHORN

In **April 1998** get ready to catch the bouquet. Join in the excitement as these bestselling authors lead us down the aisle with three heartwarming tales of love and matrimony in Big Sky country.

A very engaged lady is having second thoughts about her intended; a pregnant librarian is wooed by the town bad boy; a cowgirl meets up with her first love. Which Maverick will be the next one to get hitched?

Available in **April 1998**.

Silhouette's beloved **MONTANA MAVERICKS** returns in Special Edition and Harlequin Historicals starting in February 1998, with brand-new stories from your favorite authors.

Round up these great new stories at your favorite retail outlet.

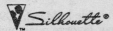